MONSTER WHISPERER

MONSTER WHISPERER

NOBILIS REED

CIRCLET PRESS, INC.
CAMBRIDGE, MA

Monster Whisperer
by Nobilis Reed

Copyright © 2016 Nobilis Reed
Cover art by Starla Huchton

ISBN paperback 978-1-61390-174-8

Published by Circlet Press, Inc.
39 Hurlbut Street
Cambridge, MA 02138

An audio version of "Monster Whisperer" was offered to supporters of the No-bilis Erotica podcast as bonus material available through the podcast mobile app. It was also briefly for sale on the scribl.com website, without the addition of the "Birth of a Monster Whisperer" material.

CONTENTS

Chapter One: Lending a Hand   7

Chapter Two: Up in Arms   27

Chapter Three: Time on Their Hands   67

Chapter Four: On Hold   85

Chapter Five: Disaster Bound   93

Chapter Six: Sleight of Hand   110

Chapter Seven: Losing Grip   127

Chapter Eight: Holding a Grudge   154

Chapter Nine: Fingerhold   170

Chapter Ten: Within Reach   188

Chapter Eleven: Out of Reach   210

Chapter Twelve: On the Other Hand   222

Epilogue   230

Bonus: Birth of a Monster Whisperer   236

About the Author   248

CHAPTER ONE
LENDING A HAND

A calm voice sounded in the darkness of Dale's room. "Ma'am?"

There was a stirring among the blankets, but nothing more.

"Ma'am," said the voice, somewhat more stridently, "You need to wake up." A small red light appeared over the door.

"Ten minutes." Blankets muffled the words.

"I'm sorry, Dale. I'm afraid I can't do that."

Every light in the room suddenly turned on, accompanied by blaring trumpets and thundering drums. Dale sat upright in her bed.

"I'm up! I'm up!"

The noise stopped, and the lights dimmed except for an indirect glow from the ceiling.

"My apologies, ma'am, but it is my responsibility to make sure you do not break your appointments."

She groaned and tried to burrow back under the covers. "They can't wait for me to get a decent sleep? What's the rush?"

"We will be landing at New New Amsterdam Four in approximately ninety minutes. Three clients have requested your services. One of them is the Governor's wife, ma'am. She has paid extra for an expedited appointment, and she can be particularly troublesome if people are not seen to be making all haste in fulfilling her demands. I thought it best to awaken you."

Dale yawned, stretched, blinked, and rubbed her eyes. "I see. Do I have time for a workout?" Dressed only in a thin nightdress, Dale felt goosebumps prick up on her skin, but she paid them no attention. She would be warming up shortly.

"I have taken the liberty of preparing the Nalcheka, ma'am. I have concluded that it would be the best choice."

The woman rolled out of bed, and began windmilling her arms and rolling her head.

"Thank you, Vi. Why the Nalcheka?" she asked as she stepped

out the door. As she walked along the curving corridor, the voice followed her, coming from whatever console was closest.

"While the Storazoid is in greater need of your attention, a typical session takes fifty minutes or more, and I decided to let you sleep. I have scheduled the Storazoid for your evening workout. The Nalcheka has been somewhat agitated lately, so I picked it instead."

Dale looked through the transparent panels making up the wall to her right as she passed, surveying the creatures on display. "Excellent choice, Vi."

She stopped at a large, circular opening in the transparent wall, and stretched her back, arms and legs in a series of gymnastic poses. Her deep splits and graceful arabesques were performed with remarkable ease.

"Should I activate the cameras, ma'am?"

"Of course, Vi. We never know when we're going to get something exceptional."

After finishing her routine, Dale touched the control plate next to the door. It rotated a quarter turn and then rose out of the way.

Instantly, tentacles shot out of the opening, grabbed Dale around her abdomen, wrists, and ankles, and pulled her in. She shrieked as her flimsy nightdress was ripped from her body and the shreds thrown to the spongy floor beneath her.

The creature holding her was a three-meter sphere, covered with crater-pocked stony plates. From the gaps between the plates, long green tentacles emerged, each with a specialized organ at the end. Some, like the ones gripping Dale's body, split into clusters of smaller tentacles and served as hands. The ones stabilizing its body against the floor and walls were thicker, ending in heavy paddle feet. A few terminated in large eyeballs, unblinking orbs with star-shaped pupils in their livid red irises.

Dale struggled against the monster's grip, thrashing her arms and legs and shouting at the top of her lungs. Suspended in midair, however, her struggles had no impact on the beast. Its powerful limbs held her spread-eagled while three of the creature's eyes moved in to inspect her from only centimeters away. Their attention darted from landmark to landmark, focusing for one moment on her dainty, elegant face, the next on her shoulder-length black hair, then on a jiggling, chocolate-tipped breast, then on the narrow triangle of pubic hair between her thighs.

After a few minutes of wandering, one of the eyes stopped moving, staring directly into Dale's eyes, so close that she could see little else beyond its staring orb. In her peripheral vision, she could just barely see the meandering of the other two eyes focusing on the lower part of her body.

The arms coiled around her body, drawing her closer as they shifted their coils, freeing some of their length to allow the tentacle-tips to roam over her body. The ones on her arms crept toward her shoulders and then down onto her breasts, squeezing and pinching until they found her nipples, soft-peaked in the chill air. The one around her waist slid down her spine to settle between her buttocks, making its way between the warm globes toward the delicate pucker of her anus.

The tentacles wrapped around her legs shifted and rolled to bring their dexterous tips into contact with her sex. They slid in and around her cleft, stroking the delicate flesh with tender but insistent grace. Her cries, which had been full of alarm when she was first snared, shifted to gasps and moans as the numerous arms continued their varied stimulations.

She heard a grinding sound as the creature's plates shifted, and a new tentacle emerged. This one was simpler than the others, a simple cylindrical shape that tapered down to a small egg-shaped bulb. The green color gradually faded into an eggplant purple toward the sphincter-pierced tip. As it stretched upward, the Nalcheka drew her body down upon it, until the end bumped up against Dale's naked pussy lips.

She thrashed even harder as the creature fumbled for entrance, but her struggles succeeded only in delaying the inevitable. The two manipulators focused on her pussy drew her outer lips apart, and the bulb slid inside.

For a moment, Dale froze, except for the heaving of her chest as she panted for air. The creature's tentacle-cock was deep within her, pulsing and squirming as if seeking a way to push even further. She squealed again, tensing her muscles as if to force the invader out, but every time she managed to eject it the slightest bit it slid right back in as soon as she relaxed.

As she gradually quieted, exertion and ecstasy combining to drain her of every ounce of energy, the beast became even more agitated. The pulses and thrusts of its penetration took on a frantic pace, and a quivering energy ran through the entire creature. Its arms positively vibrated with tension, making its touch even more stimulating to Dale's overpowered nervous system. She cried out as a climax convulsed her body.

The event triggered something in the Nalcheka. It stiffened, and a deep rumble, like the sound of a distant avalanche, resonated in the chamber. Its tentacles stopped mid-grope, and the pupils of the creature's staring eyes narrowed to tiny pinpricks of black. One second passed. Two. The only sound was the gradually fading echo of Dale's orgasm.

Then a flood of pale green goo squirted out from around its stalk, running down Dale's legs and the creature's shaft to dribble a sloppy puddle onto the floor beneath her. The flow surged, then slackened and stopped. The tentacles retreated under the stony shell and the plates clamped shut with a snap, leaving a surface indistinguishable from any common boulder. Dale dropped into the slime and fell onto her back, splashing more of her body with the viscous substance.

She lay there for a few seconds, trembling breaths shaking her body, then sat up and squeezed the junk out of her hair. "Cut!" she said sharply.

"Video stored, Ma'am," said Vi. "An excellent performance."

"Oh, don't flatter me," she said as she picked herself up and gingerly made her way back to the door. "I only got one of the 'positor arms to come out. The fans expect a double, at minimum." She sighed, and flicked a wad of goop against the wall. "Oh, well.

Hold onto it. We'll see what we can make of it once the appointments are handled."

Freshly showered and styled, Dale walked down the gangway into the brightly-lit VIP terminal of Oliver Wendell Holmes spaceport. She was dressed in a spotless, skin-tight, pale blue coverall with white boots, and a pair of white gloves tucked into her belt. The unmistakable "Monster Whisperer" logo was blazoned over her left breast, as well as on the small khaki athletics bag slung over her shoulder. Behind her, a camera-bot hovered silently, its wide lens aimed over her shoulder.

A woman in a conservatively-cut, shining gold business suit stood alone in the middle of the room. As soon as she caught sight of Dale, she frowned.

"Miz Ventura?" said Dale, "Is there something wrong?"

The woman sighed. "I'm Miz Ventura's assistant. Shannon James." She offered her hand for a dead-fish handshake. "Pleased to meet you, Miz Clearwater. We were hoping that you would be able to help without the, mm..." she glanced up at the hovering camera-bot, "...publicity?"

"Ah, I see. You must understand that an operation like mine won't run without significant funding. If we aren't able to record, then I am forced to request reimbursement for the lost revenue." There were still places where enjoying the company of a tentacle beast was considered vulgar or deviant. New New Amsterdam Four must be one of them. Dale made a note to herself to instruct Vi to inform her of such details when arriving at a new planet.

"Of course. Miz Ventura will cover your losses." She glanced meaningfully at the camera-bot.

Dale instructed the bot to return to the ship, and gave the payment details to Miz James, who authorized the exorbitant amount without blinking an eye. With the financial business settled, the assistant led her to a limousine parked on the roof.

They took off, heading for a low range of mountains visible in the distance. Miz James remained silent, leaving her passenger to watch out the window as the terrain transformed from urban to rural to wilderness. After crossing the mountains, the craft finally descended to land on the roof of a large structure perched high on a rocky mountainside, surrounded by trees and scrub.

Dale took a moment to enjoy the smell of clean, natural air, the breeze ruffling her hair, and the broad, unspoiled vista stretching out around her. There were no roads that she could see, no power lines, no evidence that mankind had touched the land except to build this one structure.

"This way," said Miz James, indicating an open elevator at one corner of the roof.

The elevator took them down several floors, opening into a balcony overlooking a vast chamber carved out of the rock. Under thousands of lights strung over the roof, a private jungle of trees and vines grew in a tangled riot, crisscrossed with meandering sandy paths.

A woman rose from leaning against the curved railing at one end of the balcony, and walked toward them with a measured stride. She appeared fortyish, with mild creases at the corners of her mouth and on her brow that gave her a permanent look of disapproval, even as she made a professional smile. She was dressed in an informal blouse and shorts, with a pair of hiking boots.

Dale held out her hand. "Miz Ventura."

"Pleased to meet you, Miz Clearwater. Please, call me Ellen." She turned to her assistant and dismissed her with a nod. "Thank you, Francis." The younger woman disappeared into the elevator.

"Thank you. Ellen. Call me Dale. So what's the problem? Your request didn't include any details."

"It's my Orichalc. It has been rather listless lately. The veterinarian hasn't found anything medically wrong; she says it must be something psychological. I was hoping you could help."

Dale nodded. It made sense; one would need a place like this to keep an Orichalc healthy and happy. "Shall we take a look?"

"The stairs are right over there. I hope you don't mind if I return to my office?"

"I don't treat tentacle monsters, Ellen. I teach people how to be better tentacle monster owners, so your presence is required. I need to see how you interact with it."

She sighed. "Oh, very well."

Dale set down her bag at the top of the stairs, and the two women descended into the trees and walked along the packed sand leading deeper into the chamber. "It'll be just up the way a bit."

Dale scanned the trees that overhung the path. "Orichalcs are stealth hunters, normally. Are you sure you know where it is?"

"Yes."

The trail opened into a wide open space, surrounding a single large tree festooned with vines and creepers. Ellen walked up to the tree and thumped it several times with her fist. Slowly, a glittering line, looking like nothing so much as a long gold necklace, descended from one of the lower branches.

"You see?" said Ellen. "No energy at all." She swatted at the line with the back of her hand, causing it to twitch briefly. Dale smiled and looked up into the branches, visually tracing the shining cord.

"You're a confident woman. Self-assured. Calm. You know what you want, and you go get it."

"Yes, of course."

"Well, that kind of calm, assertive attitude isn't going to help your relationship with your Orichalc. What it needs more than anything is terror—or, at least, a reasonable facsimile. Excitement, at the very least."

"Are you saying I'm supposed to be afraid of this?" She gave the tendril a yank. It was no more responsive than before. Dale spread her hands.

"I know it doesn't seem very frightening right now, but if we take a few simple steps, we'll have it back to its usual self. Take a nice deep breath, and scream as loud as you can."

Ellen glared up into the tree, frowned, and let out a guttural scream. The Orichalc barely twitched.

"No, no," said Dale, "Too angry. Again, what we need is fear."

Ellen tried again. The result was a bit higher pitched, but not much different than the first.

"Like this." Dale took a deep breath, clutched her arms to her chest, crouched in a protective pose and let out a high-pitched squeal of terror. "Oh, mercy! It's an Orichalc! Those things are terrible!"

The glittering tentacle twitched, shuddered, and retracted back up into the tree.

"Oh no!" she continued, "I can't see it anymore! It's going to get me, I just know!" Dale ran around the base of the tree, glancing up into the branches with exaggerated anxiety. The edge of Ellen's mouth twitched with the beginning of a smile as she watched the performance.

"I know it seems a little silly. Just play along," Dale whispered.

Ellen shrugged. "You're the expert." With a shriek, she grabbed Dale and held her close. "Save me! It's going to get me!"

"Much better," Dale whispered, returning the embrace.

"Thanks."

"The panicked hug was a nice touch."

"I thought so."

Faster than the eye could follow, there was a flash of gold. Even though she knew what was coming, Dale squeaked as she felt the rush of movement down the back and up the sleeves of her coveralls. With a jerk, the metallic tendrils drew tight, wrapping around thighs and arms, hauling them up off their feet.

Their faces were only inches apart, but even at that range Dale could see excitement charge Ellen's expression. "It worked!" she gasped, clutching Dale's body closer. "My God, it worked!"

The thin, metallic tendrils would have bitten cruelly into their skin if the women's entire weight were suspended by them, but with the creature's levitation field active, each of them only weighed a fraction of what they usually did, and they rose like tangled marionettes from the mossy ground under the tree.

More tendrils invaded their clothes as the creature followed its usual hunting procedure. They were smooth and hard like metal, but not uncomfortably cold.

Dale could feel a faint buzz in her pelvic muscles as the beast began sending a rapidly pulsing electric current back and forth between the arms holding her thighs. More tendrils snaked down her cleavage to wrap around her breasts and tickle her nipples, each touch bringing yet another tingling jolt. The shocks were mild, causing only a slight twinge of pain, but they supercharged the nerves they passed through and made even the slightest touch incredibly erotic.

Dale's professional demeanor quickly succumbed to the Orichalc's electrically-charged attentions, and within minutes she could barely speak as the creature stimulated her helpless body. She could only clutch Ellen close as the current surged through her skin.

Yet another tendril appeared, wrapping around the others, drawing them together into a glimmering amber cable. When it passed Dale's field of view, she caught sight of a golden, two-centimeter spike on its tip.

"Ellen," she said, as calmly as she could, which is to say, hardly at all, "How long has it been since you've had a successful, uh, encounter with the Orichalc?"

"Three—three months."

"You didn't have it de-spiked."

"De-spiked? Oh, god—What—what's that?"

In contrast to the other tendrils, the one carrying the spike moved slowly, its chain links rattling against the other tentacles as it plunged down Ellen's neckline.

"If you don't take care of it, it grows a—oh—sharp tip on its breeding stalk."

An edge of honest panic crept into Ellen's voice. "What's it going to do?"

"Don't—oh—don't worry. It's not going... to do anything to you."

Dale felt the organ pass over her belly on its way further south, and tried to summon the concentration to prepare herself, but the chaos of pain and pleasure jangling through her mind made it impossible. She could only wait in horrified expectancy as it homed in on her moist, hungry sex. More tendrils shifted position, spreading her legs wide to either side of Ellen's body.

"I'm the one it wants."

There was a pause as the electrical current faded away, leaving Dale with just two fast heartbeats to collect her wits, and then it struck. Her head flew back and a loud grunt escaped her clenched teeth as she felt the needle-sharp spike pierce her clitoral hood. The electricity surged back, and Dale's respite was over. Her screams echoed from the distant ceiling as she convulsed in the throes of a powerful orgasm.

As her cries faded, so did the electricity, until they were left panting and gasping but still hanging in the creature's clutches.

"I'm sorry," said Ellen, when she had gotten her wind back. "I didn't know."

Dale took a deep breath and let it out slowly, calming her still-trembling body. "It's all right. I've never been marked by an Orichalc before. I'll have something to show my viewers when I get back to the ship."

"Still, I never wanted to put you through that kind of pain."

"If I didn't like a little pain with my sex I wouldn't have gotten into this business. Think nothing of it."

Ellen glanced up into the branches, where the golden cords disappeared into the canopy. "Why isn't it letting us go?"

"After three months? Miz Ventura, your tentacle monster isn't even close to being done." As if on cue, the electricity came on again, thrumming through her body with no less power than before.

"Oh God," whispered the older woman, and her grip tightened around Dale's body. "Here it comes."

Dale splashed cool water over her abused genitalia. A path led down to the little grotto, which was surrounded by beautiful flowers and greenery. She spoke to a communications unit sitting on top of the pile of her clothes on the side of the pool, loud enough to be heard over the burbling artificial spring feeding it.

"It's really not a problem, Vi. I've had rougher days. I can handle it."

"Ma'am, you were held by that Orichalc for three solid hours on top of the piercing. You must be exhausted."

"I'm fine. Look, the bleeding has completely stopped." She bent over, peering at the little curl of gold running through her flesh. The sharp point had already dropped off, leaving a smooth gold dumbbell. The only parts that were visible were the two thick knobs at either end. "Put out a call, see if anyone is willing to host an Orichalc embryo. We'll get it transplanted. These things are rare enough; I'd hate to have to destroy it."

"I've already got three offers. Are you certain about the appointment? Remember, there's also the Storazoid tonight. You want to be at your best for that."

"Don't worry! The girls will be a real easy case. I've read the dossier; it should be no trouble. I'll get set up over there, maybe get some dinner. See if we can get someone in to do a transplant on the Orichalc embryo tonight, so we don't imprint it on me when I exercise the Storazoid."

The AI made an audible sigh. "Very well. When should I inform Omicron Theta Psi you will be arriving?"

Dale peered at the time display on her comm unit. "Have they all transmitted the appropriate releases?"

"Enthusiastically, ma'am. They seem quite excited at the prospect."

"Good." She waded out into deeper water and lay back, floating in the warm, clear pool. "Tell them I'll be there around four."

A robot descended to the side of the pool, carrying a tray of elegantly-prepared sandwiches, a bottle of wine, and a pair of crystal goblets. Ellen appeared shortly thereafter, her matronly body gloriously naked, and slipped down into the water next to the tray.

"Oh, thank you! You shouldn't have."

"It's the least I could do. You've given me my old monster back." The robot poured the wine and, as Dale came alongside, Ellen handed a glass to her. "Cheers."

"Cheers."

"I'm so happy you came out to see us," said the blonde with the perfect teeth and the sorority crest on her flawlessly-tailored blouse. "I know that what we have isn't technically a tentacle monster."

"Well, that depends on who you talk to. Certainly, in behavior and temperament, under-the-bed monsters are similar."

They walked through the arched doorway, underneath the bright pink holographic letters proclaiming the sorority's allegiance, followed by her trusty camera-bot.

Dale looked over her shoulder to address the camera directly. "I'm here on New New Amsterdam Four at the Central University, talking with Miz Cindy Cooper, president of the Omicron Theta Psi sorority." She turned back to the blonde and smiled. "So, where does it normally stay?"

The blonde stopped at the foot of a set of elaborately-carved marble stairs, where eleven women had lined up with their perfect hair and perfect teeth and perfect bodies to smile for Dale's camera-bot. The machine scanned over them dutifully, catching each of them in turn until it focused on the very last one, a redhead, standing at the top of the stairs.

"Under my bed," she said. "I'm the one who brought it here."

Cindy walked alongside Dale, climbing the long stairs. "Miz Clearwater, may I introduce Miz Ursula Tebbins, one of our new members this year."

"Call me Dale. Let's go take a look."

The large bedroom had three immaculately-made beds lined up along one wall with a comfortable meter-wide space between them. Chiffon curtains framed the windows, and holograms of famous cities and spaceports around the galaxy adorned the walls.

"My bed's the one on the end, this one." Ursula did a reasonable imitation of a game-show model presenting a prize.

Dale nodded, and got down on hands and knees, unclipping a flashlight from her pocket. She lifted the bed-skirt and shone it through the gap, peering into the darkness. A soft chittering sound, like paper rustling and creaking wooden beams, came from a cluster of fur and randomly jumbled eyeballs hunched into the corner.

"It looks pretty healthy," she said, sitting back on her heels. "So, what's the problem?" Dale already knew what it was from the communications she'd already received, but she needed to get it all recorded for the show.

"The problem," said a blonde, coming into the room and sitting down on the central bed, "Is that her little friend isn't content with just grabbing ankles. I don't care what she does with her own monster, but I can't get a decent night's sleep with that thing under there. I never know when I'm going to wake up with the thing's hands under my covers instead of hers. It's crazy."

"You're Christine, right? Have you ever had an under-the-bed monster before?"

"No, and I don't care to, either. Anyways, I thought those things are supposed to go away when a kid grows up."

Dale shrugged. "They usually do find a different bed to lurk under once a girl gets past a certain age. They're attracted to innocence as well as a certain emotional vulnerability." She cocked an eyebrow and shot the woman a meaningful look. "Does that make any sense to you? Any reason the monster might think you were more innocent than Ursula?"

Christine looked around nervously, her eyes darting to Ursula, the bed, and back to Dale. A slight flush of color darkened her cheeks. "No."

"All right. Well, let's get some cameras set up so we can see what happens tonight. Cut!"

The little red light on the side of the camera-bot went out, and Dale stood up to unclip some smaller lens-pods from the machine's undercarriage.

Christine watched dubiously as Dale attached the little devices high on the walls, aimed down at Ursula's bed. "Um, can't we just, like, get rid of it, or something?"

"I understand your concern, but under-the-bed monsters are quite manageable creatures once you understand them. They're a lot tamer than, say, a Storazoid or a Mumzer. Mostly harmless." Dale placed the last of the cameras underneath Ursula's bed, pointed at the quiescent monster in the corner.

Christine nodded thoughtfully. "So, um... what now?"

"Nothing to do until bedtime."

Cindy appeared at the bedroom door. "Miz Clearwater? Dale? We'd like to take you out to dinner—that is, if you don't mind cafeteria food."

"I'd be honored."

Dale sat with her feet up on her desk, holographic monitor screens displaying six different views of the empty bedroom at the sorority house. Her crotch was still a bit sore, and it felt good to have her weight on her tailbone. She studied the latest scholarship on Orichalcs from a tablet propped up on her thighs.

The women of Omicron Theta Psi had peppered her with questions about tentacle monsters, show business, and the story that had appeared in the holotabloids a year back about her relationship with that monster hunter, Vince Klieberman. They had been polite, friendly company in spite of their exuberant enthusiasm but, in the end, she had to excuse herself to take care of business.

If she was lucky, she could transplant the Orichalc embryo, work out the Storazoid, and still get a few hours' nap before the girls went to bed around midnight. She would want to be awake to monitor the cameras at the sorority, hopefully from somewhere nearby.

That is, if her appointment would show up. She glared in frustration at the chronometer. The woman was already a half-hour late, and hadn't even called to cancel. Dale suspected that she had lost courage at the last minute, and didn't even have the spine to call up to tell her. Time was running out, and it looked like she would have to either destroy the embryo, or exercise the Storazoid with it in place. Neither prospect was particularly attractive.

Vi's voice broke the silence. "Ma'am, there is a Miz Christine Delavos at the airlock."

"From Omicron Theta Psi?"

"Yes, ma'am."

"Let her in, by all means." Dale put her tablet aside and jogged down to the airlock to meet her guest.

"Christine! Welcome to my ship. Has there been some kind of trouble?"

"No, no. It's nothing like that." The young woman fidgeted, clearly at a complete loss about what to do with her hands.

"What can I do for you?"

"I've been, um… thinking. About changing my major. Xenomedicine."

"Let me guess—specializing in tentacle monsters?"

Christine nodded. "Yeah. I was wondering if you could show me? Your collection, I mean."

Dale gave her a knowing smile. "I'd be happy to. Follow me." She led her guest up to the observation balcony, and walked slowly along it, describing the various creatures in the chambers below them. She carefully chose their route, to arrive at one particular cage last of all.

"And this one is the Storazoid."

Christine peered down into the space, where something that looked like a two-meter orange mushroom stumped around the floor on six stubby legs. "It doesn't look like much."

"Oh, it's got what it takes, believe me. You'd like to try it out, I bet."

Christine looked up, a wave of tension crossing her face, followed by wide-eyed hope. "Could I, really?"

"That's really what you came for, isn't it? A session with one of my monsters?"

Christine blushed and dropped her gaze, shrugging her shoulders. "Was it that obvious?"

"For one thing, I could see the look on your face when we were talking over dinner. When I described the Mumzer's hunting methods you blushed even redder than you are now. I guessed that you were getting pretty turned on."

"Well, yeah..." A little tremble was creeping into Christine's voice.

"And I bet you're expecting that, if you submit to a tentacle monster, you won't be as tempting to that under-the-bed monster. You could look forward to a good night's sleep for once."

"That, too."

Dale chuckled. "So. Do you have a spare set of clothes?"

"Uh, no. I guess I didn't think that far ahead."

"That's all right. I've got something you can wear. The Storazoid likes a challenge, and I want to make sure to give it a good workout." Dale walked to a stairway and descended to the access level.

After a few minutes, Christine stood at the entrance to the Storazoid's chamber, dressed in a baggy "Monster Whisperer" coverall and heavy black boots. She closed her eyes and took deep breaths.

"Don't do that," said Dale. "Don't calm yourself down. Worst thing you can do. You need to amp it up. Feel the panic. You're about to step into the lair of a monster! A creature that's more than capable of having its way with you six ways a night. You've got a right to feel panic!"

"What do I do once I'm in there?"

"Whatever comes naturally." Dale nodded in the direction of the door controls. "Go ahead."

Christine touched the controls, and the door rotated and slid up. Gingerly, she stepped in, and let the door close behind her. As soon as it was sealed, Dale ran for the stairs, back up to the observation deck.

"You getting this, Vi?"

"All cameras operating normally, ma'am."

"Good work." Dale reached her perch and looked down into the chamber. Inside, Christine approached the Storazoid tentatively. Dale could just barely hear her muttering to herself, trying to steel her courage. The Storazoid stopped in the center of the room, settling its trunk down into a little patch of dirt, as if offering itself to her.

Christine drew closer. By now, she would be smelling the creature's sweet scent, the mixture of cinnamon and barbecue sauce that was unmistakably unique to the species. Her hands trembling with fear, she reached out to touch the tough orange skin.

Dale hadn't warned her about the Storazoid's hunting strategy. It would be better for her to learn on her own. About now, Christine would be feeling the Storazoid's compulsions beginning to take hold, and the hunt would begin. Dale's hand ran over her coverall, anticipation driving her to caress her own body.

The Storazoid's body rippled and convulsed, and Christine screamed as she tried to pull her hand away, but she was stuck fast. When she tried to get leverage with her other hand, it became stuck as well, and the more she struggled, the more stuck she became, until both of her arms were enmeshed right up to the elbows.

From her position at the balcony, she could see the look of puzzlement on Christine's face, the disbelief and horror that her body was no longer under her control.

Slowly, spots darkened on the Storazoid's skin, rising up out of the flesh like big brown pimples. They slowly elongated, each one producing a swaying, fifty-centimeter protuberance. As they made contact with Christine's body, they wrapped themselves around whatever body part they encountered and slowly drew her in.

"Here it comes," Dale whispered to herself. There was no reason to be quiet, as Christine certainly couldn't hear her, but she couldn't manage any more voice than that.

When a dozen or so tentacles had grabbed hold of Christine's body, the adhesive holding her arms suddenly let go. She squirmed, trying to get free of the creature's grip, but nothing would dislodge the woody stems. Her movements became more and more desperate as the helplessness of her situation truly set in.

"That's right," said Dale. "Fight it. Try to get free. It won't help, but it makes you look so much more beautiful."

More tentacles grew from the creature's surface, hauling Christine up onto its dome-shaped top. Inch by inch, they dragged her up onto the rubbery surface, deftly rolling her onto her back as they went. At every moment, every part of her body was under the creature's firm control.

No other creature in her menagerie could induce such a supreme feeling of helplessness. Its movements were so slow, so deliberate, that the victim would hardly notice the subtle chemicals sinking into every exposed patch of skin. It took nearly five minutes for the creature to get Christine into position, spread-eagled at the very apex of its body. By the time it was done, her screams had faded to whimpers and quiet moans.

The tentacles changed behaviors. Their tips secreted adhesive, sticking fast to Christine's coveralls and boots, and then pulled. The fabric strained, stretched, and finally failed. Huge rips opened in the fabric, and within moments the garment was in rags. The boots took some seconds, but the slow strength of the tendrils could not be resisted for long. When the tendrils discarded the shreds of fabric and returned to her body, they found only tender flesh.

Dale knew well how that felt. The thick stems were smooth and firm, like well-polished wood. They were done excreting the adhesive. Next, they oozed a thin, slippery substance that made the skin tingle wherever it touched. As she watched the tendrils descend upon the woman's firm, young body, she slid down the closure on her own coverall and ran her hand over her own naked flesh. Her fingertips found the little metallic knob on her own sex just as one of the Storazoid's tendrils found Christine's and pushed its way inside.

It felt good. The flesh should have been sore, but it wasn't; there was something about the Orichalc's presence in her skin that salved the soreness of the wound without dampening any of the pleasure. If anything, it felt better to play with it than if her labia had been untouched, and she found herself flicking the little stud with gusto as she watched the scene below.

A double dozen tendrils crisscrossed Christine's body, binding her firmly to the Storazoid's back, while more of them stroked the sensitive places on her body and another plunged in and out of her channel with maddening slowness. Christine was crying out again now, but instead of screams of terror, these were cries of ecstasy, ripped from her body by effects of the hyper-sensitizing ooze that was spread all over her body.

Dale clutched the balcony railing with her free hand as her muscles began to tremble. Her imagination replayed the sensations that were rocking Christine's body, the ones she had experienced dozens of times before when exercising the Storazoid. This was why she did what she did. This was why she was the Monster Whisperer: to bring this incredible, unique pleasure to as many people as she could.

Her legs failed her and she sank to her knees. Dale's eyes would no longer stay open, her mind flooded with the waves of pleasure radiating through her. With her fingers still dancing over the baby Orichalc, her mind still filled with the image of Christine slowly being fucked insensible, she collapsed into a twitching ball on the cold metal balcony floor.

Less than an hour before midnight, Christine and Dale arrived at the Omicron Theta Psi sorority house. The holovision was on in the common room, and popcorn popping in the kitchen, but many of the sisters were in their pajamas and there was a general air of sleepiness hanging about the place. Christine excused herself as soon as they arrived, and Dale found a quiet corner to set up a makeshift control room where she could monitor the cameras waiting for the under-the-bed monster to come out.

It was still an open question about whether the under-the-bed monster would prefer Ursula or Christine, tonight. It might be that Christine's experience in the Storazoid's chamber had rendered her so unpalatable that the monster would escape to find the bed of a child to lurk under, as it should have done already. It might be that its behavior would be unchanged, though Dale doubted it. More likely, the creature had a special attachment to Ursula, and with Christine's purity somewhat sullied, it would go back to tormenting its owner rather than her owner's room-mate. Time, and the cameras, would tell.

No matter how it happened, however, Dale knew she would be able to handle it.

After all—she was the Monster Whisperer.

CHAPTER TWO
UP IN ARMS

Dale double-checked the file one last time, then saved it in the outgoing data store.

"Vi, send that off to the network, please." The show wasn't nearly as explicit as usual, as the Under-the-Bed monster never did anything more intimate than grabbing an ankle or pulling at the covers but, unlike what the critics claimed, her show really was just as much about learning about these monsters as it was getting to see people getting fucked hard by huge scary monsters.

"Sent," said Vi. "Incoming message from Vince Klieberman."

"Do I really want to take it?"

"He says it's important."

"He would."

"He says it's a business proposition."

Dale took a deep breath. "All right," she said. "Put him through."

A couple hours later, Dale found herself stepping through her airlock onto Vince's ship. She waved him off from an overly affectionate hug, and demanded he get down to business.

"You and me," he said, "Together, again. Everyone will be watching." The rugged man with the impressive mustache sat back in the chair extruded by his ship specifically for his body shape. He took a puff on his expensive, real-tobacco cigar and blew the smoke in the direction of the ventilation intake near the ceiling. Ordinarily, it was bad form to smoke on board a starship, but as it was his own craft there were no grounds to complain. Those were his awards on the wall: Best Reality Holoseries, Most Eligible Bachelor three years running. Those were his covers from holomagazines like *Personal Artillery Monthly*, *Gotta Catch Em All*, and *Playbeing*. A well-polished glass cabinet in the corner held trophies from galaxy-wide competitions in marksmanship, wilderness survival, and machismo. The whole room practically sang hymns to Vince Klieberman, Monster Hunter Extraordinaire.

As he tapped off the ash, he swirled a snifter of brandy in the other hand, smiling the smile that had broken hearts across the galaxy. He was tall, fit, and wore his leather utility kilt and tight-but-not-too-tight informal shirt like he was born to them. His mustache was groomed three months ahead of galactic fashion, eschewing the narrow cut everyone else was wearing for a full growth extending back in a sweeping curve to his sideburns. His dark hair was cut short, except for one forelock that emphasized his prominent widow's peak, arching down over his face in a sweeping, architectural curve.

Dale Clearwater reminded herself that hers was one of the hearts he had broken. Ordinarily, negotiations like these would be handled between intermediaries. It was only because of their short-lived romance that she'd taken time out of her schedule to come to his ship. But, that was as much slack as she was willing to cut him.

She gave him a cocked eyebrow. "It's not my area of expertise. I don't deal with wild tentacle monsters."

"You're the Monster Whisperer," he replied, capital letters evident in his tone. "Most of the creatures you deal with started off quote-unquote 'wild' and you know it. If anyone understands the mind of a tentacle monster, it's you. You certainly know it better than those hacks at the University of New Boston."

Dale waved her hand as if to blow away a bad smell. "All right, fine. But sometimes the planets you visit don't even have spaceports, Vince. You of all people should know I don't like that lifestyle."

"I promise you'll never be more than a kilometer from a comfortable bed. Just hear me out, all right?"

Dale sighed, shaking her head. "And how do I know this isn't a ploy to boost your ratings?"

"My ratings are doing just fine, thank you." His gaze swept the wardroom, with its luxurious furnishings and prominently-displayed numerous mementos and awards, as if to say, *And here's the evidence all around you.*

"Not worried about Penny Angstrom?"

Vince waved the cigar dismissively. "She doesn't have what it takes. She'll disappear in a year or two, and I'll still be here."

"I don't know. Last I heard, she had just signed a big distribution deal with GBS."

"Pfft." Vince took another puff on the cigar. "Gone in two years. You can count on it."

"She already turned you down on this, didn't she? Too bad, she's really cute."

He shrugged. "Like I said. She doesn't have what it takes."

"Dude, that doesn't say much for your teaching skills. How long was she your protégé?"

Vince shrugged. "A year. Not long enough."

"So the rumors—"

Vince cut Dale off with a growl. "I'm not here to talk about Penny Angstrom. She's a kid. She doesn't know what she's doing. That's all I'm saying about it."

Dale double-face-palmed, then shook her head. "She's not a kid, Vince. She's twenty-one, a full adult on every Human planet."

"Yeah, well, seeing as how I taught her everything she knows, I guess I have a hard time seeing her as anything else. Anyway, I need your help. This is not a one-hunter job."

"So what is it you're hunting?"

"The starliner *Star of Mandragora* got a Phase Looper last week. They're looking for someone to clear it out."

"A Phase Looper? Are you insane? Those things can't be contained, much less domesticated. They should follow standard protocol: write off the ship and tow it into a convenient star."

"The client's techies say they've got that all worked out," said Vince. "They got this thing called a 'reality anchor' to keep the thing from shifting back and forth to hyperspace. They just need someone to prove it works."

"Great. Untested technology, the most dangerous tentacle

monster in the galaxy, and unresolved daddy issues. What part of 'fuck no' do you not understand?"

"The bounty is seven million credits."

Dale sat, merely blinking, for a few seconds. "Seven million?"

"I'll split it fifty-fifty. Plus you keep the rights to anything you record there. You know the gossip shows are going to eat it up with a power shovel."

"Ugh, don't remind me. Good reason to turn you down."

"All right. Well... you've always wanted to open that sanctuary for abandoned tentacle monsters."

Dale blinked a few more times, sighed, and said, "When do we start?"

"I shouldn't be gone longer than a couple of days. The only one that needs exercising is the Yartroan, and it's an easy one. You did great with the Storazoid, so the Yartroan shouldn't present any difficulties." Dale leaned back in the pilot's couch of Vince's ship. It was more of a cockpit than a bridge: just a tiny room filled with switches and readouts, much more hands-on than her fully automated ship. She hadn't visited Vi's bridge even once after the day it was purchased. For a moment, she envied him his interest in these details of interstellar travel. She paid little attention to sensors and navigation and all the other little technical bits, leaving them to Vi and her collection of robot drones. She would never have that much need to control her environment. Her ship was a necessary convenience, not a point of pride.

A short, high-pitched squeal erupted from the comm system. "You can count on me, Miz Clearwater. I won't let you down." The sorority girl's enthusiasm was practically dripping from the console.

"If you have any questions, just ask Vi."

Another squeal brought a crooked smile to Dale's lips. "Eee! I can't believe I'm actually doing this!"

"Believe it, Christine. But I need your head in the game, here. Glee isn't going to help with the Yartroan. Remember—"

The young woman's voice took on an enforced seriousness. "Right. Fear. Terror. Excitement. Got it."

"All right, I'm going to talk to my ship now. You go relax, maybe study up on the Yartroan."

"Yes, ma'am."

There was a click and a beep, and the measured voice of Vi, the ship's computer, came on the line. "The call is now private. What can I do for you, ma'am?"

"Two things. First: offer to show Miz Delavos the holo where I introduce the Yartroan. That's a damn hot one, and it'll give her an idea of what's in store. Then, immediately before she goes in, offer her a broadcast contract. Offer twenty percent of gross receipts on sales and licensing of her session. If she negotiates, go as high as thirty, but no more."

"She is from a fairly wealthy family, ma'am, and not one of the more liberal-minded ones, either."

"Yes, and those sheltered scions of privilege are also the most rebellious. I know the type, Vi. Trust me. She'll take it just to say she did."

"And if she doesn't accept a contract?"

Dale pursed her lips. "Record the session anyways. We'll give her a copy as a souvenir."

"Yes, ma'am. Anything else?"

"Right. Second thing: if I don't come back, and Christine ends up looking after the monsters for longer than she had originally signed up for, I want you to offer her the Yartroan in the will. It should go to a good home."

"Yes, ma'am. I've made note of it."

"See you in a couple days, Vi."

"I'm sure you will, ma'am."

Dale cut the connection. With a deep breath and a stretch, she rose from the chair and walked through the hatch into the common area of Vince's ship. He was still there, though the cigar was little more than ashes and the brandy snifter was empty.

"All set?" he said.

Dale nodded. "Schedule's clear for a few days."

"Good. The cargo pod with your luggage arrived at the airlock while you were on the comm." He leaned his elbow on the arm of the chair, then rested his chin lightly in his fingers. One eyebrow twitched ever-so-slightly upward. "Can I carry your bags somewhere for you?"

Dale strode to the airlock, and the hatch irised open. "You mean to your room?"

"Why not? We had some good times, you and I, didn't we? Maybe we'll make the scandal mags again." He held his hands up and spread apart, as if appreciating an orbital advertisement projected into the sky. "Together Again? Or Just a Fling?"

"Oh, wouldn't that be wonderful," Dale called out, unable to suppress the sarcasm. She opened the hatch to the cargo pod and retrieved her day-pack. "If there's one thing I like about being a very minor celebrity in a very niche market, it's that I don't get media snoopers poking around in my private life." She activated her camera-bot, and the ovoid machine with its numerous sensors and lenses rose up into the air, its antigrav unit humming softly.

"No such thing as bad publicity," Vince said, poking his head into the airlock.

"Yes, there is," she said, shouldering her day-pack and striding purposefully down the passageway toward the guest quarters. "And the publicity wasn't the only reason we broke up, either. As I have explained to you on multiple occasions, we're just not sexually compatible."

He followed, and leaned on the door-frame. "You can't say we didn't have some good times," he said. "Certainly seemed that way to me."

She tossed her day-pack onto the bunk, turned, and crossed her arms over her chest. "I was younger then, and naive. I didn't know who I was, or what I wanted. I had just learned what it meant to be a sexual submissive, just learned that it didn't mean being weak or shy. I hadn't learned that being a sexual dominant wasn't the same as being strong or bold."

"You won't give me a chance? I can be dominant. Watch me."
He stepped into the room and grabbed Dale around the waist,
pulling her body to his.

Dale put her arms between them, keeping him from holding
her close. Her body responded to the embrace, but she mastered
it and maintained a calm demeanor. "No, Vince. You can't be
something you're not. You throw yourself into whatever you do
fully and entirely. You never hold back, you never back down. It
makes you a great monster hunter, and it makes you a great
lover—for someone who likes that kind of thing. But it doesn't
make you a good dominant. A good dom knows when to hold
back, knows when to tease, knows when to hold his sub on a knife
edge. That's not your thing. You can try to fake it, but it's not the
same. I'm sorry. But the answer is still no." She pushed, forcing
him to either fight her, or let her go.

"And your monsters give you that?" he asked, taking her wrists
in his hands.

"It takes training, but yes. They do. It comes naturally to them."

"I'll be your monster, then. Have my way with you, fuck you
silly, and then leave you when I'm done. How about that? Train
me. Show me what you need."

Dale laughed, letting him push her arms back against the
bulkhead, letting him bring his fierce expression nose to nose.
"Oh, Vince. You will never be domesticated. Not ever. You are wild
and untamed, just like the worlds where you are most comfortable.
I would never want you to be one of my monsters. It would be a
betrayal of who you are."

Vince stared into Dale's eyes, jaw muscles clenching.

"You know I'm right," she said. "Deep down, you know it. And
if we fuck that way, it would be a betrayal of who I am, as well."

He let go and pushed away, his face shadowed. "You're a real
piece of work, you know that?"

"I know it better than you ever will, Vince."

"I will never stop wanting you, Dale Clearwater."

"Just because you want something, doesn't mean you should have it."

Dale woke to Vince's voice on the other side of her door. "Wake up, Monster Girl. We'll be out of hyperspace in about an hour, and we need to get prepped."

"Okay."

"Oh, no. Don't give me that. I know how you wake up. Out of bed."

"Five more minutes."

A series of beeps came from the door, and it opened.

"You used the override," Dale mumbled, rolling onto her back. She cracked her eyes open to see Vince staring down at her, and she realized that perhaps sleeping in the nude hadn't been a great idea as his face broke out in a huge grin.

"I used the override." Taking one last look, Vince sighed, and turned away. He grabbed a robe from the room's little closet and tossed it over his back onto the bed. "Get dressed and meet me in the common room so I can show you the gear."

Dale pulled the blanket over her body. "I hate you."

"Or you can just meet me in the common room. All the same to me." Vince strutted down the passageway, turning his back on Dale's grumbled insults.

When she finally arrived, Vince greeted her with a cup of coffee and a hot breakfast. Dale accepted both, gratefully. The easy chairs had been replaced with a dining set, extruded from the programmable plastic of the floor. Even in this somewhat more practical mode, the furniture was quite comfortable, adapting to Dale's body as she sat down.

After the last morsels disappeared, she said, "Damn you for being such a good cook."

He laughed. "Why is that?"

"Because for the first time in a year and a half, I love you right now."

His face brightened. "Really?"

"Don't worry, it won't last. You said you had some gear to show me?"

"Ah, right." Vince snapped his fingers and stood up briefly, retrieved a backpack-sized device, and laid it on the table. The thing looked like an oversized tablet computer, except it was at least ten centimeters thick, with a carrying handle on one end, and straps so it could be carried like a backpack. "This is a portable reality anchor. It's got a short-range force field generator, tuned to project into both normal space and hyperspace. It can also raise a barrier between the two dimensions, preventing any movement back and forth."

"Great," said Dale. "Let's try it out."

"We can't. It won't work while we're anywhere near an active hyperspace engine. But there's a simulation mode we can use." Vince flipped a switch, and a hologram appeared in midair over the device. It showed a schematic of the room they were in, a good portion of the rest of the ship, and figures representing Dale and Vince, all outlined in green light.

"It's pretty simple. You're looking at the short range scanner. It shows everything going on in normal space, and hyperspace, within about a twenty meter radius. Anything in green is normal space, red is hyperspace. These controls here—" he said, indicating spots on the touchscreen, "—activate the basic protections. This one activates a barrier that prevents travel to or from hyperspace within its range. This one activates a spherical barrier that prevents movement in or out of the device's range, whether in hyperspace or not."

"Sounds like a pretty effective capture tool right there. Just bring it to within range, activate both of those, and it's trapped."

"It might be that easy if it were well-behaved, but it's a wild monster. For one thing, the barrier won't form if there's a material object in the way. It'll just leave a hole: a hole that a Phase Looper could slip out of. That means we have to have the whole thing inside the field in order to capture it. That means distracting it, getting its attention."

"Wait a minute. Hold on—get its attention? I see where this is going. I'm going to be bait?"

"I can't think of anyone better."

Dale shook her head. "I should have asked you the plan before I got on board."

"Don't worry, I'm not done. Here, for one thing..." he reached into the hologram and snapped his fingers inside one of the figures. It immediately glowed red, then expanded into a sphere. "That's a failsafe. It creates a skin-tight force field, then expands outwards into a sphere. Anything that's got you would have to immediately let go."

"That's a little better, assuming you can actually operate the thing. What if it's got both of us?"

"You know how these things work. Tentacle monsters aren't attracted to people like me. I just don't get afraid enough for them. That's what makes me a good hunter."

"You say that like every monster's the same."

"That's been my experience, and I've seen as many different kinds as you. Possibly more. Here, look; there's more tricks in here, too." Vince clapped his hands within the projection, and a plane of light appeared where his hands came together. Then, as he pushed and prodded at the plane, it curled into a tube, rolled into a ball, and stretched into a long spike. "Whatever shape I need to capture the thing, I can make."

"All right," said Dale, "I can see how this can work. It's risky, but it can work. One thing, though-Vince, I'm putting my life in your hands here. You know that, right?"

"Don't worry," he said. "Nothing's going to go wrong."

Dale swore and shook her head. "You had to go and say that, didn't you?"

"What?"

Dale returned to her room and powered up her camera-bot. The white ovoid followed her as she walked backwards toward the cockpit.

"Hey, folks, we've got a special treat for you today. I've been invited by renowned monster hunter, Vince Klieberman, to assist with a very delicate operation. The starliner *Star of Mandragora* has fallen victim to a Phase Looper, one of the most dangerous tentacle monsters known."

Arriving at the bridge, the camera-bot turned its lenses toward the window, beyond which the massive, cigar-shaped hull of their destination loomed. It was sleek and shiny, studded with numerous windows and observation decks, each of which sparkled with illumination.

Vince scowled at one of his many screens.

Dale sat down next to him in the copilot's couch. "What's wrong?"

"According to the client, the *Star of Mandragora* is supposed to be powered down. Gave me codes to transmit to the computer to restart gravity and life support."

"They're not working?"

"No, it looks like they've already been used. Ship's powered up, and looks like it has been for a while."

"Maybe they forgot to shut them off when the ship was evacuated?"

"Or maybe someone got here before us."

Vince piloted his little ship along the ship's hull, past the rings of hyperdrive engines, then angled it toward the broad opening of the port docking bay. He swore. Dale shook her head, making a note to herself to edit that out before the recording went to the network. "What's wrong?"

"That's what's wrong," he said. As the aft docking bay of the *Star of Mandragora* swung into view, Vince pointed to the sleek little cutter nestled into one of the docking cradles. "That's Penny's ship."

"And does she have one of these fancy reality anchor things?"

Vince piloted his ship into place alongside Penny's, hastily enough that Dale was almost rocked out of the couch. "Doesn't matter. As far as I'm concerned, this just changed from a hunt to a rescue."

He started to jump out of his seat, but Dale put her hand on his arm. "Vince, I've met Penny. Several times, in fact, back when she was your protégé. She seemed pretty sharp to me. Does she have a reality anchor?"

"No. Well... maybe."

"Then why don't we see if she's activated it. That's a huge ship out there. Searching the whole thing is going to be impossible."

Vince took a deep breath, and returned to his seat uneasily. He fiddled with the ship's controls, bringing up a new display on one of the monitors.

"Hyperwave scan," he said. "Not very good resolution, I'm afraid. This thing is made to detect starships, not tiny little hand-held devices."

Dale pointed to the screen. "There. That dot. Is that a reality anchor?"

Vince typed in a few more commands, and the screen magnified the spot. "Yeah, might be."

"And it's moving. That means Penny has activated it, and she's mobile, right?"

"Most likely."

"Then there's no reason to panic. We can assume that she's relatively safe."

"For now," said Vince, with a dark edge to his voice. He brought up a schematic of the Star of Mandragora and overlaid it on the scanner. "Looks like she's on her way to the auxiliary control center. If we hurry, we can catch up with her there."

He rose from the seat and proceeded to the airlock, grabbing a belt heavy with a dozen different devices, and slung the reality anchor over his shoulder. His own camera-bot, a smaller and less versatile model than Dale's, rose from a cradle in the airlock to follow him as the hatch opened onto a broad hallway lit by red emergency lights.

Dale followed, hurrying to match his long strides. "So how

did Penny know about this job? And how did she get a reality anchor? You gave me the impression this was brand new tech."

He shrugged. "Maybe the client went to her, too."

"Vince. What are you not telling me?"

"Okay! Okay... maybe she came to me with this job in the first place. And maybe I told her she shouldn't do it."

"So we're basically stabbing her in the back, here."

Vince turned, grim-faced, and held a finger in Dale's face. "No. She is not up to this. Not alone. And if I went behind her back to the client, it's for her own safety." His little camera bot hovered just over his shoulder, as if joining his admonition.

Dale pushed his finger away. "I'm beginning to see why Penny struck out on her own."

Vince whirled and continued down the corridor, grumbling to himself. Dale followed, giving him a few meters of space.

"Great. The most dangerous tentacle monster in known space, untested technology, unresolved daddy issues, and outright lies. What else could go wrong?"

Vince rounded a corner, entering a wide, canyon-like plaza with elevators running up each side. Storefronts covered the walls. With their lights off and signs darkened, there was little to differentiate them from each other, but Dale could see clothing shops, a pharmacy, a day spa, and, toward the far end of the concourse, a *Monster Massage* franchise.

She stopped and addressed her camera bot, pointing at the sign. "What do you want to bet they made no provisions at all for the welfare of their tentacle monster?"

"Dale!" shouted Vince, rapidly widening the space between them. "Keep up. We don't have time for your soapbox."

"Yeah? And how many Kritzoans have you caught for *Monster Massage*, huh? Don't think I didn't hear about it when they started sponsoring your show."

"Yes, and I dropped them again, if you hadn't noticed. As a matter of fact, it was Penny who told me about the investigation into their handling practices. Remember Penny? Now come on!"

Vince proceeded down another broad corridor, then stopped in front of a heavy duty hatch, its sturdy utilitarian shape completely at odds with the smooth, sculpted look of the rest of the deck. "This emergency seal isn't supposed to be closed." He strode to the wall and punched the buttons on a small control console next to the hatch. It made a soft buzz, but nothing happened. He tried again, with the same result. "I don't understand," he said. "That's the override code. Why isn't it working?"

A panicked female voice echoed through the concourse. "I don't know! They're not working for me, either. I think the Phase Looper did something to the ship's computer!"

Vince growled and punched more keys on the panel, then slammed the side of his fist against the bulkhead. "Penny! Where are you?"

"Auxiliary control room," replied the disembodied voice. "A few levels above you. Can you make it back to your ship? I'm on the Phase Looper's trail, I but I don't have time to fiddle around with the computer."

Dale took Vince's arm in her hands. "You have to admit, she doesn't seem to need rescuing."

He pulled away, hunted along the wall until he found a flip-handle, and pulled a maintenance panel away from the wall. "We're getting through this door, one way or another." Among the maze of pipes and conduits, he found a red lever labeled MANUAL EMERGENCY SEAL OPERATION and DANGER: DO NOT UNSEAL HATCH IF HULL BREACH ALARM IS ACTIVE. He grabbed it, pulled it out of its bracket, and pumped it up and down.

Dale put her hand on Vince's shoulder. "Stop a moment."

"Fuck you."

"No, seriously, stop. I think I heard something."

Vince stopped, cocking an ear toward the concourse. "I don't hear anything." Then his eyebrow cocked as a faint, distant thunk echoed through the little plaza. "What was that?"

"Sounded like another hatch opening. Penny? Are you opening hatches somewhere?"

"No! They're coming open by themselves. Vince, you have to get back to your ship. I think it's releasing the Kritzoan from the *Monster Massage*."

Another thunk echoed, this one louder, closer; after that, a low thrumming vibration in the air, a moan that was halfway between heard and felt.

"Oh, no," said Dale.

A shape lurched into view, lights shimmering off of a viscous surface that flowed out into the concourse, and the humming grew louder. Spheres floated in its semi-transparent flesh, shifting about as it oozed forward on massive pseudopods.

"I got this," said Vince, unslinging the reality anchor from his shoulder and activating it. He touched the control to activate the outer barrier, and a field of force snapped into place, holding the amorphous monster out of their little piece of corridor. "Dale, stay here and make sure this thing doesn't get to us while I get this door open." He set the device on the floor.

"That's not a Phase Looper," said Dale as she knelt down with the reality anchor. "That's just an ordinary Kritzoan. Hardly a danger to anyone." She felt a tingle go through her body as she watched the beast gathering its body against the force field.

"Yeah, well, whisper to it if you like, but I doubt it's in much of a good mood after being left alone for four days. Sorry to spoil your fun, but I think we're better off if we can get on the other side of this door from it. That barrier field will hold it back just as well as it will the Phase Looper, but we can't have it tagging along."

The Kritzoan surged up against the barrier, its protoplasmic body undulating like flowing molasses. "At least it seems healthy," said Dale, watching it throw pseudopods against the barrier, seeking any hole or breach to ooze through to its prey.

The reality anchor beeped, zorped, and buzzed. A warning message appeared on its screen. "Uh, Vince? What does 'cross-phase interference' mean?"

"What?" shouted Vince. He knelt at the reality anchor and tapped on the screen, bringing up a display of incomprehensible technobabble. "There's a hyperspace field coming up. I think it's the *Star of Mandragora's*. Must be malfunctioning, along with the doors."

Dale stood up, fighting the sexual anticipation that the sight of the monster was bringing on. "Vince, you're the big bad monster-hunter. Don't you have something to deal with it?"

The answer never came. With a pop, the force barrier fell and the Kritzoan's amorphous flesh surged into the corridor, sweeping over Dale and Vince, engulfing them in thick pseudopods. Vince screamed, though it sounded more like frustration and anger than terror.

"Try to stay calm!" Dale shouted. "It's looking for agitation."

"I know what it wants!" Vince growled.

The ooze slid under Dale's coverall, causing the baggy fabric to balloon outwards. The goo was chilly enough that she shivered as it flowed up her thighs and over her breasts. The creature hummed, squeezing her body rhythmically, sensuously, flowing over the muscles of her arms and legs in waves.

In what seemed like middle distance, she could hear Vince shouting at the creature, commanding it to get off him, leave him alone, but Dale was completely immobilized. She was helpless to prevent it wrapping one long arm after another around his body, wrapping itself around him, layer upon layer.

Then she lost sight of him. She was immersed in the Kritzoan, with just her face above its surface, as the creature squeezed and caressed every inch of her body. She tried to focus, to remember any detail that might help them out of its grasp, but its rubbery embrace was too distracting, too intense to ignore.

A deep hum filled her ears as the Kritzoan entered the second phase of its routine, producing strong, low-frequency vibrations against her skin, focused on the most sensitive places. It could taste her sweat, she knew, smell her breath, feel her arousal building. It reacted, shifting its attentions, strengthening them, intensifying the stimulation. A ring of its flesh formed around each nipple, throbbing in time with her heartbeat, and a hard knob formed between her legs, pressed against her sex. More knots formed, sucking her toes, rubbing the backs of her knees, kneading the muscles between her shoulder blades. Some of them faded away, moving elsewhere, but the ones that found a positive response intensified. Nothing else felt like a Kritzoan, nothing else held its prey so securely, so completely. No other monster was so gentle while being so inexorable.

She could hear Vince growling and struggling, fighting to keep free of the creature, but the thought didn't penetrate far into her consciousness. The sensations were just too intense to ignore. *He'll be okay*, she told herself. *He'll be okay.* The creature's vibrations echoed inside her like she was empty, as if she were the pipes of an organ, and the Kritzoan was the bellows, blowing out any other thought.

Vibration—there was something about that. Something about sound, or was it something else? Hard to remember. Hard to think. She had slipped into that insidious bliss to which she was so prone when she was the sexual plaything of a creature whose power could not be denied. Orgasm convulsed her body, ripping a cry of ecstasy from her throat, but the Kritzoan did not relent. Instead, its grip intensified, stretching her arms and legs back behind her. The monster was the only thing she felt. She was totally helpless in its grip.

There was something, she was sure of it. In fact, she had taught it to people. Back before the show, back when she was a monster trainer. What was it? The thought darted about the dark recesses of her mind, just out of reach.

Above her, the camera bots buzzed and hovered, their lenses and microphones recording everything, tantalizingly out of reach, and useless to assist in any event. Neither of them were capable of broadcasting a signal outside of the ship, or had any kind of manipulator with which it could render assistance. They triggered Dale's exhibitionist streak, making the whole situation even more complicated.

Penny's voice came over the PA system again, hoarse and throaty. "Listen, you guys aren't in any danger at the moment."

Her words came slowly, distractedly. "I got the hyperdrives shut down, but I need to make sure the Phase Looper isn't going to get you. My reality anchor should start up properly now, and once I have dealt with the beast, I'll—Gnrk!" The woman's voice cut off suddenly, with a choking noise that chilled Dale's ardor in a moment.

"Penny!" shouted Vince. "Penny!"

A faint hum played from the intercom, evidence of an open circuit, but no voice came across it. Dale's eyes snapped open.

The Kritzoan should have noticed the change in Dale's response; it should have been a signal to it that it was not going to get the kind of result it wanted, but it increased its efforts instead. She tried to relax, tried to go limp in its grip, but Dale knew the most likely reason for Penny to have suddenly gone silent was that the Phase Looper—one that had never been trained, a wild intelligence whose motives could only be guessed—had gotten her. Chilled to her deepest core, she found it impossible not to give the Kritzoan the kind of terrified feedback that its true nature craved, and its grip never wavered.

"Vince! Stop shouting!"

"It's got Penny!" he screamed, panic bringing it nearly to a shriek.

"You have to calm down! The Kritzoan is feeding on your fear!"

"I can't help it! It could be killing her and it's my fault!" Dale felt the flesh of the Kritzoan shake as Vince thrashed and fought against its immense bulk. "I have to do something!"

Dale's mind cleared, and she remembered, finally, the detail that had eluded her. She was in the grip of a Kritzoan, an amorphous variety of tentacle monster favored by the *Monster Massage* franchise for its ravenous sexual appetite and trainable nature.

"Vince, have you got an arm free? Can you reach the wall?"

"Yes," he grunted, "But not for much longer!"

"Bang something against the wall," she said, "Even if it's just your fist. Use a rhythm of three and two. That's the usual stand-down signal they teach to Kritzoans."

Dale heard faint thumps, but they had no organization to them, no pattern.

"Like this!" Dale shouted. "One two three... five six... one two three... five six." The Kritzoan continued its ministrations, fighting her agitation with its attempts to stimulate her, but nothing she did could get it to let go.

"Bloody amateurs," she grumbled, "Don't know how to train a simple Kritzoan right!" It was a crime, really, that this tentacle monster had been left in such a state.

The thumps on the wall took on the correct rhythm on the fifth or sixth try, and the Kritzoan retreated, leaving Dale and Vince in separate piles of ruined clothing. The pressure of its body invading their coveralls had ripped them wide open, leaving the garments virtually useless.

Dale knelt, catching her breath, while Vince finished ratcheting the door open. She decided not to comment on his frankly impressive hard-on. No good would come of it, and she had always known he was a danger junkie. Still, she couldn't help taking a moment to check him out. They had been naked together many times, of course, but the sight hadn't lost any appeal. His body didn't have the extreme bulk from shaper nanotreatments. His muscles had that honest, straightforward look that came from using them in real work. There was even something honest about his thick patch of pubic hair, especially about the way it thinned out and ran up his belly into his chest hair.

Dale grabbed the reality anchor and followed him through the heavy hatch. "What about your other equipment?" she asked.

Vince waved a palm-sized disk in his left hand. "This is the only one that will be of any use," he said. They came to a maintenance hatch and found a ladder behind it. "Communicator," he said setting one hand and both feet to climbing. "We'll use it if we have to."

"If we have to? To me, this sounds like a terrific time to call for help." Dale slipped the reality anchor's straps over her shoulders and started up behind him, with the camera bot preceding her up the shaft. It was only just barely narrow enough to fit in the narrow space, which was crowded with pipes and conduits. Still, it kept its holographic eyes dutifully pointed down at her, catching every move she made for posterity.

"We wouldn't be calling for help," he said. "We would be calling the Patrol for a quick tow into the nearest star. It would mean that not only had it gotten Penny, but us too."

"The authorities won't help us?"

"Not when there's a Phase Looper loose. We're well outside of standard operating procedure here." He tapped one of the pipes running up the wall. "We're getting closer."

"Why do you say that?" said Dale, starting to feel a little winded from the climb. Her camera focused on her heaving chest, but Vince's was pointed upwards, over his shoulder.

Vince glanced down and touched a pipe on the side of the shaft with his toe. The metal was crumpled, squeezed off by an incredibly powerful grip. "Phase Loopers do that," he said. "If you see that kind of damage, it almost certainly means a Phase Looper has been by."

As they climbed, Dale saw more and more of the crushed pipes. The thought that the shaft she was climbing in could also be thought of as another kind of pipe brought on an uncomfortable feeling in her stomach. She swallowed it down, eyeing the metal walls around her and hoping they were a good deal stronger than the power conduits.

After climbing another three or four levels, Dale's arms were burning with exertion. "Vince, can you carry this thing for a while? It's getting heavy."

"A little farther," he said, opening a hatch in the side of the shaft. "We're here. This is where the sensors said that Penny was operating her reality anchor." He stepped through, then turned to help Dale in.

"This doesn't look good," said Dale, surveying the room. The auxiliary control center had six consoles arranged in an inward-facing circle, with a holographic display column in the center. The column was smashed and useless, and the consoles sparked and smoked. A reality anchor, no doubt Penny's, sat on top of one of the consoles, its screen reading "Reset complete. Resume program?"

"No, it doesn't." Vince activated Penny's reality anchor, immediately throwing up the perimeter barrier, and then widened the perspective on the holographic display, scanning for Penny.

"What does a Phase Looper look like on one of these things?" Dale asked.

"Don't know," said Vince. "But I think we'll know it when we see...There." He pointed to a spot a few dozen meters away down the main corridor. "There she is. In that observation lounge."

The figure was indistinct, but Dale could make out a human shape outlined in green, with lines of red running to a bulbous form nearby. The shape struggled in the creature's grip.

"What are you waiting for?" she said. "Save her. Do that snappy thing."

"We're not in range. Come on." He grabbed the second reality anchor and ran for the door. For a moment, Dale worried that the portal wouldn't open for him, but it functioned well enough for him to get through, and the two of them raced down the corridor.

Still not completely recovered from the climb, Dale was completely exhausted by the time they caught up to Penny and the Phase Looper. The lithe young woman was naked, suspended between the carpeted floor and a domed skylight showing the star-scattered blackness of space. Dozens of glowing bands wrapped tightly around her legs, ankles, arms, and torso. There were even circles of light wrapped around her breasts and, more worrying, around her neck. The rings were not being gentle. She screamed in panic as they squeezed and shook her violently. Her long, platinum-blond hair waved around her head as she fought, uselessly, against the creature's remorseless grip. Bruises showed on her pale skin around the places where the bands had grabbed her.

"I'm going to have to lower the barrier to get her into range," said Vince, setting the reality anchor down.

"No. Wait, look." She pointed to the display. "That thing has lots more arms it could be using. Here." She clapped her hands inside the display, creating a flat barrier in front of them, then used her hands to form it into a second bubble inside the first. "There. Now we can lower the outer barrier and get her into range."

Vince lowered the outermost barrier and slid the device along the floor. In the display, the red lines probed at the barriers with what seemed like frantic intent. When Penny's body was fully within range, Vince snapped his fingers and a white bloom of light appeared around her body, and Penny dropped to the deck, sucking in air. Dale immediately erected the outermost barrier, and the Phase Looper withdrew, scooting rapidly out of range of the reality anchor's sensors. Vince ran to Penny's side.

"I'm okay," she said, in between gasps. "Just a little, heh, shaken up. Thank you." She wrapped her arms around him and squeezed.

Vince nearly jumped out of Penny's grasp. "Dude! You're naked. No naked hugs."

Dale fiddled with the reality anchor, making sure the barriers were secure, then turned to help Penny onto one of the lounge chairs that projected from the walls. Under normal circumstances the elaborately upholstered chairs gave passengers a comfortable view of space through the skylight windows overhead. Dale was more worried about any injuries Penny might have. "You sure you're okay? Nothing broken or strained?"

The young woman stretched and probed. "Just bruises. Nothing serious."

"All right." Dale straightened up and glanced at Vince to include him in the conversation. "I think we need to get back to our ships. We're safe now, but I don't know for how long, and that thing's still out there."

"No," said Vince and Penny, in unison.

"I'm going to catch that thing," said Vince.

"The hell you are!" said Penny, sitting up. "It was my contract in the first place. I had everything under control until you butted in."

"Oh, like you had the Kritzoan? And the emergency seals?"

Penny leaped up from the chair and gave Vince a shove in the chest that didn't move him very much. "Are you even listening?

This is my business. Mine. I'm the one Galactic came to. I invited you because I thought you could help, not because I wanted you to take it over."

"Help! You need help, Missy, but I'm not a psych-med. The help you need, I can't give. You get back to your ship and let me handle this."

"If you hadn't noticed, I was the one that thing was shaking like a chew-toy! You're the one who's going to clear out." Her eyes narrowed and she peered at the reality anchor's display. "That thing and I have unfinished business."

"That's exactly why you need to get off this ship," said Vince. "Your head's not in the game. You're letting your temper get to you."

Penny gave him a cruel sneer. "Ha! You're not exactly mister self-control, Mister K."

Dale growled with exasperation and stepped between them. "All right. Before you two lovebirds need to get a room, I've got some observations to make that might bear on your decisions. So, why don't you both calm down for a few, listen, and we'll make a plan that all three of us can agree on, huh?"

The two backed away from each other and turned to face Dale. "All right," said Vince, after a moment. "What have you got?"

Dale took a deep breath and lowered her voice, using a quieter tone to calm down the conversation. "First, the Phase Looper was acting strangely, at least for tentacle monsters in general. The damage to the ship, for example. It looks severe, but we still have power, and heat, and air. It clearly has the ability to wreck the whole ship, but it didn't."

"It smashed the hell out of the control room," said Penny.

"Well, you said it had taken control of the doors." Dale observed. "How did it do that?"

Penny shook her head. "I don't know. I didn't see it."

"Well, we don't know a lot about Phase Loopers. It's possible it has some way to interface directly with the computers. If it didn't know exactly what it was doing, that wouldn't have been a gentle process."

Vince squinted and looked back in the direction of the control room. "That should take a bit more sophistication than you'd find in a tentacle monster."

"I don't know how it happened, it just did," said Penny.

"It makes sense to me," said Dale. "Tentacle monsters are a lot more intelligent than we often give them credit for, which brings me to my second observation. For all of its fury, it could have done a lot worse. It could have snapped your neck, or suffocated you, but it didn't."

Vince shrugged and shook his head. "That doesn't tell us much."

"It tells us it wants something from us. One thing that's true of tentacle monsters across the galaxy, is that they gain energy from human emotions. Most of them feed off of a form of sexual ecstasy, usually found only in certain kinds of submissives, but there are also variations, like Under-the-Bed monsters and their preference for scaring innocents."

Vince rolled his eyes. "We're all experts, here, Dale."

"In that case you noticed, as I did, that the Phase Looper, with all three of us available for its attentions, went after the sexual dominant among us, rather than the submissive."

"What?" Vince looked from Dale to Penny and back again. "What are you talking about?"

"Trust a sub," said Dale. "I know one when I see one." She nodded in Penny's direction. "Didn't you hear the arousal in her voice as she watched the Kritzoan have its way with me?"

Penny shrugged. "Guilty as charged. I mean, it's even in my profile on Fetish Galaxy. Not exactly a secret."

"Fetish Galaxy?" Vince shook his head. "I don't want to hear this. Besides, all this psychic energy stuff is nonsense. Completely unscientific."

"No, she's right," said Penny. "If only in terms of an as-if construct. It may not be an actual measurable force, but thinking about it as if it were makes it easier to understand. Thing is, though, that monster definitely wasn't acting submissive."

Dale raised a finger. "I think it was. I think it was being a brat.

Acting out, trying to get you to punish it. It knew you were psychically capable of giving it the kind of energy it wanted, but that was the only way it knew to tell you."

"Huh." The corner of Penny's mouth turned up. "A submissive tentacle monster. I kind of like the sound of that."

"None of this changes anything," said Vince.

"I think it does," said Penny. "I think it's pretty clear that my original plan makes all kinds of sense. With a functional reality anchor, I'll be able to draw the creature out, confine it, and make it my bitch. Just like it wants."

"Oh, no. There's no way I'm letting you go into this alone," said Vince.

"She won't be," said Dale. A shiver of anticipation ran down her spine.

"You?" asked Vince, making a sour face. "You and her?"

Dale glanced at Penny. "If it's all right with you."

Penny blinked. "Uh, who, me? Oh, yeah. Sure, that's fine."

"I'm going to be the example. Show the creature what's what, how it all works."

"Wait, wait. You two are going to have kinky sex in order to get the Phase Looper to attack?" Vince shook his head. "This is bugnuts."

"It makes perfect sense," said Penny. "It's the best way to draw it out."

"I understand, Vince," said Dale. "You're upset because you don't like to think of Penny in a sexual way. You don't have to be part of this if you don't want to."

Vince growled and tangled his fingers in his hair, as if to yank it out by the roots.

"You know I'm right," said Dale.

"Fine. Fine!" he shouted, stomping over to where his reality anchor lay. "But I'm going to be keeping an eye on you. If anything goes wrong, I'm stepping in and stopping this." He sat cross-legged, with his back to Penny and Dale, facing the holographic display.

Penny scooped up her own reality anchor and looked around.

The observation lounge was a fairly large room, elliptical in shape, with rows of comfortable chairs and small tables with tasteful abstract sculptures. She walked toward the other end of the room, and when she came to the shimmering outer barrier, she said, "All right, let us out, Vic."

Without a word from the man, another barrier formed inside the first, and then the outer one popped out of existence.

The two women hurried toward the far end of the room, where Penny set her reality anchor down on a low table and knelt down in front of it. She powered it up quickly, and erected a spherical barrier around both of them.

"Safe-word?" she asked.

"Mandrake," said Dale. She shuddered and wrapped her arms around her belly. "Not that I usually need one." She gestured to her camera-bot, directing it to a spot where it would get a good view of the proceedings.

"Good to have one anyways. So—I imagine bondage is one of your things, right?"

"Yeah, but we don't really have anything we can use."

Penny tapped the reality anchor. "Oh, yes we do. I've been thinking about the possibilities ever since I got hold of this, believe me."

Dale purred, her own imagination sparking. "Ah, then yes. Definitely bondage."

"Pain?"

"A bit," said Dale. "Not too much. Slaps, spanks. That kind of thing."

"Humiliation?"

"No. Not my thing."

"Ah, too bad. I want to try that someday."

"Someday?" Dale cocked her head. "How many times have you done this?"

An anguished growl came from across the room. "Argh! I can't listen to this. I'm going to watch for the Looper somewhere I can't hear you!" Vince scooped up his reality anchor and stormed out.

Dale and Penny shrugged to each other. On Penny's reality anchor display, the bubble representing the fields projected by Vince's unit slid out one of the corridors and into one of the nearby staterooms.

"His loss," said Dale. "So. You've done this before, right?"

"Yeah. Of course."

"You've been the dominant in a BDSM scene, I mean."

"Well..."

Dale's smile spread across her face. "You haven't."

"I have!" She put her fists on her hips. "Just not with a woman. Or anyone older than me. Or," she looked up at the ceiling and finished softly, "...with someone like you."

"Like me?"

"Stars, this is embarrassing."

"Best to just say it. If we're going to be putting on a bondage show it's best not to have this kind of secret."

Penny closed her eyes, took a deep breath, and then blurted out, "I had a crush on you."

"When Vince and I were a couple?"

"Yeah. I was just nineteen, crazy about tentacle monsters, and here you were knowing everything there was to know about them, and I thought you were pretty and smart and daring and I wanted to be you so bad but you were with Vince and okay I'm going to shut up now." She shook her head, blushing.

"And you don't have that crush now?"

"Yes! Yes, I do."

Dale bent down, put her hand on Penny's shoulder, and whispered in her ear. "And now you get to do all the things you imagined doing."

Penny moaned.

"Tell me what you want me to do."

Penny took another deep breath, flexed her hands, and pointed to a spot across the table from her. "Stand there."

Dale took the spot, standing at attention.

"Raise your hands. Spread them out a bit, wider than shoulder width apart."

Dale lifted her arms over her head. When Penny clapped her hands in the reality anchor display, Dale felt a force field pop into existence at the level of her wrists. She looked up, and saw the shimmering semi-transparent energy field shrink down until it was no more than a rectangular bar with two holes exactly the right size for her wrists. It didn't feel like a physical object. It didn't have well-defined edges, for one thing, and it went far enough up her wrists that she couldn't bend or twist her lower arms at all. It was simultaneously more immobilizing than it should have been, and less constricting. There was no pressure, just an even force that perfectly matched any motion she tried to make.

Penny giggled. "Oh, this is perfect. Spread your legs."

Without protest, Dale widened her stance until her feet were as far to the sides as they would go. Penny clapped her hands, and shortly there was another force field holding her ankles in place just as firmly as her hands.

"Do you think he can feel it through the force fields?" Penny asked.

"You mean the Looper? I don't know. Maybe he can smell arousal. The force fields are gas-permeable."

Penny worked some more with the reality anchor, connecting the two bars she had created with vertical pillars, forging them into a single shape. Dale could see herself, in miniature, directly in front of her in the holographic display.

"Oh, look," said Penny, pointing to the holographic display. "I think he's interested."

On the very edge of the scanner's detection range, a few threads of red could be seen tentatively moving about in hyperspace, in the direction opposite the one Vince had sulked off to.

"Let's see if this will draw him out." Penny rose to her feet, and walked around the table to stand behind Dale. "Everything comfortable?" she asked. "Nothing binding or pinching?"

"It's fine."

"Good. Because I wouldn't want to cause you any unintended pain."

A sharp sound reached Dale's ears a moment before the sharp

pain of a hard smack on the buttocks, followed by another, and another in quick succession, until Dale cried out. "Ow!"

"It's too bad I don't have a gag for you," said Penny, delivering another swat. "And stop wiggling."

"If you gagged me, we'd need a different safe word. And you're hitting the same spot over and over."

"Quiet! No insolence from the sub."

Dale sighed. "Mandrake." Penny came back around into Dale's field of view with a disappointed look on her face.

"It's okay," said Dale. "I just need to explain a few things."

"You can tell I don't know what I'm doing, can't you."

"How will you know if nobody tells you? I think you should mix up the sensations more. Caresses in with the spankings. If I know what you're going to do next, I can prepare for it. Also, it's not just about causing pain, it's pain mixed with pleasure. So, there needs to be some nice things in there too, caresses and other kinds of touch." Dale felt a little funny giving a lecture like this when spread-eagled and naked, but she carried on anyways. "For me, the big turn-on is being helpless, a toy for you to do whatever nasty things you want to do to me."

"So—you need me to do things."

"Right! I'm okay with a lot of things, but some of them need to feel good too, you know?"

"Gotcha."

"Look at it this way: here I am, the object of your crush, on display for you. You can have your way with me. Don't you want to do anything else but hit me?"

"Right. Okay. Anything else?"

"That covers it for now. If I think of anything else, I'll safe word again, and we can talk some more."

Penny nodded. "Can I start again?"

"Yes, please do."

"All right." She squinted a bit, thoughtfully. "From now on, I don't want you to say anything, not a word or a sound, unless it's your safe word. Understood?"

Dale couldn't help smiling. "Yes."

"Ah! You couldn't even make it five seconds." Penny stepped to the side and gave Dale another swat, this time on her left cheek, and then followed it up with a gentle caress. "Let's not try to earn another one of those, eh?"

This time, Dale nodded.

"Good. I'm sure you'll fail, but it's good of you to try." Penny put her arm around Dale's belly and pulled herself close. Dale could feel Penny's warm body all along her back, and relaxed into the embrace, suppressing a purr of contentment.

"You were right," Penny purred, stroking her hand up Dale's stomach and ribs. "I have wanted to do this since I first met you." Her other arm joined the first, sliding down. "I wished I was a monster so I could hold you all over."

Dale bit her lip as Penny's fingertips brushed one nipple, bringing it to tight peak. The other hand swept down over her shaved mons and stroked Dale's outer lips, making silence even more difficult.

"You're holding back," Penny whispered in her ear. "Good." Then the caress on her breast turned into a deep squeeze narrowing down to a sharp pinch, just as the fingers lower down slipped into the folds of Dale's sex.

She couldn't hold back any more. She let out a soft moan.

The hand between her legs delivered a sudden slap to her pubic mound, eliciting a gasp of surprise. The slaps to her bottom had been painful, but this hurt more, and the surprise of it made it even more shocking.

"You were doing so well," whispered Penny, one hand still gripping the flesh of Dale's breast, "But here you are making more noise." The next slap came on Dale's flank, a hard, full-force smack. "You're going to make my hand sore if you keep this up."

Dale choked back another cry, holding as still as she could. Inside, waves of emotion coursed through her. She was falling into a bit of a familiar receptive trance but, at the same time, she felt a surge of pride that she had guided her young lover to this point.

Perhaps she wasn't a complete innocent, but Dale had no doubt that this moment would be a significant one in Penny's sexual life. The slaps and spanks, the caresses and gropes, none of it had half the effect of that one thought. "Yes," she wanted to say, "Take me, you wonderful little domme." But she held it in, letting the thought permeate her mind as Penny's hands took possession of her body.

Yet there was still something missing. This was nice, this was very nice, but Dale knew there could be much more going on. "Mandrake."

Penny let out a disappointed groan. "What's wrong?"

"Nothing wrong, precisely," said Dale. "But I think you're not taking every advantage you could. Standing up, there's not a whole lot of ways for you to use your body, but you could be using your mouth, too."

"Ah, I see your point." She looked around. "Maybe if we lay you down on one of these chairs?"

"That would probably work better. In my experience, you bind someone standing up for a heavy pain workout; if you're going to do other things, it's better to be in other positions."

"I'll remember that, thanks." Penny bent over the reality anchor to remove Dale's force-field restrictions. "Oh, look—our Phase Looper has come out of hiding."

Dale paused a moment to watch. "He's interested. I think he can sense what's going on here."

Penny looked up with a lascivious smile. "Let's see if we can get him even more interested."

Dale allowed herself to be led over to one of the couches, where she lay back and placed her hands over her head, and her ankles at the lower corners of the cushion. This time, Penny encased her wrists and ankles in immobile spheres of force that held her even more securely than ropes would have done. She was nearly immobile, able only to squirm against the soft fabric of the cushions beneath her.

"Everything comfortable?" Penny asked.

"Yep, this is good."

Penny bent over Dale's recumbent form and laid a gentle hand on her thigh. "Ready to get started again?"

"Let's go."

"Good. Okay. Same restriction as before; don't make a sound except to say your safe word. Got it?"

Dale smiled and nodded enthusiastically.

Penny walked casually up along Dale's side. "Oh, so you're being careful, are you?"

Dale nodded.

"All right, then. Let's try this." Penny knelt at Dale's side, laying one hand lightly on Dale's breast, and placed a line of kisses along the woman's collarbone. As she got closer to Dale's ear, her hand went from soft caresses to deep squeezes, forcing soft flesh between her spread fingers.

"You like that?" she said.

Dale nodded again, swallowing a moan of pleasure. Monsters were good for many things, but they couldn't really kiss. Penny could kiss. Her lips were soft, her tongue hard and ready, and she alternated licks and sucks, feather-light pecks and the occasional, fierce soul-kiss on Dale's mouth. The whole time, her hand was on Dale's breast, squeezing, pinching, and running her fingers lightly over the sensitive skin. It wasn't long before Dale couldn't hold it in any longer, and let out a long, loud moan.

Penny's hand came down in a vicious slap on the inside of Dale's thigh, bringing out a new squeal of pain. She tensed and squirmed as another slap came down, higher this time, and in a more sensitive place.

"Quiet," Penny whispered, "Or you won't like what happens."

The implication was clear: if she made too much noise, a slap was going to come down directly on her sex. While she liked a bit of pain, that was probably more than she wanted. She closed her eyes, willing herself to silence, but that only heightened her focus on the sensations coursing through her body. The places Penny had spanked her still tingled, and the memory of her tender lips and cruel hand was too fresh to ignore.

Then Penny's hands gently pushed Dale's knees apart, and she nearly cried out in anticipation. Surely she didn't expect Dale to stay quiet for that? But of course she didn't. That was the whole point.

Somehow, Dale managed to stay silent as the first kiss arrived on her outer lips. She discovered she could hold back a bit better if she allowed herself to breathe freely, panting rather than moaning, and she maintained her silence as Penny's tongue ran up the length of her slit. But her control dissolved when Penny gently pulled her lips apart and deftly explored Dale's sex with her tongue. She moaned long and loud, until she was silenced by another slap on the inner thigh, dangerously close to her pussy.

At this point there was nothing she could do. Each touch brought forth another moan, each slap another squawk, and the strikes were getting closer and closer to the one that would really hurt. And the thought was driving her mad with anticipation and dread.

Then Penny let out a squeal. "It's here!"

Dale opened her eyes, shaking herself out of the erotic haze, and looked over at the reality anchor, where Penny touched its controls and stared up at the display hanging in midair. Threads of red light flitted through the air, passing through the walls and people there as if they didn't exist. Just at the edge of the globe of glowing lines, there was an amorphous smudge where all the threads came together. The threads moved frantically, waving about.

"It's trying to reach in," said Dale. "Trying to get into our dimension from hyperspace."

"I know," said Penny. "I'm setting it up. Just a little closer..." The young woman's lips spread in a feral, close-set smile that chilled Dale to the core.

"What are you doing?" she asked.

"Giving it what it needs," said Penny, "And giving it what it deserves." Penny worked quickly, forming a cylinder of force in the space over the table. Shimmering curves and planes come into being as Penny worked. "Come on, you know what I have for you..." she breathed, barely above a whisper.

The creature responded. Dale couldn't tell if it could actually hear her, if it sensed her thoughts, or what, but it responded, coiling its long, thready limbs and sliding into the cylinder. In the display, the threads changed from red to green, but the reality was far more interesting. Appearing as if from nothing, the cylindrical chamber, only about a meter and a half in any dimension, filled as if from nowhere with thick, glowing loops, like a bundle of loosely-gathered multicolored rubber bands rolling over and around each other, swelling to fill the space. They seemed quiet, but in Penny's display they pulsed with a faint red light.

Penny slammed her hand down on the console, then clapped her hands and bounced. "I did it! It's caught! Dale, look!" She pointed, still bouncing. "The barrier to hyperspace is up. It can't get away! And I caught it!"

Dale was willing to let Penny take the credit for the capture. After all, Penny was the monster hunter, and Dale was the primary lure, a helper. Still, she couldn't help scowling. "So, now what are you going to do with it?"

Penny's smile took on an even more feral aspect. "It's been a very bad monster. All that damage it's done, plus attacking me? It needs to be punished."

The Looper squeezed and a visible shudder ran through it in response to Penny's pronouncement. "You're right," said Dale. "It does."

It was more than Dale could have hoped for. The plan had worked flawlessly. Penny gave Dale an intense glance, eyes sparkling. "Watch," she said, gesturing with the controls to open a tiny hole in the top of the cylinder.

A single loop of the creature's rubbery flesh ventured through the opening, feeling around the edge tentatively, opening and closing as if looking for something to grab onto. Penny stepped up onto the table and took a firm hold of the loop, holding it closed between her hands and carefully controlling its movements. It seemed to relax in her grip, moving where she guided it, caressing her body, running over her stomach and back.

Dale felt a certain voyeuristic thrill go through her, watching this exchange, but even more than that, she marveled at the communication going on between Penny and the monster. She was training it how to please her, showing it how she would be touched. When the Looper tried to encircle one of her breasts, Penny slapped it, and the tendril quivered in response. A flash of light drew Dale's attention back to the holographic display of the reality anchor. While the creature's outline was still bright green, red particles swirled within it, growing in number, size, and brightness.

"What's that?" Dale asked.

"Quiet," said Penny, not looking away from the beast. "You're not supposed to be talking."

"Mandrake. Seriously, something is happening."

Penny glanced over her shoulder at the display, then waved her hand dismissively. "Doesn't matter. I'm busy. Shut up and watch."

"I'm not playing anymore. I think it's absorbing and transforming the energy."

"Awesome. Now stop distracting me or I'll gag you." Penny guided the Looper's tentacle down to her crotch, rubbing the smooth flesh over her sex. "Yes, like that," she crooned. "Just like that."

Second by second, the red particles in the holographic display multiplied, swirling along the Phase Looper's coils. Dale wished she knew more about the reality anchor's operation. What did those red dots mean? From what she understood, red things were in hyperspace rather than the normal universe, but that couldn't be right because Penny had put a barrier between the two dimensions using the reality anchor. Were those particles something else in hyperspace, something that wasn't the Phase Looper itself but was something attracted to it? Whatever it was, the effect was getting stronger.

Dale bit her lip. "Penny, I really think you should check this. Something is happening."

Penny ignored her, instead guiding the Phase Looper's flesh inside her body. At her command, it thrust in and out, jerkily at first but more smoothly as Penny's firm grip showed it what she wanted.

Then something changed. The arm retreated, slipping back toward the cylinder. In the display, the red particles drained inwards, finding a bright spot in its core. It seemed to be done with Penny, and was preparing itself for something else.

But Penny didn't let it go. "I'm not done with you. Come back." She grabbed the Phase Looper's arm and pulled, dragging it back out of the container. When it resisted, she pulled harder, and when its muscles bunched and tensed, Penny braced a foot against its prison and yanked it, hard. Inside the prison, the Phase Looper extended its body to brace itself against the walls, but Penny had the advantage. She pulled again and again, stretching the arm mercilessly. The red particles dispersed with each yank, swirling through the Phase Looper's tentacles.

Dale shouted helplessly. "Penny!" Dale shouted helplessly. "Something's happening, and I don't think it's good. Take a break."

With a frustrated huff, Penny shoved the Phase Looper's arm away from her and hopped off the table. "That's it. You asked for it." With a grunt, she ripped a thick satin cord from one of the chairs, tied a knot in it, and stretched it between her hands. "This will make a good ball gag; don't you think?"

"Penny, let me up. Mandrake. Really. You don't want to do this."

"Yes, I do," said Penny. "Now hold still."

Dale thrashed, keeping her mouth away from the gag. "Vince!" she shouted, as loud as her voice could stand. "Viiiince!"

"Hold still!" Penny slapped her, hard enough to make Dale see stars for a moment, but it didn't stop her from struggling.

Then, suddenly, a circle of flesh slipped over Penny's head and dragged her back. The Phase Looper's free tentacle had wrapped around her neck, and it was her turn to struggle, fighting not to get free, but just to get enough air to breathe.

"VIIINCE!" Dale screamed. "Get your hairy ass in here!"

Penny wrestled with the Phase Looper, her strength barely sufficient to keep herself conscious. Angry red particles streamed in the reality anchor's display, swirling deeper and deeper into its body. The seconds passed like hours before Vince finally ran into the room and snapped his fingers in the hologram, freeing Penny from the monster's grip in a flash of white. She collapsed to the floor as her rescuer sealed the Phase Looper's prison.

"Vince. Let me loose."

"Of course." With a wave of his hand, he banished the force constructs that held Dale's hands and feet.

"Kill it," growled Penny, clawing her way to her feet. "Crush it. Destroy it! That thing tried to kill me!" She lunged for the reality anchor, but Vince held her back easily with one arm.

"It wasn't trying to kill you." said Dale. "It was just trying to get your attention. We've already established that." She waved her hand at the display. "What is that red stuff inside the Phase Looper?"

Vince knelt at the reality anchor and tapped some commands. "It says they're miniature wormholes. I think it's coalescing them into a single, large one."

"Wormholes? Aren't they researching those for faster interstellar travel? Is it trying to go somewhere?" asked Dale.

"Not interstellar; interdimensional. If it's going to a home, it's not a home planet, it's a home dimension. I'm not an expert on these things, and the sensors in the reality anchor aren't that sophisticated, but one thing's clear. The wormholes are forming in hyperspace, and it's still here in our dimension. It's trapped."

Penny tried to shove Vince out of the way, but he grabbed her wrist and twisted it behind her back.

"Don't be a fool. This thing's worth a lot more alive than dead," he said. They wrestled that way for a moment, then Vince tripped over a corner of the table and went down with Penny on top of him.

There was no time to consider. Dale jumped forward and brought up the reality anchor's main controls. The words FULL RESET appeared in the holographic display, along with numbers counting down from ten.

"Stop her!" shouted Penny. "She's letting it loose!" She grabbed for the device, but she and Vince were still tangled up together and neither of them were moving easily.

7... 6...

"I don't think so," said Dale. "I think it just wants to go home."

3... 2...

The holographic display disappeared, the force fields vanished simultaneously, and a moment later the Phase Looper followed. The holographic display flashed back on a moment later, showing the Phase Looper, now bright red and surrounded by a nimbus of red energy, its numerous strands churning the space around it.

"See?" said Dale. "It's going home. Nothing to be afraid of."

Penny punched Dale viciously in the jaw, then kicked her in the stomach, causing her to double over in pain. "You've ruined everything, you monster-loving freak!"

Dale curled her arms protectively over her head as Penny rained blows on her back, until Vince pulled her away.

"Nothing to do about it now," he said. "We'll never recapture it."

Penny screamed with rage and frustration. "I hate you! I hate you both! You had to come here. You had to escape the Kritzoan. You had to get through the doors—"

"Wait," Vince interrupted. "You set the Kritzoan loose?" He spun her around to confront her face to face.

"Of course I did, you moron! And it would have worked, too!" She stomped her feet and screamed again, shaking with rage.

The red aura grew brighter and broader as the Phase Looper's body seemed to contract in on itself, knotting tighter and tighter. Abruptly, one loop lashed out, briefly turning green before the entire creature vanished from the display.

Penny's scream ended in a soft pop as she disappeared, as well.

Vince looked around in alarm. "Penny!" He dove for the reality anchor, desperately working the controls. Then his eyes narrowed as he looked up at Dale. "She's gone," he said. "It took her. It took her, and it's. Your. Fault."

Dale's mouth fell open. "I didn't... It—it's a wild creature,

Vince. They're unpredictable. It had to be set free, don't you understand? But she wanted to kill it."

Vince flipped his communicator disc to her. "Talk to the patrol. Maybe they will give you a ride back to your ship." He turned to his camera-bot. "We're done here. CUT."

Dale shuffled from her airlock into the corridor of her ship, taking only cursory glances at the tentacle monsters in their enclosures to her left. Her camera-bot hung from a carrying-strap over her shoulder, inert, and she wore a borrowed Patrol coverall.

"Welcome aboard, ma'am," came the voice of her ship's operating system.

"Thank you, Vi. How did things go with Miz Delavos?"

"Quite well, ma'am. She signed the contract, and we have a full hour of recordings of her encounter with the Yartroan. After a shower and rest, she asked if there were any other creatures that needed tending, so she spent another seventy minutes with the Chocondris. And then the Kritzoan, and after that the Whombar. I had to stop her, or else she'd disrupt the schedules of every tentacle monster on the ship."

"Wow, she's got quite the appetite. Where is she?"

"Sleeping, ma'am."

"I would be, too." Dale slotted the camera-bot into its recharging station. "Vi, rebuild the operating system on the camera-bot. While you're at it, see if you can recover any of the recordings. The Patrol are usually pretty thorough, but you never know."

"Yes, ma'am. The Patrol confiscated your recordings?"

Dale proceeded down the hallway toward her quarters. "They've decided that since the incident involved a death, it can't be broadcast until a full inquiry is concluded, next of kin alerted, that kind of thing."

"A death, ma'am?"

"Well, she might as well be. The Phase Looper pulled Penny

Angstrom into hyperspace. Took her with it to... wherever it is they come from. That was a major point they kept asking during the questioning."

"Questioning, ma'am?"

Dale sighed, stopping for a moment to peer into the enclosure where her own Kritzoan lay, quiescent, in a shallow pool, only the barest ripples running across its surface.

"Four hours isn't an especially long interrogation, as I understand it, but it certainly seemed that way after the ordeal on the *Mandragora*. But yeah, after looking over all the evidence they decided that it counted as a death."

"I'm sorry to hear that, ma'am."

"Well, at least it's been ruled an accident, so no charges were filed, but," she shook her head, "I've been asked not to leave the system for a while. I think it helped that I paid half of my share of the bounty to Penny's estate."

Dale opened her bedroom door to find the covers rumpled, and a very naked, very nubile university student sprawled beneath the sheets. She watched for a moment as the young woman's chest rose and fell with an untroubled rhythm. "Someone deserves a good night's rest," she said, and closed the door. "Certainly isn't me."

"Is there anything I can do, ma'am?"

Dale turned and continued down the hall. "Have a bottle of wine ready for me in the wardroom."

"Yes, ma'am. Any particular one?"

"Whichever one has the most alcohol," she said. "Aside from that, it doesn't matter."

CHAPTER THREE
TIME ON THEIR HANDS

Dale Clearwater stumbled into her galley, squinting at the bright illumination.

"Good morning, Miz Clearwater!" said the gorgeous young woman standing at the control console. "Coffee?" Her blonde hair was pulled into a ponytail, emphasizing her perfectly smooth, pale skin. She wore a blue *Monster Whisperer* tee-shirt and a pair of sensible briefs that were much less fancy or fashionable than Dale would have expected. The scanty attire showed off an equally perfect figure, the product of carefully engineered genetics and nanoform treatments.

Ordinarily, Dale would have paused to appreciate the sight but, instead, she winced and pressed her fingers to her temples. "Christine, please. My head is killing me."

Christine put delicate fingers over her lips. "Oh, sorry."

Dale seated herself at the little table opposite the food console. "Coffee would be fine, thank you. Black. And you can call me 'Dale.'"

A flat, matter-of-fact voice came from the console. "Shall I add a hangover treatment to the coffee, ma'am?"

"Yes, Vi. Please. And lower the lights fifty percent."

"Yes, ma'am." The lights dimmed immediately.

The cute co-ed brought two mugs to the table. The contents of the mug in front of Dale was as black as space; the one in front of Christine was just slightly darker than milk.

"I take it things didn't go well on that mission yesterday?"

Dale sipped her coffee, letting the elixir seep into her. "You might say that."

"What happened?"

"We lost someone. Penny Angstrom."

Christine's jaw fell open. "Lost?"

"Missing, and presumed dead. The Phase Looper took her away

somewhere. Nobody's really sure where, but it's not likely she survived." Dale took a long drink from her coffee. "I'd rather not talk about it."

After a pause, Christine asked, "Should I go?"

"Probably a good idea. When the news-hunters get a hint of this, they're going to be all over me."

"Speaking of which, ma'am..." said the computer.

"Yes, Vi?"

"I have just received a message from the Interstellar Patrol. They have concluded their investigation, and the travel interdict has been lifted. We are now free to leave New New Amsterdam. Also, in the past ten seconds I have received requests for interviews from every news organization on New New Amsterdam."

Dale groaned. "I do not need this."

"In addition, there are two visitors at the airlock."

"Great. The paparazzi have showed up." Dale looked up from her coffee and sighed. "As fabulous as it has been to have you here, Christine, it's time for you to go. You've got to get back to your studies. Is there someone from Omicron Theta Psi that can come out to pick you up? The sooner, the better, really. The reporters are going to be all over you if you just walk out the airlock."

"Reporters?" Christine's smile froze into a worried frown.

"It's not a secret that you're here, is it? You agreed to the distribution contracts on the holos you made. But if you want to get out quietly..."

"I would rather not face them, really. My friend Kitty has a shuttle—maybe she can meet us in orbit?"

"We can do that. And I tell you what: I'll sit on those holos you made until things quiet down."

Christine smiled. "Thank you. I'd appreciate that."

Dale looked up toward the ceiling. "Vi, are we sufficiently stocked and supplied for takeoff?"

"Yes, ma'am."

"Good. Vi, take us into orbit, and transmit the elements to..." Dale glanced at Christine.

"Cath Naker."

"Transmit the elements to Cath Naker at Omicron Theta Psi."

"Yes ma'am. Space traffic control has given us an orbit, and the orbital elements have been forwarded to Cath Naker at Omicron Theta Psi. We are ready to lift off at your mark."

"No reason to wait, Vi. Go ahead and get us off the ground."

A subtle vibration ran through the ship. "Docking clamps disengaged. Atomic batteries to power. Turbines to speed. Lifting off." A deep hum rose to audibility, underlining the silence in the little galley.

Dale sat, sipping her coffee, for a few minutes. Just as her brain was starting to clear up enough for a real conversation, the computer announced, "Miz Delavos, I am receiving a call for you, ma'am."

Christine addressed the ceiling. "Who's it from?"

"The incoming call is from a Miz Arkadia Delavos."

Christine swore.

"Your mother?" asked Dale. She finished the coffee. Her headache faded with every swallow.

"Yeah."

"Do you want to take it in private? You can use my quarters."

"No, I'll take it here."

"Vi? Open the channel, please."

"Yes, ma'am."

After a brief pause, the console by the door lit up, projecting the image of a mature, stern-looking woman in a dark, austere business suit into the middle of the room.

The image glanced only briefly at Dale before focusing an intense look on Christine, who stood up to her full height and returned the stare, lifting her chin defiantly.

The older woman's voice was calm, but stern. "Young lady, I am made to understand that you have violated your curfew. Is this true?"

Christine took a deep breath. "Yes. And I am willing to accept my sisters' punishment for that."

The woman's eyes narrowed. "Your sisters' punishment? They are not the only ones concerned about your conduct, young lady."

"I'm sure they will be quite strict, mother."

"Don't lie to me! That ship is leaving the planet! You turn around and come right back down. I'll send the car to pick you up. I believe a weekend at home is in order."

"No."

The woman's eyes sprung wide. "What?"

"I'm having a friend pick me up in orbit. There are too many reporters on the ground."

Christine's mother sliced the air with a stiff-handed gesture. "No. Unacceptable. I'm bringing you home until we straighten this all out. If you don't come back down right this minute, I'm going to call the university. I can have you out on your ear within the hour. You will have nothing. Do you hear me? Nothing!"

Christine looked over at Dale, then back to her mother, and back to Dale. Her fists clenched behind her back. "Can we suspend the call for a moment?"

Dale nodded. "Vi, please put Miz Delavos on hold."

"Yes, ma'am." The hologram winked out, cutting off the woman's protest mid-sentence.

"She's serious," said Christine, her voice trembling. "She'll do it. Can I—can I stay with you?"

Dale's eyebrows rose. "Uh...."

"Please? I don't have anywhere else to go. Just until I can convince her that this is what I really want?"

Dale considered. Christine was a cute kid. She had the perfect skin and perfect teeth and perfect eyes that expensive genetic engineering could give to someone born to wealthy parents. That wasn't the core of the attraction, though. What was most intriguing about Christine was her spirit. She had ambition, and it didn't seem like the sort that used and manipulated people. The kid might not be the brightest woman she'd ever met, but she was honest about her enthusiasm for tentacle monsters.

"All right," said Dale. "For a few days. Until you get this straightened out."

Christine squealed, clapping her hands and hopping in place.

Her enthusiasm and bralessness made Dale aware that her hangover had faded adequately enough to get turned on, and she had to smile. Dale held up her hands in a calming gesture. "All right, all right—your mom has been waiting a while. Do you want to just cut her off?"

Christine's eyes narrowed gleefully. "Oh, I want to tell her to her face."

"Vi, resume the call please."

"Yes, ma'am."

The hologram bipped back into view and caught the elder Miz Delavos mid-shout.

"—don't care what you have to do, bring that ship back here immediately!" She was facing away, waving her hands at someone or something outside her comm system's field of view. "Call Parsons and Rappaport on the finance committee. They—"

"Mother!" snapped Christine.

The woman's attention refocused on her daughter. She stomped a foot and crossed her arms, her lips drawn tight. "Young lady, you do not put me on hold, and you do not speak to me in that outrageous tone of voice!"

"Mother, if you want to get me thrown out of university, go ahead. I'm not going to give in to your threats."

The holographic eyes narrowed. "It's that *Monster Whisperer* woman, isn't it? She's seduced you or something. One of her creatures has you in a mind trap. I've heard about those things."

"Tell me, mother. Do I go back to the university, or do I stay here? Your choice. Either way, I'm not going home with you. You couldn't pay me enough to give in to your threats."

"Don't call my bluff, young lady. You won't like what happens."

Christine crossed her arms. "I'm waiting."

The woman's face hardened. "I cannot conscience paying good money to support a lifestyle of debauchery."

"Then we are done," said Christine, and turned her back.

Dale shook her head. "Vi, close the channel."

"Yes, ma'am." The hologram disappeared.

"Well, that was fun," said Dale, trying hard not to roll her eyes. "Can we call Kitty and have her bring up my things?"

"Of course."

Three hours later, Dale's guest had said her goodbyes to her sorority sisters, and moved into the ship's guest quarters after learning that her mother had carried through on her threat. Dale had sent out a press release explaining her perspective on the events on the Star of Mandragora, and polite refusals to everyone requesting an interview. There had been a good deal of tension as Christine had spoken first to the New New Amsterdam police, and then to the Space Patrol, to explain that, no, she wasn't being kidnapped, and she was aboard Dale's ship completely voluntarily. The latter had even insisted on boarding the ship to scan Christine for mind-control drugs and nanomachines.

"Your parents are really going all out to try to get you home," said Dale, as she sat down to lunch with Christine. It wasn't anything special, just beefalo stew out of the synthesizer.

"Mother has been like that ever since my younger brother turned eighteen and left home to study martial arts. They wanted him to get a law degree and take up the family business. Now he lives at a dojo on Yartro."

"Yartro! Really. That's where Yartroans come from."

Christine smiled. "Yes, I know."

Dale pursed her lips, considering. "Last I knew, it was a wilderness planet. I didn't know there were any human colonies there."

"It's not very old. Just got established a couple years ago. Glen was one of the first to arrive. I think it's kind of a monastery."

"How'd you like to go visit him?"

Christine's eyes lit up. "Could we?"

"I don't see why not. A brand new colony seems like just the kind of place to get away from it all, don't you think? Vi, plot a course for the planet Yartro."

"Course plotted," said Vi. "Space traffic control has been notified, and have given us clearance for immediate departure from New New Amsterdam."

"Go ahead, Vi. No reason to wait."

A distant hum rose in pitch. "Engines engaged. We will reach the hyperspace entry point in two hours; total travel time is estimated at three days, seven hours."

"Really?" asked Christine. "That seems like a long time."

"This isn't a particularly fast ship," said Dale. "But it does the job. Besides., it'll give us time to get you started on your studies."

"Studies?"

"If you're going to travel with me, you're going to work, and if you're going to work, you're going to learn."

After lunch was eaten and cleared away, Dale set Christine up with a series of electronic texts, holos, and simulations on various topics related to tentacle monsters. Then she sat down at the desk in her quarters to handle her correspondence, as any messages would have to be sent before the ship went into hyperspace. She started by recording a special thank-you message for the women at Omicron Theta Psi, with an assurance that she'd take care of their sister while she was away. Next up was another message for Ellen Venture, thanking her for the opportunity to work with her rare monster, and expressing hope that all was well with both of them. Finally, she sent a personal thank-you message to the woman who had received her Orichalc embryo, again expressing hope that both of them were well, and explaining that she was leaving the system for a while, but hoped she could come back to visit them at a later date.

Then, she tackled the inbox. Many of the incoming messages were requests for her to visit other star systems to handle tentacle monster issues. Those would have been sent before the *Star of Mandragora* incident, but it wouldn't be good business to assume they'd change their mind. She sorted out the good prospects, sent them a standard package of information, and instructed them to forward their responses to Yartro. Given the speed of message traffic on the express-boat system, some replies might well be waiting for them there.

Shortly after Dale finished a message to her lawyer on New

New London, Vi announced, "Ma'am, we have reached the hyperspace transit point."

"Are there any more critical items in the inbox?"

"No, ma'am; not that I can see. There are four hundred eighty-two new messages containing expressions of appreciation; six hundred ninety-eight messages containing complaints, unfounded accusations, or threats; five thousand four hundred ninety-eight unsolicited advertisements; and ten thousand one hundred forty-two highly suspicious notifications of inheritance, bequest, grants, and miscellaneous windfalls. None of them contain any noteworthy information."

Dale sighed. Most of the time, the positive messages outnumbered the negative ones. Whenever her name hit the media, however, that vocal minority of people who hated everything she stood for didn't take long to act when they got stirred up. "Vi, next time I want to go on some grand adventure, remind me about the *Star of Mandragora*, please?"

"So noted, ma'am. Do you wish to reply to any more messages before the transition to hyperspace?"

"Yes. Please send standard text thank-you messages to all the positive ones, and set them aside. I'll look through them to see if any warrant personal replies while we're in hyperspace. Archive the rest."

"Yes, ma'am. Messages sent, and the express system has acknowledged receipt. Total charges are five hundred forty-six credits."

"Have you asked Christine if she wants to send any messages before we transit?"

"Yes, ma'am. She has no message traffic pending."

"Very well. Transit to hyperspace."

"Yes, ma'am." The hum of the ship's engines changed pitch, winding up briefly and then sharply down again as the ship pierced the barrier between dimensions. "Hyperspace transition achieved. We are on course for Yartro."

"Excellent." Dale stood up from her desk and headed out into the corridor. "I'm going to go have a look at the monsters. Is there anything in particular I should know about?"

"No, ma'am. They've been rather quiet today. All vital signs and behaviors within normal parameters."

"Good to hear," she said. She walked along the gently curving corridor, looking into the transparent enclosures to her right. The Nalchecka had pulled its shell tight around its body, appearing to be no more than a crater-pocked boulder. The Storazoid sat quietly in the middle of its loamy environment, content to absorb completely mundane nutrients through its root-feet. The Yartroan hung limply from the ceiling, its dozen or so arms dangling, its single monstrous eye lidded and drowsy. The Kritzoan lay motionless, its surface as placid as a reflecting pool.

She found Christine at the door to the Chocondris' forest-like enclosure, sitting on a chair pulled in from the galley and reading from a tablet computer. The creature was camouflaged as a gnarled tree branch, but Dale knew its habits, knew where to look for it.

"What do you think of this article?" asked Christine, angling the tablet up so Dale could read. The headline read, "New Theory of Tentacle Monster Intelligence"

"I haven't seen that one yet. Was it on the list I gave you?"

"No, Vi pointed it out. It arrived just before we went to hyperspace." Christine paged through the article. "It says that scientists at the University of New Boston think that tentacle monsters, specifically the Chocondris, have a non-symbolic intellect."

"Non-symbolic?"

"Yeah. Their minds don't work with symbols, but with concrete representations that they communicate to each other with... well, they're not sure exactly how, but it seems to work like touch-based telepathy. Like, they don't need to distill thoughts down into symbols because they can send the whole thought straight into another's mind."

"That would explain why they've had so much trouble," said Dale. "Tentacle monsters don't touch each other very often. They tend to be solitary."

"Except the Chocondris," said Christine, nodding at the enclosure. "It says here that when several of them are hunting in the same area, they cooperate, coordinating their actions."

Dale grunted dismissively. "I could have told them that."

"It says they can also work together to solve puzzles. But, they haven't been able to teach them any sort of language."

Dale glanced down at the tablet. "They aren't going to get very far keeping Chocondris in a place like that," she said, pointing to an illustration of a plain white laboratory enclosure. "Too clean and sterile. Chocondris like the woods. Won't be happy anywhere else."

"So, how did you manage to get a miniature forest in your ship?"

"Specially engineered trees," said Dale. "The trunks go from the lower bulkhead to the upper one, where they're connected to this bio-matrix thingy that takes the place of the rest of the plant. That way I don't need room for whole trees. I'm not really sure how it all works, but I know one thing: anyone who keeps a Chocondris should have trees."

Christine squinted up at Dale thoughtfully. "So, is that why you don't give any of your monsters names? The non-symbolic intelligence thing?"

"Something like that. It's kind of pointless, if you think about it. It's not like I'm going to call them for dinner. They react to the emotional content of what we say—screams and shrieks or moans and groans, but the actual meaning of the words doesn't carry over. So why give them names?"

"That makes sense." Christine set the tablet aside and stood up, making a mild grunt of pain as she carefully climbed to her feet. "Thinking of having a go?"

"Nah. It'll be satisfied for a few more days. Sore?"

"A bit."

"I'd be more than a bit sore if I'd spent three hours having sex with tentacle monsters."

Christine shrugged. "Aren't Kritzoans always up for a session?"

"Oh, I could wake it up, but then I'd be imposing my needs on it."

Christine's eyebrows knitted. "Isn't that what they're here for? You give them food, shelter, et cetera, and they are, well... there for you, when you need them?"

"There's some of that, yes," said Dale. "But the relationship is more mutual than that. Yes, having sex with them is a lot of fun, but for them it's a need that goes beyond anything a human feels. They hunger for us in a way that we can only experience second-hand. So, offering myself to the Kritzoan right now, so soon after you've done such an obviously thorough job of sating it, would be like offering another main course after the dessert of a lavish banquet. It could take me, no doubt, but it wouldn't be the same." Dale caught Christine blushing.

"I guess I got a little carried away," she said. "I'm sorry. I guess I kind of took some things that didn't belong to me."

Dale smiled. "Don't worry about it. With two of us on board, though, we're going to have to be somewhat more restrained than we'd like. But trust me, every meal tastes better if you're a little hungry."

Christine nodded. "I don't think I'm going to be up for anything today anyways." She rubbed her behind. "Or maybe tomorrow."

Dale laughed. "Serves you right." She took the tablet and selected a different document. "Here. Read up on the basics of the Chocondris. You can hit the advanced stuff once you've got that material mastered."

Christine saluted with a double-flip flourish. "Yes, sar. Any particular reason to study up on this one?"

"Unless they surprise me, which happens once in a while, that's the one that's going to need exercising next."

"When will that be?"

"Not too long, but you'll have time to recover."

Dale enjoyed watching Christine wait. It was almost cute. She only took a day to finish recovering from the tentacle sex marathon, and shortly thereafter she showed every sign of being ready for another one. She spent every spare moment looking into the Chocondris enclosure, and Dale didn't need Vi to tell her that Christine was slipping away to masturbate regularly.

Not that Dale wasn't in a fair bit of need, herself. Editing the holos Vi had recorded put her into a decidedly sexy state of mind, but she refrained from slipping away for a wank. For one thing, she knew it wouldn't do much good, and for another the orgasms she had after denying herself for a while could be mind-blowing. Instead, she savored the sexy, itchy feeling and reminded herself how good it would be when the time came.

Christine didn't take the pressure as well. Breakfast on the second day of waiting brought her to the galley with hair mussed and bags under her eyes, brewing her coffee double-strong and taking it black.

"Rough night?" asked Dale.

"Uh-huh."

"Nightmares?"

Christine took a sip of coffee. "Something like that."

Dale hid a smile behind her own coffee. "It's too bad. You really should be well-rested to have a session with the Chocondris. It's not gentle."

The woman's face brightened in an instant. "It's ready?"

"It's showing signs of agitation. It's moving from tree to tree, and releasing a lot more pheromones."

"I'm ready too," said Christine.

Dale cocked an eyebrow. "You sure? We can wait until tomorrow if you're not up to it."

"Don't be mean! I'm ready!"

"All right. Go get a performance nightie from the replicator and meet me at the entrance."

"Performance nightie?"

"Didn't Vi tell you about those? I use them so the monster has something to rip off. Regular clothes are too durable. They can hurt coming off."

Christine blinked. "I just went in naked."

"Yes, I know."

"So, just the nightie, then?" She arched a perfect eyebrow.

Dale held back a smile. "Yes, just the nightie. Go on. Show time in ten minutes."

Christine slurped down her coffee and dashed from the room. Dale just managed to contain the dark chuckle bubbling up in her throat until the door closed behind her.

"Dale Clearwater," she said to herself, "You are so bad."

After a leisurely breakfast that included a healthy serving of anticipation, Dale strolled out to the main hallway. She was looking forward to this so hard that her teeth were tingling. How long had it been since she had initiated someone like this? A year? Two? It was a very rare treat. Even though she had watched Christine with four different tentacle monsters now, only the first had been in person and, as good as the holograms were, there was something about being there that just couldn't be replicated electronically. Maybe it was the pheromones.

Best of all, the monster of the day was the Chocondris. Dale tried not to play favorites with her tentacle monsters but, if she were forced to say, that one would be her favorite. It had been the first one she had for herself, acquired before she had gotten her starship, back on Montana Prime. There was a special place in her heart for this one.

Christine stood outside the door, bouncing on her toes in the flimsy, thigh-length nightie. She had chosen a bright red color that went well with her creamy skin, and had done up a bit of makeup, expertly covering up the fatigue that had made her seem a bit more human earlier on. Her hair was pulled back into a loose ponytail with a matching lace scrunchie. Under the semi-transparent fabric, she was succulently naked. The Chocondris wouldn't care, but Dale appreciated the packaging.

"Anything special I should know?" she asked.

"Just the usual," said Dale. "Fear. Excitement. Don't hold back if you feel like struggling or screaming. It's all part of the experience. Ready?"

Christine nodded, face already growing flushed.

"And we're okay to record this? Same contract as before?"

"Yes. Yes, of course. Please?" The young woman bounced a little closer to the door.

"Vi, start recording, please."

"All cameras operating normally, ma'am." said the computer.

"Then it's show-time." Dale touched the door controls, and the heavy circular hatch rotated and slid up out of the way with a gentle hiss. A heavy scent floated through the door, redolent of moss and pine, but with a hint of flowers as well. Christine took a deep breath and stepped gingerly onto the loamy soil of the enclosure, peering up into the tree branches as she went.

Dale wished she could follow, but instead she closed the door and watched through the glass. Ordinarily the Chocondris could be anywhere in the enclosure, but when it was truly needy, it waited somewhere near the entrance. Dale felt confident she would have a good view of the proceedings, in spite of the dense foliage of the enclosure.

Christine picked her way gingerly across the bits of forest detritus littering the ground, eyes scanning the branches overhead, tension and excitement evident in every tentative footstep.

"Ooh, yes," Dale growled to herself. She had spotted the Chocondris, and it wasn't up in the trees. The beast was on the ground, masquerading as gnarled roots lying across the path. As soon as Christine stepped over it, the root sprang out of the soft earth, wrapping its thick, woody length around her ankle.

She stumbled, then fell back on her posterior, kicking at the root with her other foot.

"It's got me!" she shrieked, "Let go, you brute! Help!"

More woody stems erupted from the ground, securing both arms and both legs. With unanswerable strength they ripped the flimsy nightie from her body and pulled her, spread-eagled, toward the nearest tree.

Christine thrashed uselessly against the monster's grip, wailing and shouting. Its strength was far beyond anything the girl could muster. It had her entirely at its mercy. There was nothing she could do to prevent it from binding her to the meter-wide trunk, limbs stretched behind her, completely open and vulnerable.

More roots appeared, trailing loamy earth as they rose from the ground. Green buds grew in dense rows along their length, each onion-shaped orb a couple centimeters across. These didn't wrap around Christine's body, but instead hovered near her, quivering, until the buds popped open, petals bursting forth like tiny fireworks and spraying pale pink pollen in an enveloping cloud.

Most of the dust drifted down to the ground, but even so the substance covered Christine's skin in a thin layer that sparkled even in the shaded light of the forest-like enclosure.

Dale could almost feel the enervating tingle that pollen evoked on the skin, and the heightening effect that breathing it created internally. She almost wished she had chosen to be the one who went in with the Chocondris. Its pale green tendrils, each no thicker than a pinky finger but almost a half-meter long, uncoiled from within the blossoms and reached out for Christine's body. The very first touch was enough to transform her last cry of fear into a choking moan.

"Vi?" Dale asked, hugging her arms around her midsection to keep them still.

"Yes, ma'am?" answered the computer.

"Which one of the monsters is in greatest need of exercise right now?"

"I believe that would be the Kritzoan, ma'am. Its activity level has increased somewhat."

Dale wanted to stay and watch her apprentice being taken by the Chocondris, but the stimulation was growing beyond what she could contain.

The monster's tendrils traced lines in the pollen stuck to Christine's skin, waves and whorls leading to all the spots where her nerve endings were densest: ears, neck, lips, nipples, feet, and the crooks of her knees and elbows. But, more than any other part, the trails led to her hairless mons. Dale wanted to stay and watch her apprentice being taken by the Chocondris, but the stimulation was growing beyond what she could contain.

"How much has it increased?" Dale asked.

"Four percent, ma'am. It has not reached the thresholds you've set for exercise readiness."

Dale sighed. "Oh, well. I can wait."

Christine cried out as the first tendril entered her pussy, then moaned louder as more of the tendrils twined with it, while others stroked and squeezed elsewhere. A drop of moisture rolled down Christine's thigh, turning deep pink as it cleared a trail of pollen on its way. The Chocondris scooped it up with one of its tendrils, on its way to its captive's posterior.

"Damn," Dale whispered to herself. She needed something inside her, and the Kritzoan wouldn't do that. Its body wasn't built for that sort of experience. The Storazoid would give that to her, but after the lecture she had given about imposing her needs on the beasts? No. She would contain herself. Dale leaned against the transparent wall of the enclosure, one arm cushioning her forehead from the hard transparent aluminum, the other tugging at the closure of her coverall. *Discipline*, she thought as she slipped a hand inside and down into her underwear.

The cluster of tendrils sliding in and out of Christine's body had increased its speed and power enough that each thrust now visibly shook her torso. Vines wrapped around her breasts squeezed, pulled and twisted, and another cluster prepared to enter her mouth, dosing her with even more of the sensitizing pollen.

Dale kicked herself for allowing her young apprentice to be the one to exercise the Chocondris. She should have done it herself, made Christine be the one to squirm and wait for the next opportunity. Her breath fogged the wall in front of her, partially obscuring her view, but it didn't matter anymore. Her imagination and memory filled in the missing pieces. She knew the sensations Christine would be feeling, knew the reactions, knew how spent and satisfied the beast would leave her. As the Chocondris muffled Christine's cries of pleasure with its tendrils in her mouth, Dale replaced them with her own. She sank to her knees, no longer able to support herself.

"Be strong," she whispered to herself, her mind drifting toward the other monsters on board her ship. "Need to set a good example." The self-exhortation did no good. Eyes closed now, her imagination evoked the Nalcheka, its long green tentacles full of power, promising exactly the kind of release she needed. She could almost feel its arms around her, lifting her into the air, while its ovipositors positioned themselves at every entrance to her body, filling her helpless form with its unquenchable, alien lust. She wanted it so badly it hurt. The groaning, spasmodic orgasm that clenched its way through her did nothing to quench that need.

The spasms faded, leaving her body drained but her mind no more satisfied than before. Her eyes opened at the sound of Christine dropping to the soft forest floor. She was covered head to toe in pink pollen, twitching and moaning with the aftershocks of more orgasms than could be counted. Dale picked herself up, took a few breaths to steady herself, and zipped up her coverall.

Dale entered the enclosure and bent down to help Christine to her feet. "Come on," she said, "Let's get you into the shower."

"By the Stars," Christine murmured.

Dale's hands tingled where they came into contact with the pollen on Christine's skin, and she regretted not preparing herself with some gloves. At least her coverall would protect her from contact with the pollen all over the woman's body. Slowly, they made their way down the corridor to Christine's quarters and into the bathroom.

Inside, Dale said, "Vi, please activate the shower seat."

"Yes, ma'am," came the obedient computer's voice.

A low platform extended from the shower wall. Dale set Christine down on it and the spray turned on. The young woman twitched and moaned as the spray struck her hyper-sensitized body. Her eyes opened half-way, and a goofy grin spread across her face.

"So, that's the Chocondris," she said.

Dale turned to wash her hands in the sink. She had only gotten a tiny dose of the pollen, at least compared to Christine, but it wasn't helping her mental state any. She grabbed a washcloth and tossed it onto Christine's lap. "Any thoughts?"

"Nope," she replied, a dreamy look in her eyes. "None at all."

Dale made every effort to maintain her facade of professional patience. She made sure not to check on the monster's status when Christine would see or hear, and tried to keep from squirming too much when her thoughts drifted in that direction.

She distracted herself with entirely mundane, nonsexual business. Unfortunately, there was little of that to do. Vi handled the maintenance of her ship, her local financial accounts, and most of her correspondence. Ordinarily, she'd read up on recent developments in the business or edit holos, but anything relating to the monsters made her frustrated distraction even worse. Exercise worked for a while, but there was a limit to how much time she could spend in the ship's little gym before sheer exhaustion forced her to find some other way to pass her time.

Having Christine around, radiating an aura of complete sexual satisfaction, did nothing for Dale's mood. After sleeping off the effects of her session with the Chocondris, she had put on another performance nightie to wear while studying. After an evening meal spent trying and failing to think of things to say that weren't either crabby, bitchy, or laden with unintended innuendo, Dale decided to go to bed early. Maybe tomorrow morning one of the monsters would be in the mood for a romp.

But, sleep just wouldn't come, and she knew that taking medication to induce it would not be a good idea. Finally, Dale was reduced to going through the unsolicited commercial messages Vi had archived. She sat in the ship's lounge, deleting them one by one, wondering if her life was really this one-sided. Was there something wrong with her, that she built her whole life around tentacle monsters? Was she obsessed? Maybe, but wasn't it also true that it took this kind of focus to accomplish something great?

Ads for nanosurgery, security cyberneticists, questionable investments and, of course, the usual raft of sexual enhancements drifted through her vision in a blur, each one pretty much the same as the one before, until she paused, staring.

"Complete control," it said, "An experience programmed to your specifications." Underneath the words, it displayed a device that looked like a reclining couch with coiled mechanical tentacles hanging in clusters underneath. The chair rotated to show every angle.

Dale's heart thudded as she stared at the hologram. She knew such devices existed, of course, but they lacked something, in her opinion. They seemed cold, heartless devices, no better than masturbating. There was no interplay, no back-and-forth. No mind there to interact with. What was the point of giving yourself to a machine if you never really lost control? No, such things were for people who couldn't handle the real risk of interacting with a living, breathing monster.

Or so she had always told herself. But now, with her body crying out for release, she wondered if maybe there was a use for such a thing. Maybe if she had someone else program it, maybe even control it in real time? She imagined herself lying on that couch, its manipulators clenched around her wrists and ankles, thrashing, while more arms explored her body, giving her what she needed oh, so badly.

With a shake of her head she threw off the vision. There was no way she could get this machine, not without turning around and flying back to New New Amsterdam. She wasn't that desperate. Not yet.

"Vi?"

"Yes, ma'am?"

"Attach this message to my to-do list, please."

"Yes, ma'am."

"Add in any other messages with related content, and make a note to download company details next opportunity we get."

"Yes, ma'am. Anything else, ma'am?"

Dale yawned. "No. Dim the lights; I think I'm finally sleepy enough for bed."

"Good night, ma'am. Sleep well."

The first thing the following morning, Dale checked all the monsters personally. The Nalcheka sat in a corner, its stony, crater-pocked shell clamped shut. The mushroom-shaped Storazoid stood in the center of its space, as immobile as the mushroom it resembled. The Kritzoan looked like a placid pool, only the slightest ripples disturbing its surface. The same was true of the Yartroan, the Chocondris, and the Whombar. Not a single creature showed any sign of agitation.

Dale still felt the emptiness in her gut, the hunger that had driven her so crazy the day before. The sexy dream she'd had the night before hadn't helped matters any. She couldn't remember many details, but there had been a table involved, and faceless giants passing her around like a shared bottle of wine, each one tasting her, and talking to each other in a language she didn't understand. Did the dream mean something? Did the giants represent tentacle monsters? Or maybe it referred to one of those Kritzoans the *Monster Massage* boutiques kept for people to hire out by the hour? She wished she could remember more.

"Vi, has there ever been a period of time when the tentacle monsters been this quiet, all at the same time?"

"No, ma'am."

Dale scowled, thinking. "Is there anything different in their environment?"

"Not that I have been able to detect, ma'am. All environmental systems are operating at correct levels. There are no contaminants in the system."

"Well, there's one difference. Christine. Maybe there's something about her body chemistry that's affecting them?"

"I do not believe we are equipped to detect that kind of influence, ma'am."

"Christine was genetically engineered," Dale mused, mostly to herself. "Maybe her body has been altered to cause tentacle monsters to become quiescent after having sex with her? No, that doesn't make any sense. That would require understanding of tentacle monster arousal that they don't have. If there was a way to dampen their hungers, then there'd be a way to amplify it as well, and the *Monster Massage* franchise would be using it. We'll just have to keep watching."

"Yes, ma'am," replied Vi. "Will there be anything else, ma'am?"

"How much longer until we come out of hyperspace?"

"We will arrive at Yartro system in approximately twelve hours, ma'am."

"And then it will be a couple hours after that until we get to the planet itself."

"Yes, ma'am. Approximately."

"Looks like a good time to start a new hobby."

CHAPTER FOUR
ON HOLD

Over a lunch of beefalo steak strips served over green salad, Christine said, "Monsters have been quiet again today, huh?"

"Yes, and it's beginning to worry me. This isn't usual for them. Normally there'd be enough activity for me to get two workouts a day. I'm starting to wonder if there's something wrong."

"I didn't, like, break them or anything, did I?"

Dale smiled comfortingly. "No, don't worry. You are the big change in their environment lately, so you may have played a role, but I don't think they're broken. My gut says they're adapting. Thinking. Figuring something out." After taking one last mouthful, Dale stood to carry her dishes to the recycler.

"I'm going to go into the Nalcheka's enclosure for a closer look. I'd like to know what's going on. Plus I'm going to take the camerabot and get some detailed scans, just in case I need to send an inquiry off to a XenoMed. Want to join me? This will give you a chance to have a look at them in less distracting circumstances."

"Oh, yes please! I'd like that."

A few minutes later, the two of them entered the Nalcheka's chamber followed by Dale's trusty camera-bot. It hovered just over her shoulder, its multiple lenses focused on the roughly circular body sitting silently in the corner of the chamber. As they crossed the spongy, cushioned floor, Dale gestured toward the creature. The camerabot responded by zipping up to it and humming quietly as its lenses spun and rotated. An emitter on the underside splayed a fine red beam over its surface, angling toward the cracks that crisscrossed its surface.

Christine followed, resting her hand on the stony surface. "I hadn't really understood just how big it is," she whispered.

"Really?" Dale asked. "You were in here just a few days ago."

"As you said, I didn't get a good look at it. Maybe I don't remember that well?"

The two plates nearest the women slid apart slightly with a faint grinding noise.

"It remembers you," Dale said with a smirk.

The plates slid a bit further, and an unblinking eye with a star-shaped pupil peeked at them from the gap, shifting back and forth between Dale and Christine. More of the seams opened, and three thick limbs emerged from the underside, lifting the huge rocky orb up onto paddle-shaped feet. A tentacle with a hand-like cluster of tendrils at the end inched out, feeling along the edge of the crack.

Dale stroked the pale green flesh.

"We don't want to wake you up if you're not interested in playing," she said calmly.

"They don't understand you, do they?" asked Christine.

"No. But I think they understand the emotional tone. If they can understand terror and excitement, then they should be able to understand tenderness and caring, don't you think?"

The eye emerged on a long stalk, joined in short order by another curving down from above. The two eyeballs examined Dale and Christine closely, in equal measure. Another three-fingered arm appeared. It moved slowly toward Dale's chin, stroked it tenderly, then slipped closer, up toward her neck.

Dale tilted her head back, giving the flexible little fingers room to explore her neck, her ear, to slip inside her coverall and caress her collarbone, her shoulder, and play briefly with the strap of her bra. Another arm came out to touch Christine the same way, prompting her to turn and give her mentor a questioning look.

"Should we strip down? You said that it's not a good idea to let the monsters try to rip off normal clothes."

"That's a good idea," said Dale. "It might not do anything, but we should be prepared."

Dale pulled down the closure on her coverall, quickly slipping out of it while more arms emerged from behind the Nalcheka's stony armor. She barely had time to undo her bra before the beast's powerful limbs grabbed her wrists and lifted her into the air, leaving it hanging open from her shoulders. Christine let out a little squeal of excitement as she, too, was raised off the cushioned deck.

"This is very strange behavior," said Dale, as the creature's arms snaked slowly around her body, squeezing and releasing as it shifted its grip. "It's not nearly as violent as usual. It seems curious in a way I've never seen before."

A third eyestalk emerged and joined the other two in examining Dale and Christine's nearly naked bodies. A tendril slipped under Dale's panties and tugged, gently, then more firmly, pulling her body with them, swinging her gently in midair. Dale twisted and squirmed, finally managing to get the angle right so that the next tug pulled them off.

"What's happening?" asked Christine, who had managed to get naked before the monster picked her up. "This seems weird. Like it's just going through the motions."

"I've never seen it act this way before," said Dale.

"Have you, um..." Christine gave her another nervous look.

"Have I what?"

"Have you ever had someone else, um, in?"

"From time to time," said Dale. "Nobody ever had so many of them in one day before, though. Usually one is enough."

Christine blushed.

The squeezes and caresses of the Nalcheka's arms became somewhat more intimate, and Dale felt her body respond, heart beating faster and a warm flush coming to her cheeks. She squirmed a bit, more out of habit than anything else. "I can't think of anything that would make their behavior change this way, though. Probably best to—mm—go with it."

"It's good that it's not being too rough. I'm still a little sore."

The Nalcheka groped and squeezed, caressed and pinched, bringing a tingle to Dale's skin as the dexterous hands wandered over her. She squirmed and thrashed in response, alternating between encouraging moans and excited screams. The situation was strange enough that the fear in her voice wasn't entirely manufactured. Normally, there was a core of control, a knowledge that things were progressing according to well-understood scripts, but the Nalcheka wasn't following them.

Her heart pounding, Dale was relieved to see two arms tipped with thick bulb shapes emerge from the monster's shell. This was closer to what she expected, but instead of heading for her pussy as it usually did, the appendage presented itself to her lips. As another gasp of pleasure forced its way out, the bulb squeezed in between her lips, stretching her jaws open wide with its spongy but resilient diameter. Its earthy, salty taste was subtly different this time, having a hint of something like wood, reminding her of scotch whisky.

After a few thrusts in her mouth, the bulb withdrew, leaving Dale even more confused than before. It had never stopped in the middle of a fuck before. After a few seconds the appendage returned, again bearing that slightly woody aroma. As it withdrew, she managed to gasp out, "This means something," before her mouth was filled again.

"What does it mppph?" asked Christine, similarly interrupted.

Dale glanced over at Christine, saw the tentacle thrust a few times and withdraw, at the same time as the organ pulled out of her own mouth. She was about to speak again when she realized that the Nalcheka was alternating between them, swapping arms with each short penetration.

Without warning, the arms holding both women released them, and they fell, sprawling onto the deck. The Nalcheka's arms and feet and eyes disappeared inside its carapace, and the cracks slammed closed.

"That was odd," said Christine.

Dale swallowed, her mouth still full of the Nalcheka's altered flavor. "You said it."

The voice of the ship's computer echoed in the large space. "Ma'am?"

"Yes, Vi?"

"The Yartroan and the Storazoid have increased activity levels and are releasing arousal pheromones." A muffled vibration ran through the deck. "Ma'am, I believe that immediate attention is in order. I can release a sedative if you like."

"No, Vi, we'll handle it. Christine, you've been with the Storazoid before, so you know what to expect. If you take care of it, I'll handle the Yartroan." The two headed out the chamber's circular hatch and split up in the hallway, hustling toward their respective monsters.

Dale paused for a moment outside the Yartroan's chamber, watching. Its meter-wide body cruised around the enclosure's twenty-meter space, a pale lavender disc-shaped form floating three or four meters above the floor. It dodged back and forth, avoiding the tall pillars and walls built for the cat-and-mouse stalking games that it preferred. Its multicolored, ribbon-like tentacles quivered and danced as they hung from the perimeter, reminding Dale of a human flexing her fingers in nervous agitation.

"You and me both," she said, opening the door and entering the chamber.

The Yartroan shifted course immediately, bearing down on Dale at full speed. Its body hit her chest like a heavy pillow, almost knocking her off her feet with its suddenness. There was no stalking, no tentative touches as it worked itself up toward full embrace. The thin tentacles wrapped around her, leaving very little skin exposed anywhere but her face. The effect was like being mummified in strips of tight plastic wrap. Only a few of the monster's arms were not part of the capture. As those ribbon-like tentacles swelled, filling with fluid to look like long, slender balloons, Dale felt some relief. Hopefully, this one would proceed in its usual pattern. The thickening limbs thrust their rounded tips at her face, and Dale grunted as she fended off each attempt. Individually, the tentacles weren't terribly strong, but there were too many of them to hold off for long, and after only a few seconds of struggle her cries were muffled by a rubbery tentacle pushing its way past her lips.

Dale fell to her knees as the creature fucked her mouth, and instead of pushing away, her hands stroked the invading appendage. Another one lingered nearby, as if waiting its turn. Dale's pussy ached for it, throbbing its desire to be filled by that marvelous semi-fluid thickness, but there was no point in guiding it or trying to impose her desires on it. It would take and give pleasure in its way, on its schedule, and that's all there was to it.

Instead, she concentrated on the tentacle in her mouth, opening her throat to it at the same time as she pushed it away with her hands, giving the Yartroan what it seemed to want. As soon as it was forced out, another plunged in. She gasped for air in the rare moments that her mouth wasn't full.

Then the Yartroan let her go, peeling away from her body. It floated up toward the ceiling and hung there, suspended, its tentacles twitching slightly, not as agitated as before but not calm, either. The half dozen tentacles that had filled with fluid remained engorged, hanging heavily from the perimeter of its body.

Dale swallowed, still tasting the Yartroan's secretions: vanilla and salt and dry white wine. Rationally, she could not explain its strange behavior, but her gut told her that it was waiting for something—waiting for her to do something, or for something to happen. She picked herself up and backed out of the chamber.

She closed her eyes and took a deep breath, emptying her mind, allowing her instincts to speak to her. The monsters were waiting for something. Expecting something. They wanted her to do something. What? What could they want her to do that she hadn't before? What was happening now, that hadn't happened before?

She walked into her quarters. "Vi, turn on the shower, please. Moderately hot."

"Yes, ma'am." The water turned on, and a few wisps of steam escaped around the door.

Dale began to step under the spray, and stopped. Swallowed. The taste of vanilla and salt and white wine from the Yartroan mixed with the woody flavor of the Nalcheka. "Vi, when Christine had her sessions with the monsters while I was away, did she take a shower in between?"

"No, ma'am. She did not."

Taste. Scent. Pheromones. Many tentacle monsters used pheromones in hunting prey. Why not for other purposes? Why not for communication? Dale put a hand out to steady herself. All these years, scheduling her sessions morning and evening, showering afterwards—she had been cutting off their means of communicating with each other. They might not have even been aware that there were other monsters on the ship. Then Christine had gone in, her enthusiasm and exuberance blowing past all of Dale's habits, and now they knew. They knew and, through her and through Christine, they could talk to each other.

It was no wonder the scientists had never discovered this. The circumstances would never have happened in a laboratory, nor would they have happened with any ordinary monster enthusiast. It took Christine's unusual libido and endurance, combined with Dale's unusually large and diverse assembly of monsters, to set the stage for the discovery.

Vi spoke from the console next to the shower. "Ma'am, we have emerged from hyperspace, and we are on course for the planet Yartro. I am receiving a transmission from a ship identifying itself as the private courier ship *Edward Kenway*. They are requesting as—assist—requesting a—req—they—they—they—theyyyyy...." The computer's voice devolved into a stuttering groan. The ship went silent, the hum of its engines and the white noise of its ventilation systems suddenly, thunderingly absent.

"Vi? Vi!" Dale's throat threatened to close in panic. There was no answer. She started to run in the direction of the ship's control center, but stopped after a few steps and looked back down the hallway. What about Christine? No, she'd be fine, Dale decided. She would restart the ship's computer and if that didn't work she could activate the distress beacon. It was going to be okay. She just had to stay calm.

Stay calm, she told herself, resuming her run toward the control center.

Christine. Someone was after Christine. Her mother, no doubt, had sent the *Edward Kenway* to hijack her ship and take Christine back to New New Amsterdam. Like the customs officials and the Space

Patrol, she had no doubt lied to them to get them to come out here; if she could talk to them, they could straighten it out, let them know that Christine was here of her own free will.

Then the lights went out.

"No!" Dale cried, stumbling with the sudden disorientation. Red emergency lights flicked on for a moment, transforming the corridor into a nightmare scene, and then back out again. A thud reverberated in the darkness. Something large and solid had struck the hull, Dale felt certain. She found the wall and felt her way along it, panic gripping her chest. Were they shooting?

If she could just get to the bridge, she told herself, she'd restart the computer. Everything would be okay if she could get there. Her hand came to a doorway. Which one was this? Her quarters, she was pretty sure. There would be about four meters of wall, then the door to the mess, then the main airlock, and past that, at the end of the hall, would be the door to the bridge. If it would open. Would it open? It had to open. She had to know that it would open.

A sob forced its way from her throat. No! She couldn't give in to panic. Not now. Not with Christine and all the monsters depending on her. She stumbled forward, her hand on the wall, counting the footsteps. There; there was the door to the galley, a little further away than she expected, but it was there. She knew where she was. The bridge was just a few steps further. A few steps further—

Light burst into the corridor as the airlock door irised open. She squinted and raised her hands to block the glare. There were people in the airlock, people in space suits. Then there was a crack and a sizzle and a sharp pain ran through her whole body. Dale's muscles spasmed uncontrollably. She fell to the deck, her body twisting and convulsing as electricity robbed her of any ability to run, fight, or even move of her own volition. Then the pain was gone, and strong hands took her by the arms and lifted her to her feet.

"Dale Clearwater," said a mature woman's voice, "You are a prisoner of the Xenoform Emancipation Society. Submit peacefully, and you will not be harmed."

CHAPTER FIVE
DISASTER BOUND

Dale Clearwater had been tied up before, but that was for fun. This time, it was business, and there was no pleasure in it whatsoever. She stared back defiantly at her captor. Bound tightly to one of the chairs in her own galley and with a gag wedged in her mouth, there was little else she could do to respond to the woman's tirade.

Nobody had used the woman's name, but Dale knew who she was. Doctor Nichole Florence was notorious across the galaxy, a militant extremist working for her vision of the rights of tentacle monsters, or 'xenoforms,' as she preferred to call them. She marched back and forth, intense eyes never straying from Dale's face. A tight-fitting jumpsuit clung to her lean body, and her dark but graying hair stood out from her head in a short spacer's cut.

"Now that we've finally caught up with you, and you will receive the justice you so richly deserve. Not only have you placed six xenoforms in sexual slavery, but you have aided and abetted untold thousands more across the galaxy. This is the beginning of the end of this injustice, Dale Clearwater."

Dale grunted past the gag, unable to articulate even the slightest response. The gag was well done: not just a strip of material between her teeth, but a wad of fabric held in place by a tight nylon strap. A perverse corner of her mind wondered whether Doctor Florence had gotten her expertise in such things in the kink community.

One of the other hijackers, a burly young man with an electro-stunner strapped to his hip, came to the door. He had on the same drab jumpsuits the rest of the hijackers wore. "Doc? We can't find that Delavos woman. We think she's hiding in the maintenance passages somewhere."

"Not in front of the prisoner, idiot," hissed Doctor Florence, shoving him out into the corridor. The door failed to close behind them, and Dale strained to overhear their conversation. She caught a few words here and there, like 'ventilation' and 'carbon dioxide.' Then the young man stepped into the galley and leaned against the wall, his face flushed with embarrassment.

At least she wasn't still naked. After using some heavy tape to secure her to the chair, the hijackers had draped a blanket over her body, leaving only her head poking out at the top, to better hear Doctor Florence's lectures on the helplessness and disempowerment of the tentacle monsters.

The worst part was, after having discovered the means by which the tentacle monsters could communicate with each other, Dale found herself struggling to push away the idea that, in some sense, Doctor Florence was right. She had been, unknowingly, keeping the creatures incommunicado, by taking showers between sessions with them. By washing away the chemicals they had left on and in her skin she had isolated them in a way that would have been inhumane for a human being. But she hadn't known—nobody had known—how that communication even existed.

Not that Doctor Florence's solution to the problem would help matters any. Releasing the tentacle monsters on the wild planets where they had originally been discovered wasn't going to do them any favors. Humans were the only creatures they had any interest in, and by definition wild planets didn't have any. From what Dale now understood, the creatures would be just as mute and voiceless in their freedom as they were living with humans. She had to get free, to get the word out about what she had discovered.

Dale looked at the young man pleadingly.

"Wah-er," she managed to say past the gag. She didn't actually need water, but if she could talk to this kid, maybe she'd be able to get out of this predicament.

"Need some water?" he asked.

Dale nodded.

"All right," he said, and stepped up to the console. He brought up a manual control console and ordered up a plastic pouch and a straw. When he brought it over, he tried to slip the straw past the gag, but there was no room for it; the restraint was too well secured.

She gave him another helpless look.

"Doc's gonna get mad if I take off the gag," he said.

Dale looked down at the thick blanket covering her body and pulled at the tape holding her wrists to the armrests, trying to indicate that no, she wasn't going anywhere. The motion made the blanket slide down off of one shoulder, exposing her breast. She winced and turned her head away, as if embarrassed to have accidentally exposed herself. With her holos on sale in every market that allowed depictions of tentacle sex, she had no shame about her body, but he seemed like a nice kid and appearing more vulnerable couldn't hurt.

The guy replaced the blanket, tucking it behind her shoulder. "All right, but don't start making trouble, okay? I don't want to have to use this." He slapped the weapon at his side. Then he stepped behind her, fiddled with the strap, and then the gag was loose.

"Thank you," she said.

The kid brought the straw to her lips, and she drank, finding that she was thirsty after all. "What's your name?" she asked, taking as friendly a tone as possible.

"I'm not supposed to tell you that," he said.

"Is there anything you can tell me?"

"I'm supposed to watch you and make sure you don't try to escape."

"You're doing a good job of that."

"Thank you."

Dale looked into the lad's eyes. "You know, I'm not the terrible person your boss says I am."

"Doc says that what you do is 'beastiality.'" The boy mispronounced the word the way uninformed people had been doing ever since the twentieth century, but it didn't have a lot of venom in it. She let the long vowel go by without comment.

"If I agreed with Doc, I wouldn't do it," Dale replied. "Their behavior is natural. They don't need to be trained for it. It's part of how they communicate with each other."

He scowled. "It's not natural. They don't do it in the wild, or with other animals. Humans taught them."

Dale let it go. She wasn't going to get anywhere putting the guy on the defensive. "Could I have some more water please?"

He brought the straw to her lips. "Finish it up. I need to put the gag in before Doc gets back."

She nodded, and drank more slowly, trying to think of a way to engage the guy, get him to open up to her, give her a way to get some kind of influence with him.

The ship lurched suddenly, causing her chair to teeter precariously. Her captor caught her and set it back on four legs. "What's going on?" she asked.

"I think we landed," he said.

"Landed? On Yartro?"

"Yes, landed," said Doctor Florence, striding into the room. "We are liberating these xenoforms, returning them to the wild."

The young man jumped back as if burned, and his face lit up with another blush. "I was just, uh, giving her some water, Doc—"

"Yes, yes, whatever. Cut her loose. I want her to witness the liberation of her slaves."

"All of them?" Dale asked, as the guard took out a small folding knife and cut through her bonds. "That's insane! Even if you think they're better off in the wild, most of them aren't even native to this planet!" When she was free, Dale wrapped the blanket around herself, slinging the extra fabric up over her shoulder like a toga.

"They're not animals," she stated. "They're not slaves. They're companions! It's a mutually beneficial relationship."

Doctor Florence scoffed, "And so you keep them confined? In cells?" She turned her attention toward the young man and leveled a stern gaze. "Keep your wits about you," she said. "There's no telling what a human monster like her is capable of. Be ready to use your weapon." She turned and strode out into the hallway.

Dale followed. "I keep them in these chambers because this is how they're happiest." she explained. "They like being here. Listen to me! When we had—" Dale searched for a word that wouldn't be too inflammatory. "When we had contact with more than one monster, their behavior changed. They were thinking. They could taste each other or something. I'm certain that they use sex to communicate with each other!"

Doctor Florence ignored her. On the balcony overlooking the monster enclosures, another of Doctor Florence's confederates stood at a control console. "We're ready, Doc!" she shouted.

Doctor Florence waved and nodded to the report, and then gave Dale a brief glance over her shoulder. "I have no doubt that your so-called training has warped their psyches, but that damage cannot be undone now. We cannot heal the psychic scars you have given these poor animals, but we at least can keep you from making things any worse."

They stood outside the Kritzoan's enclosure, where the great transparent beast lay placidly in its pool, unresponsive to the turmoil going on around it.

"You call them animals," said Dale. "They're not. They're thinking, sentient beings. They have to be! Why else would we find them on dozens of planets across the galaxy? How could their biology and behavior be so similar from one type to the next, in spite of gross differences in form? They had to have had a common origin. They use sex to communicate with each other! They need us!"

"So you said," said Doctor Florence, cutting off Dale's argument with a slash of her hand. "I've heard such claims before. The science doesn't support them."

"Because the scientists are treating them like specimens! You can't treat thinking creatures like lab animals. They won't cooperate."

"Don't worry," said Doctor Florence. "We shall be dealing with those so-called scientists and their injustices as well. Today, however, we deal with yours. Open the doors!" she shouted, and the confederate on the balcony tapped the controls in front of her.

With a grinding squeal, the main cargo door, which formed one wall of the Kritzoan's enclosure, slid open, revealing a hilltop view of a forested valley where wisps of fog drifted among trees and vines with foliage in colors from deep greens to bright blue. Something large called out in a deep bellow, its cry echoing across the landscape.

The Kritzoan didn't budge. It lay in its bowl-shaped pool, surface barely rippling. "It's not moving, doctor," said the young man standing behind Dale.

"I can see that," Doctor Florence spat.

"It doesn't want to go," Dale replied. "Your mission is fundamentally flawed."

"Hush!" Doctor Florence pointed to the woman up on the balcony. "Retract the walls between the cells."

The woman acknowledged the order with a nod and tapped the control panel again, and the seldom-used but well-maintained hydraulics whined, lifting the walls separating the chambers.

"If you care about the welfare of these creatures—" Dale began.

"Quiet! Be silent or I will have you gagged again. I care for nothing as much as the welfare of xenoforms. This space is needed to rescue others."

The walls clanged one by one as they retracted flat against the upper wall of the cargo bay. The space now looked a good deal more like it had when Dale had bought the ship.

In the next space over from the Kritzoan, the Nalcheka opened one of the cracks in its stony shell and poked a single eye out. Beyond it, the Storazoid rose up on its stumpy feet and tilted slightly, a gesture that reminded Dale of a human cocking his head in puzzlement. Still further on, the Yartroan drifted lazily in the air, in no particular hurry to escape.

"Things not going according to plan?" Dale snarked.

Doctor Florence rubbed her face with both hands, muttering softly to herself. "They've become too used to captivity. We'll have to push them out. Are the freight tractors operational?" she asked.

"No," said the tech up in the balcony. "I'm sorry, we haven't gotten full control of the power systems yet. We're still on battery power."

Dale couldn't help smiling to herself. So they didn't have full control of the ship. Vi must still be operational at some level, still loyal, making trouble for the hijackers, slowing their plans. Good. There was still hope.

"Face it," said Dale. "Your whole mission is based on a misconception. These xenoforms, as you call them, they like it here. They like me. They want to stay with me, and they won't leave the ship without me."

"Is that so?" Doctor Florence growled. "Well then, I guess we're going to have to liberate you as well." She pointed to the airlock behind them. "Throw her off the ship. If she has these monsters so thoroughly brainwashed, then so be it. If she resists, hit her with the stunner and carry her to the trees."

The big guy drew his pistol and grabbed her arm with his other hand. "Come on."

"You can't be serious," said Dale. "That's a jungle. You can't expect me to survive out there!"

"No," said Doctor Florence, her voice dripping with contempt. "I don't."

Her guard pushed the button to open the airlock with the barrel of his electro-stunner. Nothing happened. He pushed it again. "Uh, Doc?"

Doctor Florence sighed. "Disengage it and use the hand pump. It's behind that panel."

"Oh, right." The big man let go of Dale's arm and fumbled with the panel one-handed.

Dale glanced at her two captors, assessing her chances of escape. If she threw the blanket over the one with the gun and ran, she might be able to get out of sight before he was able bring his weapon to bear. He didn't carry his weapon with any confidence, didn't have the bearing of a military man or a hunter like Vince. He might not be a good shot. If she could get to the maintenance passages, maybe she could locate Christine and formulate some kind of plan.

Then she looked into Doctor Florence's eyes. "On second thought, stun her now," said the doctor.

Dale tried to execute her plan, but the man swept the blanket away with his free arm and then brought the gun to bear. She crouched to jump out of his line of fire, but the bolt caught her before she could spring, and agonizing spasms paralyzed her body. She collapsed. Through the agony she felt the big man bind her ankles and wrists together with tape, and hoist her up over his shoulder.

"Sorry," he muttered.

He definitely wasn't a mercenary. He was probably some idealistic kid that had joined up with Doctor Florence full of idealism only to find out he'd become a party to piracy.

She managed to open her eyes while being carried out of the airlock. The clearing where the ship had landed was not a natural one. A deep layer of ash covered the ground, with charred tree stumps and small blackened bones poking up through it here and there. She didn't know what had done this damage, but she had no doubt that it was a weapon, and that it had been used solely to create a convenient place to land.

So much for caring about the welfare of innocent animals, Dale thought.

At the edge of the destroyed forest, where the big man laid Dale down, quite gently, with her back to a vine-covered tree. Dale looked up, eyes pleading. "You can't leave me here like this!"

He avoided eye contact. A crack of thunder rolled out from the jungle. Thick clouds promised a storm.

"Naked? Alone? Tied up? You're not even going to get the ship's survival kit out of the escape pod?" If Dale could get this man to think for just a minute about what he was doing, she might be able to get him to hesitate, get him to talk to her. "This is murder—you know that?"

Without a word, the man reached into a pocket, dropped his folding knife by her feet, and then stalked away through the ash toward her ship.

The man took a curving path toward the airlock to avoid the small herd of tentacle monsters emerging from the huge cargo bay doors. The Nalcheka was in front, walking on its great paddle-like feet, with the Yartroan flying around it like an orbiting satellite. Behind them, the Storazoid stumped along on its stubby little feet, its mushroom-shaped body waving back and forth as it negotiated the uneven ground. In the furrow driven by the more solid creatures, the Kritzoan rolled along, its semi-liquid body picking up bits of ash and detritus, turning its usually transparent body into an undulating mass of gray and black.

Behind them were the rest of her monsters. The hulking Rominek stomped on its three thick legs, its suckered tentacles dangling limply from shoulders two meters above the ground, with Chocondris wrapped around its body as if it were just another tree. Finally, the long, serpentine body of the Whombar zig-zagged at the rear of the group, its single eye lifted up above the ashes.

"No!" Dale shouted, rolling up onto her knees. "Go back! Go back inside!" She knew it was no use, but what else was there to do? Now that the ship was empty of tentacle monsters, there was nothing stopping the hijackers from taking off and stranding her here without any means of signaling for help. There was a monastery on the planet, somewhere, but there was no way to tell which direction or how far. Dale doubted the hijackers would have chosen a spot anywhere near the only spot of civilization. Panic gripped Dale's throat and squeezed, and she couldn't help choking out a sob of despair. She picked up the knife, then fumbled it when she tried to open its blade. A second try got it open, but angling it back to cut the tape wrapped around her wrists was nearly impossible. The cargo bay door descended, coming closer by the second to sealing her out, and sealing her fate.

She couldn't allow that to happen. Gripping the handle of the knife between her knees, she sawed at the tape, finally cutting through it as the cargo bay was halfway closed. Heart pounding, she cut through the tape on her ankles and sprinted for the doors. Ashes flew up in clouds around her as she pelted across the open area, stumbling over half-burned tree limbs and slipping in the loose footing. The door was closing, but she could make it inside if she ran flat out. She gripped the little blade like it was a sword. They were going to pay for hijacking her ship, one way or another. She knew her chances weren't good with only a knife but, by the stars, she was going to try.

Then she tripped. Instead of sprawling into the ashes, however, she found herself hauled up into the air. The little knife flew from her hand and disappeared into the ashes. There was a tentacle wrapped around her ankle. The Nalcheka had her.

"No!" she screamed, "Let me down! Let me down!"

The cargo doors closed with a clang and a hiss.

The Nalcheka opened its stony shell and extruded more arms, taking hold of Dale's wrists, ankles and waist, holding her spread-eagled while it inspected her with its three alien eyes. After a few seconds, it turned and lay her on the Storazoid's broad orange back. The surface had already extruded its numerous woody tendrils and had released its sweet-smelling secretions. It welcomed her with a strong, well-lubricated embrace. The aphrodisiac scent of cinnamon and barbecue sauce warred with her fear, transforming the thudding heartbeat of panic into pulses of arousal.

"Not now, not now, stars, please not now," she moaned. The Storazoid's grip did not slacken.

The other monsters did not stand idly by, either. The Nalcheka's long green tentacles, with their dexterous hand-like tendrils at the end, caressed every part of her body, joined moments later by the numerous ribbon-like appendages of the Yartroan and the gnarled, woody stems of the Chocondris. The monsters spread the Storazoid's secretions, massaging the tingle-inducing fluid into her thighs, her breasts, her arms, even into her hair. Her skin's entire surface turned into one continuous erogenous zone.

When one monster let up, another one took its place. The Rominek stood over her, clutching and squeezing with its masses of long, rope-like tendrils, while the body of the Whombar, easily as thick as her thigh, wrapped around her midsection and stroked her with the rounded tip of its tail.

The deep, mind-destroying pleasure of the creatures' attentions couldn't eliminate the fear that seethed in the rational part of Dale's mind, but the primal sexual need would not be denied. Her body responded in contrast to the tears of frustration that poured from her eyes. As one thick appendage after another thrust inside her, each monster taking turns penetrating her mouth and her pussy, the emotions swirled around into an intense, nearly indistinguishable mass. Her helplessness was complete, and the only reaction that she could muster was surrender.

Doctor Florence had won. They would steal her ship, and leave her here to die. An orgasm rose, crested, diminished, and returned again, a sympathetic undertone vibration to the pulsing rhythms the monsters played on her body. It became strangely soothing, an invitation to let go of rationality, let go of fear, let go even of consciousness, and give in to ecstasy. Why not, when reality had gone so terribly wrong?

It would be so easy. Just let those thoughts go. A climax, far too powerful to be resisted, wracked her body. In a moment when her mouth was empty, she let out a cry that was as much scream of frustration as it was a cry of pleasure. She felt her resolve weakening. The blackness of despair offered, if not comfort, then at least a release from the torment of helplessness. And this would be such orgasmic, transcendent despair.

But she couldn't. She was the leader, the responsible one, the one they needed, the only person who could get them out of their predicament. The ship had not yet departed the planet. There was still hope, and she needed to grab onto it and hold on tight. She couldn't indulge herself.

The only way out was through. The monsters would not be finished with her until she was, herself, finished: drained, exhausted. Having gone without any more sexual contact than the occasional wank for several days, there was a lot to drain.

One by one, however, the monsters took their turns and drifted away, long before they would ordinarily have been finished with her. The cacophony of pleasure slackened, until only the Storazoid still held her. After the hurried frenzy of the other creatures, its caresses soothed rather than excited. Even the slow, creaking penetration of its extended woody nodules, in contrast to the powerful fucking of the other monsters, calmed her overstimulated nerves. Then it, too, retracted its tentacles back into its body and allowed her to slide to the ground, covered head to toe in tentacle monster secretions. The green slime of the Nalcheka mixed with the Chocondris' pollen and the Storazoid's mucous, leaving her in a ten-centimeter-deep puddle of thick, sloppy fluids. She couldn't open her eyes because of the viscous ooze. If she let her arms collapse the way they wanted to, she could have slipped down into it and drowned.

She lay there for a long while. Gradually, her breathing slowed to a more normal pace, as did her heartbeat, though her head still swam and her skin still tingled. A gentle rain fell, washing away the gunk, and Dale rolled over on her back to let the warm, cascading water rinse the mess from her face.

She hoped the monsters had been talking to each other. Maybe they were just introducing themselves, or talking about Dale and the ship, but more likely the conversation would have been mostly nonsense to a human being. She was glad to have been able to give them that much, at least. It was a nice fantasy to believe that they had thought up a way to get back on board the ship, but that's all it was—a fantasy.

When she was able to open her eyes, she discovered that the water falling over her wasn't coming from the sky. She was under the trees, and the water flowed from the body of the Kritzoan. The monsters had carried her to the forest, and this one had suspended itself from a half dozen pseudopods wrapped around thick boughs and tree trunks. She stood and reached up to pat its spongy surface.

"Thank you," she said, and it quivered in response. She cleaned herself, gently. The touch of her own hand was enough to evoke post-orgasmic shudders, but she managed to get herself mostly clean in spite of it. When all the fluids were washed away, the water stopped.

Around her, she could see the other monsters in quiescent states. The Storazoid stood just a few meters away, its stumpy feet burrowed into the ground to absorb nutrients. The Nalcheka's stony shell had closed up, and the Chocondris was nowhere to be seen, camouflaging itself in the foliage. The Yartroan hung limp in midair, its ribbon-like tentacles fluttering in the breeze. The Whombar had climbed up to a tree branch to sleep, its one huge eye closed. Below it, the Rominek stood with its long tendrils wrapped around itself like twine on a spool.

Dale made her way to the edge of the clearing. The ship still stood there, silent and unmoving. They had not left yet. Whatever difficulties they were having still prevented them from taking off.

She had to get back on that ship. The doors were sealed, as was the airlock door. There was no manual override on the outside, no way to access the hand pump the hijacker had used to open the doors on her way out. If they had managed to get power restored to the doors, then they would probably have locked the controls as well.

She would have to trick the hijackers, somehow, into letting her back on board. Then, if there wasn't some way to turn the tables on them, she might at least be able to hide out somewhere and maybe find a way to alert the authorities.

Out of the corner of her eye, she caught a glimpse of movement, a flash of color among the trees. Heart thudding, she took a few steps in that direction, and then froze in place. There was a Yartroan tentacle monster cruising between the trees, meandering slowly in her direction. For a moment she thought it might have been her Yartroan, but this one was bigger, and its tentacles were not as colorful. This was a wild monster, and while it wouldn't be as dangerous as a Phase Looper or a Mumzer, getting caught in its tentacles was not going to help matters. She ducked down next to a tree and hoped that it hadn't yet caught her scent.

But the wild Yartroan spiraled closer, moving along an arcing path between the trees, gliding through the air like a meandering cloud unmoored from the wind. Every time she spotted it, it was closer. It was hunting her, Dale was sure of it.

There was nothing she could do about it. If she ran, it would catch up to her, and she was fairly certain she'd get lost in the woods. If she stayed and waited, it would catch her all the same. And without any training, she wasn't sure the creature would know how to fuck her without hurting her. Her only hope would be to play dead, to make herself as unappealing to the Yartroan as possible.

Lying on the ground, closing her eyes, Dale tried to calm herself. Fear and stress were stimuli that would excite the Yartroan, attract its interest. She had to remain calm. Yet she couldn't banish the sick feeling in the pit of her stomach that the ship was going to lift off any moment and maroon her in the middle of this vast wilderness.

Dale mentally kicked herself for coming to this planet. Hadn't she told Vince, just a few days ago , that this was his kind of planet, not hers? Now, here she was: naked and helpless, waiting for a wild tentacle monster to have its way with her. How could she have been so stupid? There were a thousand other worlds they could have gone to, a dozen or more invitations to come and record segments for her holo program.

A feather-light touch brushed against her ankle. She opened her eyes. The grayish white disc of the wild Yartroan's body hung over her like an umbrella. It was a big one, at least ten feet in diameter, with ribbon tentacles at least ten centimeters wide. She imagined what they would be like when engorged, and pushed the thought away. There was no way she could take an organ like that, not without serious injury. She had to stay still, stay calm, give it no reason to have an interest in her.

More tentacles brushed her body. Dale wished she could just sink into the ground. She fought to keep the tremble from her limbs, to keep her breathing deep and even, to keep her nerves in order. It wasn't working.

A flat tentacle worked its way under her legs and wrapped

around her ankles. Others wrapped around elbows, waist, neck, gradually encasing her in its embrace.

"Noooo," she pleaded, "Please." The cry emboldened it. It tightened its grip and hauled itself closer, while several tentacles thickened, filling with fluid. This was not going to be pleasant. It was going to hurt, and not in a good way. Dale closed her eyes, bracing herself for impalement.

This wasn't play. This wasn't fun. This was real panic, real fear of real pain and real injury. There was nothing arousing about that. This creature was going to fuck her to death, and there was nothing she could do about it.

Then there was a tug, and a jerk. For a moment, she was shaken in the Yartroan's tentacles like a marionette, and then it released her. She hit the ground and rolled, hitting the trunk of a tree hard enough to see stars. She blinked them away as she desperately gathered her legs under her to dodge if the monster came at her for another attack.

But it wasn't coming back. The big Yartroan's tentacles were bound together by a vine-like tendril of the Chocondris, which squeezed the creature mercilessly. The Yartroan struggled, freeing one arm and then another, which it used to pick up rocks and fallen tree limbs to bash at the Chocondris with all its might. It held firm until one blow struck a sensitive bud, and the Chocondris flinched and almost let go.

The crash of a falling tree heralded the arrival of the Nalcheka, using its massive bulk and strength to push through the forest. It reached out with three of its arms to grab the wild Yartroan's body, taking it from the Chocondris' grasp and wrestling its limbs into a ball. The Yartroan wasn't strong, but it had more than a dozen arms, many of them armed with rocks and sticks, and it fought back with all of its strength. Most of the blows bounced off of the Nalcheka's stony shell, but some hit home, smashing the exposed tentacles with bruising force.

The Storazoid arrived next, two tentacles holding out a large rock coated with its own adhesive secretions. The Nalcheka shoved the wild Yartroan's body against the rock, sticking it firmly to the creature's flesh. Powerful limbs then flung the Yartroan, rock and all, high above the trees, where it disappeared from sight.

Dale's mouth hung open. She had just witnessed cooperation between her monsters on a level she had never seen or even heard of before. They had recognized that she was in danger, and cooperated to neutralize the threat. The Yartroan, her Yartroan, drifted close to her and gently wrapped a few tentacles around her arm and body, then let go. She gathered up its tentacles in a huge hug.

That's when she noticed their wounds. The injury to the Chocondris' flower bud was minor, and would heal on its own, but one of the Nalcheka's three eyes had been partially crushed, one hand twisted, and its arms had many bruises and abrasions. It leaked blood from a dozen places, not badly but the injuries needed to be looked at. Dale ground her teeth, adding yet another crime to the pile of guilt heaped at the feet of Doctor Florence. This was her fault.

Dale was out of immediate danger, but the problem of getting back on board her ship had become even more acute. She needed to get to her ship's medical supplies and attend to her monster. There was nothing she could do out here. How could she get in? They'd never just open the doors, no matter what she said. Even if they took pity on the Nalcheka, they would never let her in along with it.

The Nalcheka walked, slowly, in the direction of the ship. The plates of its shell expanded and contracted, the space between them widening and narrowing, as if it were breathing. Dale knew that wasn't the case—a Nalcheka didn't breathe, didn't even need air; it could survive in the vacuum of deep space just as easily as a planet's surface. One eye turned toward Dale, and then in its direction of travel, then back again as it picked its way between the trees. It was in pain, a great deal of pain, and it knew where relief could be found.

It also knew, Dale realized, that her presence would be required to get that relief. She wished she could help it, but the moment she tried to step aboard the ship, she was certain the hijackers would simply stun her again and throw her out.

Unless they didn't know she was there.

She ran to catch up to the Nalcheka, and jumped up to squirm in through one of the cracks its armor. There was space in there, in the gap where the monster's huge leg and foot would be if it were closed up. Then the gap closed up around her, leaving only enough room for the leg to poke out at the bottom. That was how she could sneak back aboard. That was how she could get her ship back.

If they let the Nalcheka in.

If she could get away from the hijackers.

If she could stow away.

There were a dozen things that could go wrong, but now she had a plan. Now she had a chance.

She rocked gently inside that little space, the Nalcheka's body warm against hers. All she could do was trust that it understood, that it knew what was going on well enough to help.

CHAPTER SIX
SLEIGHT OF HAND

Dale Clearwater fought against panic. There was nothing she could do now but wait, watching through the narrow crack in the Nalcheka's shell for an opportunity to slip out undetected, though she wasn't sure how she could tell the massive tentacle monster that the time was right. She had to trust it.

A small patch of ground rolled past the crack, a frustratingly limited field of view. For what seemed like far too long, all she saw through that gap were ashes, charred tree stumps, and the occasional blackened bone. The apocalypse landscape was not only the result of whatever weapon the hijackers had used to create the clearing where the ship had landed. It was also evidence of the depth of the hijackers' hypocrisy. Their weapon had destroyed countless wild creatures to make a space where the ship could land, possibly even including wild tentacle monsters of the same sort they professed to defend.

The Nalcheka's gait was uneven. While the injuries it had sustained defending Dale gave the creature a very plausible reason for wanting to get back on the ship, Dale winced in sympathy with each stride of its injured foot. It was in pain, she knew, and there was little she could do about it except try to get her ship back.

The Nalcheka stopped moving, and she felt an impact through the monster's body coinciding with a dull metallic thud. They had reached the ship, and the creature was bumping its shell against the big cargo doors where it had emerged a few hours before.

"Go on, shoo," said a voice, over the ship's external speakers. "You're free. Get away from the doors." The voice belonged to Doctor Florence, the leader of the Xenoform Emancipation Society hijackers who had stolen Dale's ship. "Move along, you stupid beast! You don't live here anymore."

Another bump. And another.

There was a whine of motors, the unmistakable sound of the cargo doors rolling open. It had worked. They were admitting the monster back onto the ship. Dale's heart hammered. Timing. She had to somehow get away from the monster while they were distracted.

As if she had told it the plan, the Nalcheka opened its shell wide enough for her to slip out. She ran to the edge of the cargo doors, peering inside with one eye as the monster waited for the gap to open high enough to admit it.

"Good work," she whispered.

The hijackers would be watching it closely. If she went in too soon, they would see her. But the moment would come. It had to.

Slowly, the door slid up into its housing, until the Nalcheka could duck slightly and shuffle inside. It stopped and settled down to the deck, pulling its undamaged limbs inside its shell. Only the ones that had been hurt now showed: a damaged eye, a deeply bruised leg, a crushed tendril-hand. After long, anxious minutes, Doctor Florence and two of her followers entered the cargo bay, wheeling Dale's medical cart in front of them. The door through which they had entered stood open, no doubt to allow a quick escape if the Nalcheka turned hostile.

Their caution was warranted. The Nalcheka was the largest and strongest monster in her collection. Mishandling it could be dangerous.

Dale peered cautiously at the approaching hijackers. She hadn't been seen yet and, as the two disappeared around the curve of the Nalcheka's body, Dale felt safe to slip into the ship and make a quiet dash for the door. She expected the Nalcheka to attack as soon as she was in, providing a distraction, but instead it laid its injured limbs out on the side away from the door. *An even better distraction*, thought Dale, hurrying silently to the door. She had always considered the monsters to be intelligent beings, but this one was showing unusual planning and foresight. Had the full-on monster orgy in the woods been the trigger for that, or had it always been that bright? There would be time to investigate later.

Before she had been thrown off the ship, Dale had heard one of the hijackers tell Doctor Florence that Dale's apprentice, Christine, had retreated to the maintenance passages of the ship. She hoped that was still the case, even though she had never been in those spaces herself. She hurried into her quarters, grabbed a coverall and shoes, and found the panel that led to the maintenance passages. This was the domain of her ship's virtual intelligence, Vi, and the drones it used to perform repairs and upkeep. These tunnels snaked through every part of the ship, wrapping around the living spaces and vital systems to allow discreet access to every part.

When she popped the panel open, Dale felt a headache bloom in her temples, and a sudden need to breathe deeply. *Carbon dioxide,* she remembered one of them said. *They flooded the passages with carbon dioxide.* She closed the passage and took several deep breaths until the headache cleared. Christine couldn't hide in there, not and stay alive. Dale would have liked to believe that Christine had found somewhere else to hide, but if she had been flushed out of the maintenance tunnels, chances were good she had been captured.

Or she could be dead. If Christine didn't realize they were poisoning the air, or if she learned too late and didn't make it out—Dale pushed that thought away. Christine was alive. She wouldn't let that belief go, not yet.

Dale dressed and crept back to the door. The passageway outside was still clear, and there was no sign she had been discovered. Through the transparent aluminum wall of the cargo bay, she saw Doctor Florence and one of her crew working on the Nalcheka's wounds. It wasn't cooperating much. At every touch, it flinched, and a twitch from a creature that large carried bruising force. As she watched, it knocked the medical cart over, scattering supplies across the floor.

"Good job," she whispered. "Keep them busy."

She crept out into the hallway and had a quick glance into the lounge to make sure Christine wasn't being held there, then turned back to follow the hallway around toward the guest quarters. The transparent wall of the cargo bay was great for keeping an eye on the monsters, but Dale felt vulnerable knowing that at any moment one of the hijackers could show up and spot her.

Then Dale spotted a woman she didn't recognize leaning against the wall opposite the guest quarters, arms folded across her chest, electro-stunner. holstered on her belt. Dale ducked back out of sight around the curve of the hallway. That pretty much settled it; they had caught Christine, and were holding her in the guest quarters.

Dale was relieved, but now what? Dale couldn't hide in the maintenance passages, but she could probably find a spot out of sight in the Chocondris enclosure. The foliage was dense enough. But that was beyond this guard, and she didn't see any way to sneak past her. Overpowering her was out of the question; anything Dale did would betray her presence on the ship, and spoil the whole plan.

Nor could Dale afford to wait for an opportunity. Her spot wasn't immediately visible to the guard, but it was only a matter of time before someone came along and spotted her.

The console outside Christine's quarters chirped and a voice emerged.

"All right, everyone, I've got ship's communications back up. We're slaved to the *Kenway,* so as soon as their AI has the systems spin up we can take off." The voice echoed strangely, coming from every console on the ship at the same time.

Time was getting short. Dale had to get past that guard, quick. She looked around, desperately trying to think of a way to get to the Chocondris' section of the cargo bay, but nothing came to mind.

There was nothing to do but change the plan. Dale crouched, then sprinted around the corridor in the direction of the guard. She barreled into her at full speed, yanking the electro-stunner. out of its holder and knocking the woman to the ground. Dale aimed the weapon and pulled the trigger, but nothing happened.

Safety. Dale thought, and fumbled with the weapon while the guard scrambled to her feet.

The guard shook her head and looked up. "What do you think

you're—oh!" The hijacker figured out what was going on at the same moment Dale found the safety and fired. Blue sparks leapt down a beam of light and danced over the guard's body, making her jerk and writhe. Dale slammed her hand on the button to open the door, grabbed the guard and pulled her in.

"Miz Clearwater!" Christine squealed, Christine was dressed in exercise clothes, marked here and there with grime and dust. Her hands and feet were taped to an office chair, sitting in the center of the room. As soon as Dale had cut her free, Christine wrapped her arms around Dale for an enthusiastic hug.

"I thought they killed you."

"Not yet," said Dale. "We need to tie this one up."

"Here," said Christine, taking a roll of tape from the guard's belt. "This is what they used on me."

Together, they secured the woman's wrists and ankles, placed a strip across her mouth, then shoved the hijacker into the bathroom and closed the door.

"Amateurs," Dale muttered.

Christine gave her a quizzical look.

"Pros would have had something more sophisticated to tie people up with. Their whole operation seems only half planned."

"Now what?" said Christine.

Dale checked the charge on the electro-stunner and found it nearly full. "Now we take my ship back. Do you know how many of them there are?"

"Seven if you don't count her," said Christine, nodding toward the bathroom.

"All right, this isn't impossible. They still don't know I've gotten aboard, and if we can get you a weapon—"

The room console let out a bit of static, and then Doctor Florence's voice emerged. "Lusk, you're not at your post. Report."

Christine pressed a control on the console. "Uh, she just went into the bathroom." Dale grimaced, hoping the deception wouldn't be discovered, but her luck had run out.

The voice boomed from every speaker on the ship. "Alert! Lusk has gone missing. It's possible that Clearwater has gotten back on board the ship. Everyone come to the main corridor. If you see Clearwater or Delavos, assume they're armed."

Dale swore.

Christine put a hand on Dale's arm. "Quick, I have an idea." She stepped to the panel covering the maintenance passage and pulled it open.

"We can't go in there!" Dale exclaimed. "We'll suffocate."

"Take deep breaths, and then hold it. We should have enough time to get up to the dorsal hatch."

"Dorsal? You mean on top of the ship?"

"Right. Once we're up there we can use an escape hatch to get into the bridge. No time to explain, come on!"

Dale took deep breaths until she felt the first touch of dizziness, then held her breath and followed Christine into the cramped space. Christine took her hand, guiding her through the darkness, until she placed Dale's hand on the rung of a ladder. A moment later she found herself climbing up behind the young woman, fumbling for the rungs as she felt the first urge to take a breath.

She swallowed and clamped down tighter, holding the breath in. It couldn't be much further. They had to have climbed at least five meters, and the ship wasn't that big, top to bottom. Dull red flashed against her eyes in time with her rapidly accelerating heartbeat. She could feel it in her neck, hear it in her ears. How could the air have lasted so short a time? How could it have taken so long to take a few steps and climb a ladder?

Dale's hand landed on Christine's foot, and she fumbled for a grip on the rung, flailing in panic. The urge to take a breath squeezed her chest, and a wave of nausea suddenly gripped her insides. She wanted to shout, scream, cry, anything but wait here on the ladder for darkness to take her.

Then there was a clank and a pop and a hiss, and light and rain streamed down on her from above.

"Oh, thank the stars," she said, and the breath she took did her no good whatsoever. Blackness constricted her vision and dizziness filled her head. A hand gripped her arm, slipped on the rain-slicked fabric, finally grabbing the cuff of her sleeve. She blacked out, then came to lying on the broad curving upper hull of the ship. The storm had finally made good on its threats, and blasted wind and rain at her from what seemed like every angle.

"You all right?" asked Christine. "Almost lost you there."

Dale's skull pounded. "Headache," she groaned, and took another gulp of good air. "Stupid."

"It'll pass," said Christine. "Take deep breaths."

"Did you pull me out of the shaft there?"

"Uhm. Yeah?"

"You did. You just grabbed me and pulled me out."

Christine rubbed her arms. "I can be pretty strong when I need to be. Good genes, right?"

"Right." Dale blinked and sat up. "So where is that escape hatch you mentioned?"

"Down this way." Christine picked her way along the smooth, curving hull of the ship, down toward the blister shape of the bridge. The footing was slick and treacherous, but they managed to keep their footing in spite of the gusty wind. "I got Vi to unlock it before she was completely shut out. With luck nobody's noticed it's still unlocked."

"Vi was working? How?"

"I, uh, majored in cybernetics. You didn't have any security updates running on your comm system. The hijackers used an external pseudodrive overload attack. Totally shouldn't have worked."

"And you were able to counteract it?"

"Partially. But by the time I got to a console they had already taken control of all the major systems: communications, navigation, life support. But if we can get into the bridge, I can get Vi hooked up again. I think. If they didn't actually destroy the central unit. Which would be stupid. But these people haven't always been smart, right?"

Dale blinked. "That's really impressive, Christine. I underestimated you."

She shrugged, and crouched at a meter-square hull plate on top of the bridge. "If I had known your computer needed work, I would have done it sooner. Ready?"

Dale checked the electro-stunner in her hand and took aim at the hatch.

"Ready."

Christine opened a panel next to the hatch and touched the controls inside. There was a snap and a hiss, a whine of servomotors, and the plate popped open, revealing the ship's tiny control cabin.

Heart pounding, Dale peeked down through the opening. A hijacker sat in one of the two acceleration couches, weapon trained upwards.

"You were right, Doc!" he shouted, as he fired a blast of lightning up at her. The bolt narrowly missed her shoulder. "They're trying to come in through the escape hatch!"

Dale ducked back out of the way, spitting a curse. "Now what?"

Through the hatch, Dale heard Doctor Florence's voice from a comm panel. "Keep them from getting in. Any way you can. Get this ship off the ground."

"What about the reward for that rich girl?"

"Forget that. The ship's more important."

"Yes, sar!"

Dale angled her pistol over the edge and took a couple of random shots down into the bridge.

"No!" Christine shouted. "You'll damage the equipment."

The hull shuddered under their feet.

"If I damage the equipment they won't be able to take off and strand us here!" Dale shouted, and took a couple more shots, until a blast from inside grazed her hand and she jerked back, almost dropping the pistol. Motors whined and turbines roared, and the ship tilted slightly as it rose up from the ground. Christine spread her arms to keep her balance. Dale stumbled and had to grab the open hatch cover to avoid falling.

"No!" She shouted. "You're not taking my ship!"

Then the ship lurched and swayed, and Dale lost her grip. She slid along the hull and over the edge. She fell, screaming, toward the ash-covered clearing. But instead of hitting the ground, she landed on a soft, pillowy surface. Christine followed a moment later and landed next to her. Flat on her back, Dale watched helplessly as her ship rose and flashed away into the sky. A sonic boom echoed over the hills.

Gently, Dale's Yartroan settled down toward the ground, allowing Dale and Christine to climb down from its body. Dale slumped down onto her knees and screamed, fists raised at the sky.

"I'm sorry," said Christine. "I'm so sorry! I totally thought that would work. I thought it would work and I messed it all up. I'm so sorry."

Her energy rapidly ebbing away, Dale dropped her face into her hands. "It was a good plan," Dale said. "It's my fault we're out here in the middle of nowhere. My fault for dragging you into this mess."

"What? No!" Christine knelt down next to Dale and put an arm around her shoulder. "I wouldn't trade any of this. We'll get your ship back, you'll see."

Dale had to laugh. There just wasn't anything else to do. Even so, it was a rueful, desperate laugh, and a tear streaked down her ash-speckled face. Christine's optimism was completely unfounded, given that they were stranded on a wilderness planet, with no tools and no survival skills. Dale turned and wrapped her arms around the young woman for a big hug.

"If only that were true."

"My brother's on this planet somewhere. He'll help us."

Dale pulled back and shook her head. "Somewhere? It's a whole planet. The chances of that monastery being within even a hundred kilometers are minuscule. We've got no way to signal him, no way he'd even know we're here."

"No, he knows we were coming," Christine said, taking Dale's shoulders in her hands. "Before we left New New Amsterdam, I put a message in the relay system to tell him we were on our way.

Depending on how often they get hyperdrones, he might have heard before we even got here. He'll find us."

"Christine, he lives in a monastery." Dale stopped herself before she said anymore. If Christine still had hope, that was a good thing. Crushing it with reality wouldn't help their situation.

Lightning crashed across the sky, followed quickly by an echoing crack of thunder. "Let's get under some shelter," said Christine. "Probably not good to stand around out here in the open."

Dale sighed and followed her, slogging through ashes that mixed with the charred soil underneath to become clinging, itchy mud. The dense canopy of the forest reduced the force of the rain, though it still trickled through the leaves to ensure that there were no dry places to take refuge. With the adrenaline wearing off from the frenzied excitement aboard the ship, aches took hold in Dale's muscles, most especially in her much-abused groin, and she very much wanted to just curl up in a ball and sleep.

But that wasn't going to happen. There was little undergrowth in this forest, and thick roots seemed to spoil any spot she wanted to lie down in. Finally, she couldn't take anymore, and she sat down with her back to a massive tree, knees pulled up to her chest, and cried. Tired, cold, hungry and sore as she was, the utter hopelessness of her situation bore down heavily on her. She was going to starve, or get killed by some alien beast, probably before anyone even realized she was missing. The rain closed around her like the walls of a cold, gray prison cell, shutting off all light and sound except for the incessant hiss of the rain and the irregular bursts of thunder.

After a time, the tears ended, and she drifted off to a fitful sleep.

Morning came slowly, reaching fingers of light through the trees, ghostly sunbeams striking orange and red in the steam coming up from the sodden ground. Dale woke curled up half on Christine's lap. Her limbs felt like ice and the soreness had risen to crippling levels. She groaned, wincing, and pulled herself partly upright. Her stomach growled and she badly needed to pee.

"How are you?" Christine asked, groggily.

"Dandy," Dale groaned, leaning her head back against the tree. "I think I'll have a stroll down to the promenade, get some coffee and breakfast, and then go shopping."

Christine hung her head and sighed. "Sorry."

Dale took a deep breath. "No, I'm the one that needs to apologize. I shouldn't have snarked at you. Thank you for taking care of me last night."

Christine stood up and pulled her fingers through her hair, pulling out some of the tangles that had crept in overnight. "We should probably find some kind of shelter," she said. "I don't want another night like that."

"First, I gotta pee," said Dale, pushing up to stand. She considered the logistics required for the simple task of getting out of her coverall to squat. It wasn't much, but the idea nearly brought her to tears again, and she leaned against the tree with a mew of exhaustion. "I can't take it," she coughed as a fresh sob escaped her throat.

"Come on," said Christine. "You need help?"

"No, I don't need help peeing," she snapped, and instantly regretted it. "I'm sorry. This is all just so draining."

"If we walk downhill we'll probably find a stream," said Christine. "You'll feel better if you get cleaned up." She took Dale's hand, pulled her away from the tree, and put her arm around Dale's shoulders. "One foot in front of the other."

They made their way down the gentle slope, along a rivulet carrying ashes down from the clearing. Behind them, the monsters followed in a meandering line.

Instead of a stream, they found a broad, shallow lake, steaming in the early morning chill. Dale and Christine stripped off their clothes, and after Dale relieved herself, they rinsed out their clothes in the crystal clear water and laid them out to dry on a broad, flat rock. The water was bathwater-warm, tasted pure and felt marvelous on Dale's sore muscles.

While they bathed, the tentacle monsters settled down along the tree-line, except for the Kritzoan, which rolled down the stony lakeside to join them in the water.

The two of them floated side-by-side, watching the sun climb higher in the sky. It almost felt good enough to ignore the rumbling of her stomach. They hadn't passed anything that looked like berries, and, even if they had, they couldn't take the chance the fruit wouldn't poison them. Dale was no outdoor adventurer like Vince, but she knew better than to eat strange things on wild planets without a thorough analysis. Then water splashed on Dale's face as Christine suddenly stood up.

"Something brushed my leg!"

"That's the Kritzoan," said Dale. "It's been giving me little brushes too. If you ignore it, it should stop. Or you could panic, and it'll have its way with you. Your choice."

"Maybe it's not a good idea, right now. I mean—Eeek!" Christine jumped back, nearly falling over in the waist-deep water. The Kritzoan rose up out of the water, its transparent body resembling a huge wave. It engulfed her and carried her up onto the stony lakeside, only her head visible above its nearly transparent surface. The monster had lost all of the debris it had earlier carried into the lake, and had picked up a rather large, toothy looking fish. The predator flopped out onto the stones, limp and lifeless.

The anticipation of watching the Kritzoan pleasure Christine took a backseat to the cold realization that the monster had probably saved Dale from a very nasty bite. She couldn't tell whether it had been suffocated or crushed to death, but either way there was no doubt the thing had been dispatched efficiently.

Dale climbed up out of the water, giving the fish a comfortable margin as she followed the Kritzoan. At first, she watched to make sure that nothing went wrong. The creature was well trained, but there was no doubt it was under stress, and that could sometimes result in surprises. She sat down on the rock where her coverall lay drying.

Instead of a disaster, Dale received an astonishingly pleasant surprise instead. As Christine's face and chest took on an aroused flush and her nipples hardened under the Kritzoan's invisible manipulations, she saw stones float up from the beach and into its body. They migrated through its flesh to come into contact with the young woman's sensitive places. They didn't look like they were moving quickly but Dale knew that a Kritzoan could vibrate parts of its body with a fair degree of power. The gasp that came from Christine's throat was well earned.

Dale couldn't believe what she was seeing. The Kritzoan was using tools. She had never seen that before, never heard of it happening. Not from a Kritzoan, in any case. Her astonishment erased the disturbing sight of the fish, leaving her ready to absorb the arousing sight and sound of Christine having a rapid and powerful orgasm. A tingle of arousal spread through Dale's body. She drew a hand down from her shoulder and over her breast, feeling her hard nipple drag against her palm.

Christine did not get any respite from the Kritzoan. There wasn't a whole lot to see, really; the young woman's naked body floated within the gelid monster's form, minor distortions moving across her skin as it stroked and squeezed every inch of her. Her breasts moved strangely as the monster manipulated them. But Dale knew how that felt, and her memories colored the sight, lending it a kind of sympathetic vibration with her own body. It took a slight stretch to imagine what the half dozen or so vibrating stones felt like, but lovers had used vibrators on her when she was tied up.

Not six of them at a time, though. Christine cried and screamed and thrashed, panting for breath in between deep groans and gasps of pleasure. Dale gave her breast a squeeze, imagining the Kritzoan's grip, and then moved her hand lower, slowly crossing belly, savoring the anticipation.

Her body was still sore, and no part more than her pussy, but there was no way she could watch Christine being helplessly pleasured to one orgasm after another and not touch herself. She stroked her clit hood gently, avoiding the still-quite-sensitive flesh further down.

By the stars, she's so beautiful this way, Dale thought.

She no longer cared that Christine's looks had been engineered in a genetic design studio. She knew the woman underneath the perfect hair and skin and eyes, knew her to be sharp and caring and oh, the pretty noises she made when she came.

The Kritzoan set Christine free after only half an hour or so, but as soon as it retreated into the water, the Whombar slithered out of the trees and wrapped its serpentine body around her gasping, twitching form. Its thick, muscular tail ended in a phallic knob only slightly larger than a human male might possess, and the monster wasted no time in putting it to use. It plunged into Christine's channel, thrusting hard, its single eye staring at her face with unblinking focus. Rainbow colors played over the eyeball surface in hypnotic patterns, and as soon as Christine opened her eyes she found herself unable to look away from that terrible visage.

The Whombar had never been studied in great detail—they were too rare, only a few hundred known in the whole galaxy—but Dale was certain there was a telepathic component to the Whombar's hypnotic gaze. Even the slightest sexual arousal was enough to paralyze its victim in an inescapable mind-lock. All conscious thought erased, the mind was left empty for pure sensation.

With each thrust of its tail, Christine let out a sound halfway between a cry and a moan. The Whombar's tail was not the only sensation it provided. Undulations rippled through the creature's body, moving like caresses around Christine's entire torso.

There was something a little creepy about the way she stared into the monster's huge iridescent eye, but that just made the sight even more exciting. Dale stroked harder, uncaring of the little twinges of pain that came with it, and squeezed her breast with the other hand.

Yes, she growled to herself. *Fuck. Fuck that girl. Harder. Harder!* She grunted in time with Christine's cries, as if she were doing the fucking, holding her tight, squeezing, stroking, thrusting hard. She gripped her clit between her fingers, stroking it like a miniature cock. That particular technique had never worked well for her before, but it suddenly felt like the perfect thing. Her hips bucked against her hand, tension coursing through her limbs.

Take her. Take that human. Put your mark on her. Let them know... let them all know... Images and wisps of thought crowded into Dale's brain, flashing by too quickly to process, too bizarre to remember. *What's happening?* She increased the pressure on her clit, squeezing it hard between her fingers. *This should be scary.* Pain lanced through her mind like lightning through storm-clouds, but the storm kept building. *Oh, Stars, I'm going to come—and it's going to be a big one.*

A scream tore from her throat as the Whombar's eye closed and it stiffened with its own release. The sensation went on for heartbeat after heartbeat, much longer than usual, exhausting her with its endurance. Her vision throbbed with her heartbeat, making the blue sky pulse into deep purple, and the alien thoughts flowed out of her as quickly as they had arrived.

The Whombar released Christine from its serpentine form and slithered away, coiling up contentedly a few meters from the girl's spent body.

Dale lay back, panting, replaying the bizarre encounter. Had her rapport with the tentacle monsters grown so close that she could feel what they were feeling, or had stress and exhaustion driven her to imagine things? Was she losing her mind? She had seen so many unusual things over the past few days that it was impossible to rule out the possibility of yet another breakthrough. At the same time, the prospect of an empathic connection between human and tentacle monster was too outlandish to contemplate. Something was happening, but she didn't know whether to be excited or terrified.

A crunch of heavy footfalls against the beach stones drew her attention, and she looked up to see the Rominek shuffling out of the trees toward Christine. *Stars,* Dale thought, *Good thing she's young and fit. It's going to be a rough morning if they're all going to take turns.*

Suddenly, a shadow fell over the two of them, and Dale opened her eyes to see a large orbital shuttle slowly descending toward the middle of the lake until it hovered just a few meters off the water surface. Dale's jaw fell open and her eyes bugged. "By the Stars!" she exclaimed.

A beam of pale blue light flashed from the underside of the ship, engulfed the Rominek and lifted it off the ground. The creature flailed and squirmed in distress as it floated out over the water, rose up into a hatch and disappeared. As soon as it was swallowed up, the beam flashed out again, grabbing the Whombar.

Dale jumped up off the rock and waved her arms. "No! Stop! What are you doing?"

The ship continued its work implacably, plucking the monsters one by one from their resting places along the beach and swallowing them up.

Christine shook off the effects of the Whombar's fascination and sat up, staring in amazement at the ship. "What's going on?"

"It's a monster hunter!" Dale shouted. "It's taking the monsters!" She splashed out into the water, as if she could somehow leap up to the ship and stop its progress.

But there was nothing she could do. One by one, the ship captured the monsters and pulled them up into its hold. It even plucked the Kritzoan from under the lake's surface and drew it inside, water streaming from its transparent skin.

Without warning, two of the Chocondris' ropy, vine-like tendrils erupted from the ground, scattering stones in every direction. They grabbed Dale and Christine and pulled them toward the trees. Both of the women shrieked in surprise as it pulled them away. Where was that rapport now? The Chocondris probably thought it was saving them from capture but she couldn't bear to leave those monsters behind.

Then the shuttle settled into the water, and the forward hatch hinged downward, revealing a ladder on its inner surface. A tall, dark-skinned man with short black hair, wearing a bright green outfit, emerged and leapt into the water. He raced up onto the beach and caught up with the Chocondris in mere seconds.

He jabbed sensitive flower buds, and the Chocondris flinched and twitched. It spit spores at him, but he ducked under every little cloud without even a speck touching his skin. It tried to grab his arms and legs, but he slipped out of its coils with dizzying alacrity. On the rare occasions it could get a tentacle around one of his limbs, he twisted away, undoing its coil before it could solidify its hold.

Already injured from its fight with the native Yartroan, the Chocondris quivered with rage. It dropped Dale and Christine to bring more of its limbs to bear. The man retreated a few steps, then leapt back under a concentrated assault. He seemed to know exactly how far away to leap to stay out of its clutches as he retreated back toward the beach.

As soon as the Chocondris broke out of the cover of the trees, the shuttle's capture beam caught it, plucking it like a weed. Like the others, it quickly disappeared inside the shuttle.

The man took one deep breath, closed his eyes, and centered himself. It seemed a strange posture for a monster hunter. More like—

"Connie!" Christine shouted, stumbling forward to wrap her arms around the man. "You found us! I knew you'd find us." She squeezed him hard then stepped away to point, beaming at Dale with her perfectly bright smile. "I told you my brother would find us!"

CHAPTER SEVEN
LOSING GRIP

Dale and Christine pulled their clothes back on while the young woman gushed about how awesome it was that her brother, Constantine, had found them. Whereas Christine was pale, blonde, and curvaceous, Constantine had dark skin and a lanky frame, thin enough that his forest green gi seemed baggy. Long hands with elegant fingers emerged from his sleeves.

"I take it you're not related by blood."

"We are, sort of," said Christine. "I'm a clone of my father except for my mother's X chromosome; Constantine's a clone of my mother except for dad's Y. It's the big thing on New New Amsterdam. Or, at least, it was back then. Now, all the babies have stripes."

Dale spotted the common traits: perfect skin, perfect teeth, perfect eyes, perfect bodies. If they were simply clones of their parents, then both parents must have been from the long-standing genemod families—people who had been able to afford genetic enhancements for enough generations that there were no more improvements to be made.

He helped them up into the spacious cockpit of his ship. A little thrill run through Dale's body as his hand lent her support; he was thin, but there was unquestionable power in his grip. She found herself imagining what those hands would feel like squeezing her breasts, wrapped around her wrists, or slapping her on the ass.

"So you're the Monster Whisperer," said Constantine, as he took the pilot's seat.

"You've heard of me?" she asked, settling down next to him.

"Tentacle monsters are not outside my interests," he said, with a bit of a smile in his voice. "So those were yours?"

"Yes. They're not injured, I hope?"

Constantine checked a display on his console. "Looks like all is well. Vital signs a bit elevated, but that's to be expected." He checked several other displays, including a map, then glanced over his shoulder at Christine. "I got your message that you were on your way to Yartro, but I didn't expect to pluck you out of a lake. What happened?"

"We were hijacked!" said Christine. "Very scary."

"How did you find us?" asked Dale, sitting in the copilot's seat. Christine took the spot immediately behind her.

"We picked up a distress beacon," he said. "Or at least, a few seconds of one. It was long enough to get a general idea of your location, so I came out as quick as I could. The scanners picked up a human signature." The shuttle vibrated a little and lifted out of the water.

"I'll bet that happened when you shot the electro-stunner down into the bridge," said Christine.

"Whatever it was, we were lucky it happened, and lucky you got the signal," said Dale. "Thank you for coming out to pick us up."

"My pleasure." Constantine looked into Dale's eyes and smiled for perhaps a moment too long before turning back to the controls.

Dale chewed on her lip. "I know this is probably a huge imposition, but—the monsters you captured. They travel with me. Is there any way we can put them up somewhere safe? We've already been attacked by one of the local monsters."

"I believe we can work something out. While we return to the monastery, do you want to file a report with the Patrol? We have some communications hyperdrones. We can record your report right here, and send it ahead." The engines hummed as he brought up the power levels and the ship accelerated toward the sky. The forest fell away from the windows.

"Yes, let's do that. I want to give those bastards as little of a head start as I can."

Constantine hit some toggles, and lights came on, illuminating Dale from different angles. "Recording," he said.

Dale took a deep breath and looked into the little camera lens on the console. "My name is Dale Clearwater, owner of cargo vessel 647... uh...." She frowned and shook her head. The events of the past day were running around in her head, refusing to settle down. She took another breath and closed her eyes.

"I don't have the registration number. I'm sure it's in your records. The important thing is that Doctor Nichole Florence hijacked my ship, and tried to maroon me and my monsters on the planet Yartro. She has at least seven accomplices with her, and is holding a wounded Nalcheka. They said they were planning on using the ship to seize other tentacle monsters. Christine Delavos' mother may be involved. She doesn't like that Miz Delavos is traveling with me. I've been picked up by Constantine Delavos from the... I'm sorry, what's the name of your monastery?"

"Irairanochirasu."

"Uh, yeah. He's bringing me to the monastery on Yartro. If you need more details, you can find me there, for the time being. I'll let you know if I get a ride anywhere else. End message."

Constantine touched a control and the lights went out. "Message sent. What's this about our mother being involved?"

Christine sighed. "She's mad that I wanted to change my major. We got in an argument, and..." She shrugged.

"And she threatened to disown you," said Constantine.

"Yeah. So here I am."

Constantine shook his head. "Sounds familiar."

"I know, right? At least I got the chance to come out here and visit."

"And I'm glad of that. How are things at school?"

"Dale came and cleared out that Under-the-Bed monster that was making it so hard to sleep. That's how we met."

Constantine turned his head to give his sister an appraising look. "Oh?"

"It's not like that," she said. "We're not lovers or anything." Christine glanced over at Dale, flashed a smile, and added, "Not yet anyways."

"I see." A faint frown crossed Constantine's face, but it returned to its neutral expression as he turned back to the controls.

Dale looked down at the screen in front of her, not understanding the lines and figures dancing there. She was going to have to have a talk with Christine. That kind of teacher-student relationship had gotten her monster-hunting ex on bad terms with his protégé, Penny. Not that Dale was as clueless as Vince when it came to relationships, but still. Not a good idea. But, by the Stars, she wanted it too.

Not only that, said a voice bubbling up from Dale's subconscious, *Getting romantic with both a young woman AND her brother would be a really bad idea.*

Dale steadfastly avoided a glance in Constantine's direction and stared out the front window.

An indicator flashed on the communications console and Constantine activated the system. "Receiving. Go ahead."

A woman's voice, elderly but firm and forceful, came from the console. "Sensei Delavos, I just had a look at that report you sent us to relay to the Patrol."

"Yes, Dai-Sensei."

"And you are bringing Miz Delavos and Miz Clearwater back here?"

Constantine sat up a little straighter. "I don't see any other option, Dai-Sensei."

The woman's voice took on a darker tone. "Is there anything else I should know about?"

"Yes. I, uh..." Constantine took a deep breath. "I have five tentacle monsters in the hold. They belong to Miz Clearwater. We should prepare facilities to receive them."

"I see."

"Ma'am, these are domesticated monsters. Not wild. They need our shelter as much as Miz Clearwater does."

The Grandmistress' voice took on a darker tone. "Sensei Delavos, one might come to the conclusion that your position is beginning to engender a change of outlook. Do not forget your place."

"Yes, Dai-Sensei. I won't."

"We shall make the appropriate preparations. When you arrive, come see me immediately."

The link shut off before Constantine could say, "Yes, Dai-Sensei."

"Are you going to get in trouble for helping me?" asked Dale.

"I will need to defend my decision."

Dale reached out and put her hand on Constantine's shoulder. "Thank you. I appreciate it."

Ahead, a line of mountains cut through the dense forest. Constantine angled the ship toward a bowl-shaped valley surrounded on three sides by steep slopes, with a sheer cliff that dropped down into the trees below. A shimmering bubble of force protected most of the valley of terraced gardens and orchards. In the center, a cluster of buildings surrounded a wide plaza.

As they approached, the force field abruptly flashed out, then reappeared after they had passed its boundary. Gently, the ship touched down on a landing pad on the edge of the main compound. Constantine entered some commands in the controls, and stood from his seat as the passenger hatch opened. "If you'll follow me, I'll show you where we can set things up for your tentacle monsters. The ship will transfer them automatically to our holding facility."

Dale and Christine followed Constantine out of the ship. The landing pad was paved with colorful stones, in the same spiral pattern as Constantine bore on his tunic. A wide metal walkway extended to an arched doorway in the side of the nearest building, where two huge doors stood ajar.

Behind them, the ship's cargo bay doors opened and connected to a similarly shaped opening in the landing pad, and Dale heard the ship's capture beam operate as it transferred the monsters one by one into whatever waited below.

"You have a holding facility for keeping tentacle monsters?" Dale asked.

"As I said, they are not outside our interests. Follow me, I'll show you where we'll keep them."

"Is he being mysterious on purpose?" Dale whispered to

Christine as they followed him through the doors and onto a spiral staircase.

"He does that," said Christine, with a smile and a wink.

"You're not helping."

The stairs led to a huge open space, large enough to extend under all of the surface buildings and the courtyard as well. Thick columns supported the roof, buttressed by arches between them. Around the edges of the vast space, five-meter square alcoves had been cut into the walls. Semi-transparent force fields sealed several of them. Elsewhere, various clusters of machinery hummed and buzzed along, connected to pipes and cables that ran up through the ceiling.

"Well!" Dale exclaimed. "Not exactly the kind of facility one would expect in a monastery."

"We aren't afraid to use technology when it's essential to our mission," said Constantine, walking calmly toward a mechanism at the center of the facility.

"And what mission is that?"

"The perfection of the art of Shokushu Boei Jutsu."

Dale's mouth fell open, and she looked more closely at the spaces closed off with force fields. There were shapes inside those enclosures, drifting about, indistinct but recognizable now that she knew what to look for. There were Yartroans in those enclosures, three of them, ranging in size from merely a meter in diameter to more than three. "Shokushu! Way of the Tentacle? Really?"

Constantine let out a frustrated grunt. "That is not an accurate translation. Shokushu Boei Jutsu means *Technique for Defense against Tentacles*. Don't listen to what the media say about us. They never get things right."

"I know how true that is, believe me, but I think you misunderstand. I was surprised that you were a student of that particular art, but now that I think about it, it makes sense." A thought occurred to Dale. "You know, if I could get access to some recording equipment, I could help set things right. Give you an opportunity to present a more accurate picture."

Constantine closed his eyes and held up a hand. "You'd have to talk to the Dai-Sensei about that. For the time being, let's get your friends safely installed."

A hydraulic motor somewhere in the vast space whined, lowering a platform from overhead. It held a figure dressed in a gi similar to Constantine's, but colored a deep burgundy instead of his green. The woman's hair was steel gray, and she carried a stout walking stick.

"These monsters are not friends, Sensei Constantine," she said, in a tremulous voice. "Are you finally going soft on us?"

Constantine sighed. "No, Sensei Kiriki. They are not my friends, but they are hers. Sensei Kiriki, I present to you Dale Clearwater. Dale, this is Sensei Kiriki, our monster keeper. She'll conduct your monsters into our enclosures."

"We do not need any more tentacle monsters," said Kiriki as she stepped from the platform. Her frown accentuated the lines in her face. "Send them away."

"Respectfully, Dale and her companion monsters have been marooned here by pirates. I have offered her our hospitality until such time as transport can be arranged off-world."

"Oh, you have, have you? And you have permission from the Dai-Sensei to make this commitment?"

"I have, Sensei Kiriki. It was she who sent me to investigate the distress beacon we picked up."

Kiriki grunted with disgust. "Very well. I suppose we can always turn them out later, if we need to." She waved her hand in the direction of the elevator. "Go, go, be about your business. You have duties to attend to, I'm certain." The old woman leaned her stick up against a column and stood at a small control console that projected from it.

Constantine stepped onto the platform and stood at a little control panel. Dale and Christine followed, staying close to the center of the square. The little elevator had no sides or roof, and as it lurched upwards, she felt a little twinge of alarm in her gut.

Constantine put a hand on her upper arm, steadying her. His

grip was firm but not painful, and once again Dale felt the need to feel his hands on her. They would be strong, she knew; if he was related to Christine he'd have supremely optimized muscles. She shuddered at the images that flew through her imagination. His long fingers could enclose her wrists. He could hold her arms well above her head, or press her hands against her back as she lay face down below him. It had been a long time since a human had properly dominated her.

Then the reverie was broken, not by the platform arriving at its destination, but a sudden flash of a different image: she held him down instead, riding him, her hands on his elbows, thumbs in the joints to immobilize him with loving pain. It was an image of dominance, not submission, so vivid that it stunned her back to the real world.

Whoa.

They stood on the edge of a broad plaza paved with a gigantic mosaic depicting the same spiral emblem stitched into Constantine's gi. The mosaic ran right up to the foundations of three solidly built stone buildings, each decorated with elaborate carvings and multicolored brickwork. On the fourth side, the plaza faced out onto the green fields and orchards, and beyond that the complex's huge force field dome.

"We've got rooms for you this way," said Constantine, leading them toward one of the side buildings. "Ordinarily this wing is for candidates, but we're not full up."

The room was furnished, in a clean but utilitarian fashion, with a pair of beds, a desk, a dresser, and an upholstered chair. None of the furnishings appeared to have adaptive surfaces, but after the night spent sleeping in the forest that wouldn't matter in the least. Constantine bid them good morning, bowed, and departed.

Even more welcome were the trays of food set out on the desk. There were bowls of cut fruit, steaming oatmeal, glasses of juice, and cups of fragrant tea. It all smelled marvelous.

Dale grabbed up one of the trays and sat down on the bed. She dumped the fruit into the oatmeal, stirred it up, and ate. The simple fare tasted better than anything she could imagine. The bowl was empty before she looked up to notice that Christine, as well, had polished off the entire meal and was laying back on the bed, making little sounds of contentment.

"Dibs on the shower," said Dale, rising to her feet.

"Want some company?" asked Christine with a wry little grin.

"Uh, no. I just want to get clean and then take a nap. I don't really feel like anything sexual."

"Oh, okay." Christine tried to hide the disappointment, but it came through anyway. "I'll go in after you then."

Dale stepped into the bathroom and closed the door. As she unzipped her coverall and peeled out of her underthings, she resolved to have a word with Christine as soon as the shower was over. As tempting as the young woman was, it wouldn't do to leave this business for later.

The shower soon banished those thoughts, however. The spray soothed her abused muscles, and the soap's lack of fancy perfumes didn't detract in the slightest. She was tempted to rub out a quick orgasm, but she decided not to, instead reveling in the simple pleasure of being clean.

The door opened halfway through the shower, and Christine said, "Someone just dropped off some clean clothes for us."

"Just leave them on the counter," said Dale.

"Okay. You sure you don't... um. Okay."

After drying herself off, Dale discovered that the clothes sitting next to the sink were similar to Constantine's gi, except in white instead of green. There were drawstring pants, a wraparound tunic, and a belt with no buckle or clasp, long enough to wrap around her waist three or four times. There were no underclothes, but that didn't bother her much. She could do without.

Dale emerged from the bathroom with the tunic wrapped around herself, but with her hands holding the belt in place. "Do you have any idea how to tie one of these things?" she asked.

Christine sat at the room's computer console. "Instructions," she said with a smile, and made a gesture in the air that angled the holographic screen toward Dale. A set of diagrams filled one side of the display, and a video ran in the other, demonstrating the technique for knotting the belt.

"Wow, good thinking," said Dale. Christine really was a good deal more intelligent than she seemed. She had a bit of naiveté from her sheltered upbringing, but beneath that façade there was a sharp mind.

The younger woman scooped up a second set of clothes and walked into the washroom while Dale studied the instructions and fumbled with getting the thing to hold together properly. It took the entire ten minutes that Christine spent in the shower to get it right, but when Christine came out, hers was perfect.

"How about shoes?" asked Dale, looking around the tiny room.

"Just these," Christine said, handing Dale a pair of ankle-socks. They were thin and stretchy, with a textured sole for traction. "I don't think they're usually set up for visitors. This is what new students wear."

"Well, that would make sense, anyway." Dale sat down on the edge of the bed and gathered her thoughts.

"So what do you think of Constantine?" said Christine, sitting on the other bed, facing her.

"Oh, he's..." Dale wondered whether she should admit her feelings out loud. Wait, no, there was something more important to talk about.

"From what I hear, he was considered quite the catch at college. Some of my friends were real disappointed to hear he had gone out into the middle of nowhere to join a monastery. One of them tried to come out here to 'study' with him, if you know what I mean, but he's always been all business, and she came back after two weeks, talking about how terrible it was."

"Doesn't seem terrible so far. But listen, I think we need to talk—"

A knock sounded at the door. Christine jumped up. "I'll get it!"

At the door was a tall woman with long, gray-flecked hair tied back in a ponytail, olive skin, and thin features. Her gi was a solid, midnight black. She was a bit taller than Dale, and held herself in a self-possessed, confident manner. She bowed slightly and said, "Christine Delavos. Dale Clearwater. I am Chin Lakosta, Dai-Sensei of Irairanochirasu."

Dale stood up and returned the bow. "Thank you for all your kindness."

"We need to talk," said Lakosta. "Will you follow me please?"

"Of course."

Dale and Christine followed the teacher down the hallway and out to a small balcony looking out over the broad courtyard. The sun was bright overhead, but it didn't feel particularly oppressive. Dale guessed that the force shield dome might be blocking out some of the nastier radiation, and only letting in the visible light and enough heat to keep the interior warm. There was a stone bench near the balcony rail, but Lakosta did not sit down. Instead she stood at the rail and looked out over the courtyard. "We have gone to a great deal of trouble to remove ourselves from the distractions of galactic culture," she said. "Intrusions are not welcome."

Dale stood beside her. "I understand."

Lakosta turned her head to look Dale squarely in the eye. "Monster Whisperer," she said, with a glacial tone. "I don't think you do. Not in the slightest."

"Is there something I've done?" Dale asked. "Some rule of etiquette I missed?"

"It's not what you've done. It's who you are. What you represent."

Dale blinked and took a step back. "I—and what is that?"

"Submission. Surrender. You encourage people to give up who they are. You teach people that struggle is fun but ultimately pointless."

"Whoa," said Christine. "I think you're reading way too much into all this."

"She's entitled to her opinion," said Dale, recovering. "Tentacle monsters aren't for everyone, and I *did* ask for her thoughts, so it shouldn't come as any surprise that she expressed them. Dai-Sensei, thank you for your candor. I'm sorry you feel that way, but I'm sure you will understand if I don't give up my career because someone disapproves, even someone with as much expertise as you."

The woman nodded, crossed her arms, and looked out over the courtyard. Ten students in white gi's strode out into the space, taking up places in a half-circle. The tall, dark-skinned man in green standing in the center could only be Constantine.

"While you are here, you will not speak to students," said Lakosta. "You will not speak to teachers unless I have specifically instructed them to speak to you. There will be no interviews. There will be no recordings. You will not interfere with the operation of this monastery in any way. Is this clear?"

"Yes, ma'am. I will need to check in on my monsters."

"They will be properly taken care of."

"No offense, but—"

Lakosta cut Dale off with an icy stare. "I take offense, Dale Clearwater. Our order has kept tentacle monsters since before the people who trained the people who trained you were born. We know our business."

Dale swallowed a sharp reply. She was in no position to make demands. She took a deep breath and looked down at the courtyard.

The session started with stretches and warm-ups, and then drills of attack and defense moves, some of which Dale remembered from Constantine's fight with the Chocondris. The movements were fluid and graceful, even for the students, and once the drills were rolling, Constantine walked up and down the rows, correcting technique and offering encouragement for good form.

"I would at least like to thank Constantine for coming out to pick us up," she said.

Lakosta nodded. "I shall send him to you when his duties are completed. You may observe here, or you may return to your quarters. Now, I have duties to attend. Good day to you." And with that, the woman turned and walked from the balcony.

Christine flopped on the bench. "What a bitch!"

"We aren't exactly in a situation to demand courtesy," said Dale, sitting down next to her.

"Do you think they're helping the hijackers?" Christine whispered.

"No. Well... maybe. I wouldn't be surprised if they looked the other way. More of an enemy-of-my-enemy situation. Neither group likes me, but for different reasons."

"What are we going to do?"

"For the time being, we wait for the Star Patrol. Hijacking a ship is a major crime, they're not going to ignore it. And they're going to want to talk to me right away. The drone will take a few hours to reach the nearest planet, and the report to get into the relay network. Then it might take a day for a Patrol ship to get here, depending on how far away they are. We won't be waiting long."

"And your ship? Where do you think they're taking it?"

"I don't know. From what I gathered, they were supposed to bring you back to New New Amsterdam, but without you they'd probably get in trouble with your mother. So, I doubt they'll go there. Could be anywhere. Maybe somewhere there would be a lot of support for their cause, like New Beulah." Dale took a deep breath and swallowed down the anxiety threatening to choke off her voice. "They'll probably just dump the Nalcheka off in some asteroid field somewhere. They're vacuum dwellers. I might never see it again."

"I'm sure we'll get your ship back." Christine put her arm around Dale's shoulder and squeezed. "And the Nalcheka too."

"Thanks. I wish I shared your optimism."

The two of them sat in silence for a while, watching Constantine drill his students. After an hour or so, Constantine moved back to the center of the circle and called one of the students up to join him. The woman, fit-looking with a mature face, strode up and faced him in a ready stance.

Constantine took her wrists, guiding her through a twisting maneuver involving turning her arm in a fluid spiral while rotating her body in a 360 degree spin. It looked silly until Constantine performed the other half of the dance. He grabbed her, thumb tucked in, mimicking the motion of a tentacle wrapping around her upper arm. The student's twisting movement broke the grip of the "tentacle" and the spin threatened a nasty kick if they had not been performing it at quarter speed.

The two of them practiced the motions again and again, gradually increasing the speed, as the rest of the class watched. With the demonstration complete, Constantine coached the class through the maneuver, stepping in to guide and correct with gentle hands, and Dale felt a sting of jealousy in her gut. Why was it always the completely inappropriate guys that she fell for? This one would be a worse choice than Vince.

"It's too bad the Dai-Sensei hates me so much," she mused. "I could go for studying some of this."

"They wouldn't take you," said Christine.

"Well, of course," said Dale. "Probably worried that I'd reveal some ancient secret technique or something."

"No, it's more than that." said Christine, flatly. "When Constantine was in college, he had more than a few classmates following him around. Some of them tried to follow him here, and presented themselves as candidates. One of them came back, right away; she had been turned at the door, because she wasn't genemod. Shokushu Boei Jutsu is considered too demanding for those without the extra strength and speed."

Dale squinted at Christine in disbelief. "What? So all of these students are genemod?"

"As far as I know."

Dale looked down at the class, and saw it, finally. They were too far away to see hair and eyes and teeth, but they did have that aura of grace and strength. It was that kind of place, then. She wondered if the disdain of the elder Miz Delavos had anything to do with the fact that "Clearwater" wasn't a name that meant hundreds of years of genetic fine-tuning. She wondered if Constantine's politeness masked similar attitudes. Christine obviously didn't care, so there was hope that her brother would be as open-minded.

Then he looked up, as if noticing Dale on the balcony for the first time. It was a bit far away to tell for certain, but she thought he might be smiling.

Some hope, indeed. "Christine—the computer terminal in our room. What's it connected to?"

"I didn't look too hard at it, but it appears to be a system set up for new students. Basic information."

"Uh-huh." Dale sucked in her cheeks.

"Oooh," Christine cooed. "Are you thinking...?"

"Go on back," said Dale. "See what you can learn."

"Yes, sar." She stood and hustled from the balcony.

Dale found a stairwell and descended to the ground floor, then crossed through a wide dining hall where robots were setting up to serve what looked like about a hundred people. Given the number of forks at each place setting, she guessed it was not going to be simple fare. At the far end, she found the huge doors that led out to the courtyard, walked out far enough that she could see what was going on but not so far that she felt like she was intruding, and watched.

She decided, very quickly, that the change in viewpoint was a good one. She could see him much better from down on the ground. The grace and confidence Constantine displayed in their previous encounter had grown tenfold in front of his class. This was where he belonged and, damn, wasn't he sexy doing it.

Dale knew why he was affecting her this way. He had the same thing going for him that men who could dance had. Added to that, he was grappling with his students in ways she very much would have liked being grappled herself. Plus, he was a "man in uniform," which wasn't normally Dale's thing but, in this case? *Unf.* She could watch him all day.

Then he clapped his hands and made a circular gesture in the air. The students broke off from their drills and took off to run laps around the courtyard. After they were on their way, he took a quick glance around the courtyard and walked over to her.

"You're really not supposed to be out here," he said.

"The Dai-Sensei said she would send you to me once your duties are complete."

"I see." A thoughtful look flashed across his face. His lips barely moving, he whispered, "Find a pretext to move out of your current quarters. The room across the hall."

Dale raised an eyebrow, then nodded as slightly as she could.

Constantine raised his voice again and backed away. "Please. Find somewhere else to be. You're distracting my class."

"So who do I see about checking on my monsters?" she said, her voice also raised.

"I'm sure Sensei Kiriki is taking good care of them," he said, turning his back on her to face his students. "Harusha! Pick up your feet!"

Given what had happened, it wasn't a surprise that he would act like he was being watched. On the ship, the Dai-Sensei had said something about Constantine and his sympathies. Dale might have an ally here. Or at least someone who didn't hate her outright. Plus, he was damn hot.

Dale returned to her room to find Christine sitting at the console. "Any luck?" she asked.

"None. The system is completely isolated. No contact with any of the other systems. Anyone that wants to send a message off-planet has to submit it on data wafer to the Dai-Sensei herself, who reviews all incoming and outgoing communication. Anyone who needs something from the kitchen has to actually go there. Likewise, anything related to the robots, or the tentacle monsters. It looks like they keep all their systems isolated from each other."

"Well, it is a monastery. They're supposed to be isolated. Being able to send mail back and forth whenever they want is not part of the environment they want to promote."

Christine's brow knitted. "This is a terrible thought. If the Dai-

Sensei hates you that bad, would she have delayed your report to the Star Patrol?"

"That goes beyond looking the other way. That makes her an accomplice."

"I'm sure you're right. They would never go that far."

Dale opened her mouth to speak, but then looked at the console, and closed it again. There was no way to know whether any device in the room might be listening in on her conversation. She looked around, eyes in the corners of the room. There were no obvious lenses, but they didn't have to be obvious. There could be any number of surveillance devices in the room, and they would never know about them. She nodded to the screen. "All right, might as well shut it down, then."

Christine flicked a switch, and the holographic screen winked out.

"Now...can you disconnect it? Make sure it's really, really off?"

"I guess." Christine ducked under the desk. "Yeah, here's the main unit." Christine sat up with a small black box in her hand. "Why did you want me to do that?"

"Because I'm pretty sure the Dai-Sensei is listening in on us, when she can, though I'm not sure they'd ordinarily be set up for surveillance. So this is the best I can do." Dale went over to the window and looked out. The room faced out on green lawns dotted with well-manicured shrubs and trees, and beyond that a sheer cliff leading up to the force field dome. That precaution probably wasn't going to be enough, though. Not if Constantine wanted to meet her in another room. "If they want to keep me here, they've got a pretty effective prison."

"Constantine would never stand for that."

"He's not in charge here, that much is clear," Dale said. "Depending on how much the Dai-Sensei helped those hijackers, she may be desperate. We need to be careful."

"I guess we'll know where they stand when and if the Star Patrol arrives." Christine stood and put her arms around Dale, laid her head along her neck. "I'm scared."

Dale took a deep breath. She needed a reason to move to the room across the hall. And she needed to clarify her relationship with Christine. As attractive as this girl was, and even though their ages really weren't that far apart, getting intimate with her was a line she really shouldn't cross. It would hurt, but this was probably the best time to accomplish both of those aims.

Not only that, there were those weird thoughts that had come into her head while watching Christine having sex with the Whombar. Dale wasn't comfortable getting into bed with her until she had figured that out as well. Unfortunately, that wasn't a reason she could speak out loud. Not yet, anyways. It sounded like madness.

She turned, caught Christine's hands between her own, and looked her in the eye. "We need to talk."

"I don't want to talk. Can you just...hold me? Please?" The girl's eyes were wide and she looked like she might start crying at any moment.

Dale reluctantly put her arms around Christine.

"I'm..."

She couldn't do it. Tired, stressed, and frustrated, Dale just didn't have the energy. "I'm just not in the mood for sex right now, okay? I think I just need a nap." An image flashed in her imagination, of Christine tied to the bed, writhing in ecstasy as Dale squeezed and licked and bit her to orgasm. Dale tried to dispel the fantasy but it wouldn't go away. She wanted Christine, wanted her badly, but giving in to that desire would be a mistake. She held Christine at arm's length. "I'm going to see if I can find another place to sleep. Are you going to be okay?"

"You don't have to go. I can control myself."

Dale patted her shoulder. "I know. I trust you. But I think it would be better if it weren't even an issue." *And I don't trust myself,* she thought.

"Okay. Tomorrow?"

"We'll see."

Dale's heart felt like it was crumpling up into a ball of twisted metal. It wasn't fair, leading Christine on like this. She would fix it, as soon as she'd had some rest. After a nap, maybe, then she could tell Christine that they couldn't let sex get in the way of their relationship.

The room across the hall was identical to the one they'd been assigned, except that its window faced out on the courtyard instead of the outer grounds. Constantine was still down there, drilling his students as the shadow of the mountains crept across the paving stones. She watched him for a while, then sat down in the big easy chair.

Dale was used to solitude, or at least the kind of solitude that one had while traveling with a half dozen tentacle monsters and a virtual intelligence. What she wasn't used to, however, was idleness. Sitting alone in that room, surrounded by Stars only knew how many enemies, separated from her ship and her monsters, every shadow of Dale's past rose up around her. Sleep eluded her.

Penny Angstrom was there, screaming in rage and terror as the Phase Looper dragged her to another dimension. How did she die? It was too remote a possibility to expect that there was a breathable atmosphere where she wound up, so a quick but terrifying death from asphyxiation was most likely. If by some miracle there was air in that mysterious wherever, then it was possible she was still alive, most likely starving or else poisoned by some alien ecosystem, suffering in an even more hopeless prison than Dale was in.

Then there was Vince, the monster hunter, and her ex-lover. He had loved Penny, perhaps too much, and when Penny had vanished with the Phase Looper, he had blamed Dale. He would no doubt laugh to find her stuck this way. No, not even that; he'd consider the punishment far too lenient. The venom she'd seen in his eyes the last time they'd talked had been limitless.

And then Christine, poor Christine. The girl was clearly star-struck, worshiping an idealized image of Dale, rather than the flawed reality. She didn't deserve such devotion, such willingness to put life and future at risk for Dale's sake.

The day waned. Sunset turned to dusk, and dusk to twilight. Dale didn't bother turning on the room's lights, preferring to sit where she was, staring out the window at the stars twinkling through the force field dome. By the time the evening meal arrived, Dale had worked herself into a deep pit of self-pity. The white-clad student entered and left the tray on the dresser and left without saying anything. Dale briefly considered offering some excuse for changing rooms, but the student left without asking, so she said nothing. Dale ate without tasting the food and returned to her seat by the window.

A whisper and a gentle hand on her shoulder awakened her.

"Miz Clearwater?"

She blinked and looked around, momentarily disoriented. The room was in total darkness.

She had been dreaming. she realized. Dreaming about being out in the jungle, with all of her monsters, even the Nalcheka. She had been running through the trees, she remembered, playing tag of all things, but then she realized one of them was missing. And the others were wandering away, becoming fainter and more distant. She held onto them, pulling their tentacles tight against her even as they faded into the trees. She knew that if they left her, she would be cold and alone in the dark.

Someone stood over her, concern knitting his brow.

"Dale?" Constantine's voice.

She relaxed, and smiled. "Sorry."

"No need for apologies," he said. "I'm sure you needed the sleep. I wouldn't have woken you, except that we need to talk."

"I can't tell you how much it means to me, that you're willing to take this risk."

"Not that much of a risk. I'm not easily replaced. And, as strange as it sounds to you, I believe in the work I do here. I just don't believe in the way it gets done sometimes." Constantine stood and adjusted the curtains. "You know that tentacle monsters are used to do a lot of bad things out there."

"Yes. I'm aware."

He turned to face Dale, his lips drawn tight. "They're used to guard debt slaves on some of the corporate worlds."

"Yes. And punish them. It's sick."

"The galaxy needs the skills we teach here."

Dale stood up. "But in the course of supporting the fight against those people, your organization starts to see anyone who has tentacle monsters as an enemy, no matter what the relationship is."

"Exactly. And while it's understandable, it's not an excuse. You've been treated badly, and for that I apologize."

Dale put her hand on Constantine's arm. "I don't blame you for that. It's not your fault. You had no control over how the Dai-Sensei treated me." Beneath the thick fabric of his uniform there was iron-hard muscle.

"Perhaps. But I am complicit if I know and don't do anything about it." He put his hand over hers. "That's why I'm here."

Hunger burned in Dale's gut, and it wasn't for food. Constantine smelled marvelous. He had showered recently, and the clean scent of freshly-washed flesh made her want to throw her arms around him. She found it difficult to concentrate. Her imagination kept distracting her with images of what he might look like, feel like, in more intimate circumstances. His hand on her wrist. His arm around her body. His teeth on her neck.

Maybe the best way to put those thoughts aside, would be to indulge them. "I have a question for you," she said, her voice pitched a little lower.

"Yes?"

She moved closer, directly in front of him, and looked up into his eyes. "Are you celibate?"

He gave her that eyebrow again. It was a marvelous eyebrow, expressive of both interest and surprise. "It would be unethical to get involved with my students or the other instructors."

"I'm not either of those."

The other eyebrow went up. "No. You're not."

She put her hand behind his neck and pulled. There was, no doubt, plenty of strength to resist her, but he didn't. He allowed her to pull him down, returned her kiss, and wrapped his long arms around her body. They were just as strong as she had imagined, and her pulse thundered in response. He wasn't the best kisser, but he learned fast, matching her explorations with his own, shifting from tongue to lips to teeth and back again.

"I want you," she gasped, pulling away to slip one hand inside his gi. His chest was smooth, either shaved or naturally hairless, and his nipple was hard against her fingertips. And again, yes, muscle. A thought rose up: *This one would be perfect.*

"What would you like?" he asked, nearly in a whisper.

She spoke almost without thinking. "I want to fuck you so hard you scream."

"Really." More eyebrow.

"Silly, huh? I mean ... you're this big strong man, genemod, and well trained on top of it. And all my life I've been a submissive."

"You don't seem that submissive to me. You've got your holo program, your own ship—"

"Sexually, I mean. Usually, I like being tied up, taken. But now—" She growled and spun him around toward the bed. He let himself be maneuvered. "Now I want to hold you down and do terrible things with your body."

"And what if I said I'd be willing to try that?" He let himself be pushed onto the bed.

"Ugh, it's not the same if you *let* me. I want more than that."

Constantine deftly undid the knot in her gi, pulled it free, and stretched the belt between his hands. "Well then, restrain me."

Dale's tunic fell open, and the cool air on her nipples made them tighten. She took the belt from him, considering its possibilities. "You'd trust me that much?"

"I don't think you'd hurt me. And I'm pretty tough. I can take it."

"All right, then. Give me your hands."

He held out his hands and grinned crookedly as she wrapped the belt around each wrist, making simple overhand knots that were tight enough to keep his hands from slipping through but not so tight they would cut off circulation. The broad surface helped with this; a rope would have cut into his skin, but the wide fabric of the belt distributed the pressure more evenly. Then she laid him down, diagonally on the bed, and stretched the belt up over his head to tie the ends under the bed's corner support. She pulled that knot tight, making sure it wouldn't come out easily. His long arms stretched up over his head, elbows bent, stretching the sinews of his chest and shoulders.

"Anything pinch?" she asked.

"No, it's good."

That left his feet. She pulled the knot out of his belt and slipped it off. it was soft and supple from long use. On one end, there were small metal badges embedded in it. He was tall enough that his ankles fell almost to the end of the bed, and she spread them a bit apart, looped the belt around each one individually, and then once again tied the ends together underneath the bed. She wouldn't be able to get him completely undressed this way, but she didn't need to.

"Try that," she said, standing back to survey her work.

He squirmed against the bonds. "I could probably get out if I had to," he said.

"We don't have a safety cutter," she said. "So that's probably a good thing." She checked the knots one more time, and then climbed up onto the bed next to him.

"So, is this working for you?" he said, eyes sparkling.

Dale surveyed his body, trussed up on the bed, and purred. "Oh, yes." She swung a leg over his thighs and put her hands on his chest, kneading his muscles from his ribs up to his collarbones. "This is exactly what I had in mind." With a bit of weight on her hands, she worked them up and down his torso, curling around shoulders and waist, feeling his skin warm under her touch, his nipples harden even more. A touch to his neck revealed his rising pulse. He had given himself to her. He was hers.

"Hey there," he said, "Watch it. That's a bit rough."

Dale broke out of a reverie she hadn't remembered falling into, and leaned back, lifting her hands from around his neck. "Sorry, what was I thinking? You're going to need a safe word."

"Shokushu," he said. "Are you okay?"

"I'm fine. More than fine." She bent forward, bringing her bare chest into contact with his, nuzzling his shoulder with her cheek. Her arms wrapped around his body and hugged him close, feeling the warmth of his body. It had been too long since she'd had sex with a human being, way too long.

"Good, because you had me a little worried, there."

"Don't worry. I won't hurt you. Besides, you said you're tough, right?"

"Right, but..."

She slid down and undid the drawstring on his pants. "Then let me help you relax." With one pull, she drew his pants down to his thighs, revealing a dark brown cock just beginning to become erect, and releasing a bit of a musky scent that reached through Dale's nose to touch something primal inside her. She growled in approval and took the organ in one hand, cupping his balls with the other.

"That will work," he said, a bit of a rasp coming into his voice.

Dale stroked and kneaded the thickening organ, running her thumb up the underside when she wasn't gripping it tightly in her fingers. "Good."

What was it about this man that made her want to master him this way? He didn't show any sign of submissiveness before, and she had never really counted herself a switch. But this just seemed too right to ignore. Maybe what some folks in the BDSM community said was true; everyone had the potential to be a dom or a sub, depending on the context. Chemistry and all that.

It didn't matter. She was having too much fun to think about it. She was going to make this man hers, if only for tonight. She pulled back his foreskin and took a long lick up the underside of his cock, eliciting a delicious moan.

"There we go," she whispered. "That's what I like to hear." She patted his cock lightly. "Now you stay hard for me while I get naked."

Constantine picked his head up from the bed to watch as she quickly pulled off the white tunic and pants. "Yes, ma'am," he said.

"That's *yes, sir*," she corrected. "*Ma'am* is such an ancient word."

"Yes, sar."

"That's a good human," she said, crawling back on top of him. She knelt down and pressed his cock against his body with her pussy, rolling her hips to rub against his shaft. It felt delicious, almost as if she was fucking him. She wanted to be inside him and around him all at the same time. As her own arousal mounted, she steadied herself with a hand on his sternum, then stretched the other up to run her fingers lightly over his face. When he opened his mouth to moan, she ran a finger inside to lightly brush his tongue.

"Inside you," he gasped. "Please—Put me inside you."

Two fingers now probed inside his mouth, silencing his request. He sucked on them, breathing through his nose hard enough to make his nostrils flare.

"Silly man," she said, and ground herself against him even harder.

Something about this should have been scary, but this felt too right, too good, and that thought was small and weak. Easy to ignore. Constantine was hers to take, hers to do with as she pleased, and that power was intoxicating. Yes, she would make him spend himself like this, denying him what he thought he wanted while giving him what he truly needed.

Harder and harder she worked her body against his, each thrash and buck of his body just a new way to take pleasure from him. She wanted to laugh and scream and cry, and the sounds came out as a growl of primal triumph. Spasms shook her body from head to toe, and she wrapped her arms around him, trapping her sensitive places between their bodies.

She returned to her senses to find that he had come at some point, she didn't remember when. As she pulled away he slipped his hand out of the knotted belt and laid it on her thigh. His voice a breathy whisper, he asked, "Good?"

Dale nodded. "Good." She rose from the bed and bent to free his feet from their restraints, and then stumbled into the bathroom and turned on the shower.

What. The. Fuck.

What had just happened? She had never acted that way in bed

before. Maybe she really was cracking under the strain. That was it. Stress, the strange environment, something. Or maybe she had always been this way, but had simply told herself she was a submissive because that's what she was supposed to be?

She hardly noticed when Constantine followed her into the shower and began soaping her up with his bare hands.

"Are you okay?" he asked.

"Fine," she said. How long had she been standing there, just thinking as the water sprayed down? Long enough for him to become concerned. "Just thinking that I need to check on my monsters. I'm worried about how they are being treated."

"I'll see what I can do," he said. "That's not my responsibility, but I think I can mention it in such a way that they'll decide to let you check in on them."

"Thank you," she said, and took the soap from his hands to take her turn washing his body. They showered and dried each other off, taking the simple pleasure together. Dale took the opportunity to get back into a more normal state of mind. Too many questions that couldn't be answered right now; they would have to wait. She would let them go, and focus on the present. The thought helped quiet her nerves.

Still naked, they walked out onto the balcony, driven by some instinct Dale couldn't identify. Constantine stood behind her with his arms around her as she looked up at the stars. "Funny," she said. "With all the traveling I do, that up there, the galaxy—that's my home. But I almost never look at it."

"But you can see the same thing every day and not realize— Wait." Constantine pointed toward one of the other buildings. "See that?"

Dale peered in the direction he indicated. Starlight rendered the courtyard in ghostly shades of charcoal, but a beacon atop the middle building of the three surrounding it made the cluster of antennas stand out sharply against the black. "What am I looking at?"

"See the spire, just to the right of the big parabolic antenna? The one with the spheres on the side?"

"Yes?"

"Those are our hyperdrones. The ones we use for communications. None of them are missing. There are two there now, just like always."

"Maybe one just came in? Like a reply from the Star Patrol?"

"No, it wouldn't dock on the spire. It would deliver its message from orbit. There's only one possible explanation: The Dai-Sensei hasn't sent your report. They're not coming. Not unless we do something."

"So what do we do?"

Constantine shook his head. "I don't know. I don't have access to the communications room—only the Dai-Sensei can get in there. And the systems aren't networked. There's no way to hack in from outside. Someone would have to physically get inside the room to send your message."

"Locks can be picked."

"If you have tools. If you have skills. I don't. Do you?"

"Christine might be able to do it."

Constantine raised an eyebrow. "Really?"

"She's smarter than she looks."

"Well, she'll still need tools, and I don't know where we can get those. Everything around here is maintained by robots, including the robots. It's not like there's a maintenance shed we can raid. There might be some tools in the communications room, but that's no help."

"We'll figure something out. I'll talk to her in the morning. If I bring her in here, will we be able to talk privately?"

"I think so, as long as you don't turn on the console. That room has listening devices, but this one doesn't. At least, as far as I know." Constantine went back inside and pulled his pants on. As he tied the drawstring, the door to the corridor opened, splashing a bright rectangle of light across the floor, Christine's shadow stretching across the carpet. Her eyes fell on Constantine, then Dale.

"Tired!" she shouted. "You lied to me!"

Christine ran back across the hall, slamming the door closed behind her.

CHAPTER EIGHT
HOLDING A GRUDGE

"Christine! Wait!" Dale started to follow her protégé out of the room, but Constantine restrained her with a firm hand on her shoulder.

"Let her go," he said. "I know my sister. She won't be in any condition to listen to you tonight. She'll be calmer in the morning."

"I'm so stupid," she muttered, squeezing her eyes closed against tears of frustration. "I should have talked to her before. I— Augh! Stupid stupid stupid! I've ruined everything!"

Constantine's long arms wrapped around her, enfolding her. "I don't know all the details, but it's probably not as bad as you think it is. Let it go for now. Sleep on it. Talk to her in the morning."

Dale leaned her head back against his chest, letting his comfort seep in. They stood that way for a few minutes, as she got herself under control. Gradually, the tears dried, her breathing slowed, and her heart ceased hammering.

"You all right now?" asked Constantine.

"Yes."

"Good." He gave her a final squeeze, then let go, and finished getting dressed. "I wish I could stay with you tonight, but I can't be away from where I'm expected."

"I'll be all right," said Dale. "I'm used to sleeping alone."

"I'll talk to you again as soon as I can."

"Thank you."

Sleep didn't come easily. Her mind would not let go of Christine's shocked, hurt expression as the young woman stood in the doorway. She had known that Dale and Constantine had just had sex. Jealousy of her brother would be bad enough, but in addition Dale had told Christine that she wasn't in the mood for sex just a few hours before, and now she knew it was a lie. Why hadn't she told her the truth?, Why hadn't she just told her that she didn't want to pursue a sexual relationship with her student and protégé? That it wasn't good for them? That would have hurt a good deal less than this betrayal.

Now, too, their plan for escaping the monastery was at risk. She needed Christine's expertise with technical matters to break into the communications room to get a message off to the Star Patrol. If she mentioned that, though, then any reconciliation would seem self-centered.

That led Dale down yet another disturbing line of thought. Her relationship with Christine was one of mutual benefit, wasn't it? Dale rolled over on her back and stared at the ceiling above her, eyes unwilling to close in spite of the late hour. She wasn't using Christine, was she? Her mind played back one memory after another, where Dale had gotten off watching a tentacle monster have its way with the young woman, and what Dale had felt during those moments.

Not only that, Dale's ship, somewhere out in the galaxy, had several holographic recordings of Christine, ready to be put up for sale in the electronic marketplaces of a thousand settled worlds. And for that, Christine would get a fifteen percent share of the proceeds.

All that was just business. There was more to their relationship than that, wasn't there? Christine had saved her life out there in the wilderness, after Dale's ship had been stolen. She had carried her through the loss and despair, through sheer unbreakable positivity.

Yet now, Dale had broken that positivity. The girl who had stayed upbeat and strong through all those difficulties was now crying herself to sleep over what Dale had done. She ran her fingers through her hair, trying to think of some way to make it right, some way to fix everything, but no matter how she looked at it, the situation seemed endlessly hopeless.

After a time, Dale drifted off out of sheer exhaustion. She woke to firm, repeated knocks on her door, rescued from dreams that slipped from her mind before she could grasp them. The sweaty sheets were wrapped about her limbs like bindings, and it took her a few seconds to fight free. Those dreams had not been pleasant ones.

"Come in!" she called. She had no reason to hope that Christine was the one at the door, but she hoped for it anyways.

Instead, Master Kiriki opened the door, silhouetted in the hall light. "One of your monsters is making trouble."

Dale blinked, struggling to bring herself fully conscious. "What?"

"Your Storazoid. It's agitated. Come with me and calm it down."

Dale fumbled for her clothes. "Okay, let me just—"

"Now." Kiriki hit the light switch.

"Okay, okay." Dale stumbled to her feet, nearly blind in the sudden glare. "Let me get dressed."

Kiriki grabbed her arm and dragged her, naked, from the room. "There's no time. Let's go."

Dale didn't really awaken until they reached the stairs leading down to the containment facility. Her stomach growled, and a sour taste filled her mouth.

"What's the Storazoid doing?" she asked, pulling her arm out of Kiriki's grip.

"You'll see."

The woman led her to the containment facility control panel. There was a tool kit sitting on the floor nearby, with a pair of gloves lying incongruously over the handle. Kiriki stood back and pointed to the controls.

"Has it damaged the system?" Dale asked.

"What? Not yet, but it will if you don't calm it down."

"I see." She blinked hard, trying to banish the grogginess from her eyes.

"Look. There." Kiriki pointed to the control panel. "See?"

A video monitor showed her Storazoid from a high angle, inside a stone cell only barely big enough to hold the monster. Its woody tentacles were extruded from its mushroom-shaped body, stretching out to the walls of the cell where they wormed into cracks between the stone blocks.

"If it keeps that up," said Kiriki, "It'll bring down the whole building. Stop it."

"I'm going to need to get inside with it," said Dale. "It won't understand if I just talk to it. Also, it's going to need a bigger space. And soil. Dirt. I'm sure your robots can—"

"The control to lower the force field containing it is right there," said Kiriki. "Deal with it, or I will destroy it. It is undermining the foundations of the building."

Dale held up her hands. "Okay, all right. Hold on. I'll calm it down. But it needs dirt in there, okay? That's what it's looking for. I'll calm it down, but it needs dirt."

"I cannot access the robot control system from here," she said. "I will arrange for the soil, but you need to address this now. Open the cell."

"Right, right. Good." Dale surveyed the console. A big holographic button below the video feed was labeled *Release*. It seemed simple enough. She touched the control and the force field closing off the Storazoid's cell popped and vanished.

Kiriki nodded. "There you are."

Dale walked over to the Storazoid's cell. Its usual scent of cinnamon and barbecue sauce was muted, and she felt none of the usual arousal the aroma would provoke. She laid her hand on its body. Its skin was as smooth, hard and dry as polished wood, a sure sign that it was in no mood for sex.

She stroked its cap, then ran a hand up the thick, vine-like tentacle that stretched straight out to the wall, where it anchored deep in a wide crack between the stones. Dale knew that Storazoids were strong, but she was still impressed with what it had accomplished in just a few hours.

The tension eased a bit, and the tendril pulled out of the hole in the wall. One by one, as Dale stroked them, the tentacles ceased their assaults on the building's foundations. They did not, however, retract into the body. Instead, they drooped over it like willow boughs, arching curves constrained by the confines of the cell.

"There you go," Dale crooned, knowing that at least the gentle tone of her voice would help soothe the monster. "I'm sorry they put you in such a small space," she said. "I should have made sure they treated you better."

The Storazoid lay one tentacle across her shoulders, gently, then reached down and wrapped it around her chest just under her boobs. Its scent grew stronger, and another tentacle took a grip on her thigh and lifted her into the air. A sheen broke out on its skin. It was skipping the usual adhesive trap phase of its routine, going right to secreting the lubricant aphrodisiac. Her body responded instantly, and a shudder of anticipation ran through her.

She looked back for a moment. Kiriki watched, a nasty grin spreading on her face.

So you're going to get off on this? Dale thought. *Fine, let's give you a show then, you hypocrite.* Closing her eyes, she let the Storazoid carry her out of the cell, into the wider open area of the facility, and Dale felt a bit of tension ease from the tentacles holding her.

Creaking softly, the woody tendrils pulled Dale closer to its body, slowly stretching her over its surface. This was how it preferred to have her, spread-eagled, her back lying on its smooth, soft dome. It touched her with agonizing slowness, spreading more of its secretions over her skin, and slowly pushing one tendril and then another inside her receptive body. She struggled, but the effect of its drug combined with the lingering grogginess made them feeble at best.

It felt nice to let go, to put aside her worries about her ship, about Christine, about everything else that had gone wrong, and enjoy the moment for what it was. The Dai-Sensei had called it "surrender," and perhaps that's what it was, but there was nothing wrong with a little surrender now and then, especially when you trusted the being you were surrendering to.

Except for the quiet sounds the Storazoid made when it moved, and the sighs and moans of her own arousal, all was quiet.

A little pop and crackle came from elsewhere in the room, but Dale hardly noticed, and didn't wonder what it was. There was only her, and her monster, and the marvelous things it was doing to her body. Only when a shadow fell across her closed eyelids, did she open them to see what was going on around her.

A Yartroan floated above her, this one a pale pink with faint brown stripes. Its diaphanous tentacles reached down to wrap around the parts of her body that the Storazoid had not already grabbed. It was the largest Yartroan she had ever seen, even bigger than the one she had encountered out in the forest.

"Hey!" she shouted, "What's going on?"

Sensei Kiriki's voice cut with a sinister, sarcastic edge. "Such a shame. Against our explicit instructions, Miz Clearwater hacked the controls for the monster containment cells and released several of the beasts we keep for training purposes."

"What? No!" Dale's scream was cut off as the huge Yartroan wrapped a tentacle around her head, sealing her mouth and nose. Immediately, her heart began pounding. It had caught her with little air in her lungs and she struggled to get free.

Kiriki continued with her narrative. "You see, she was unfamiliar with their behavior, her much-vaunted skill was useless in preventing her demise. Such a tragedy."

Through vision already beginning to fade, she saw the Storazoid's tentacles attempt to reach up to push the attacking monster away, but it was too slow, and the Yartroan easily evaded it.

"But since she was there alone, there was no one to help her. Certainly, a great loss to the galaxy." Kiriki laughed. "Now if you'll excuse me, I've got an alibi to establish. Goodbye, Monster Whisperer. No more whispers from you." Then Dale heard the whine of motors as the elevator carried the woman up to the surface level.

The strength ebbed from her limbs as Dale fought for air. She pulled one arm free and clawed at the tentacle covering her mouth, managed to get the slightest of breath. The Storazoid had let go of her to bring more tentacles to bear against the Yartroan, but instead of freeing her, the Storazoid's stable weight no longer anchored her, and she floated up out of her monster's reach. More filmy tentacles wrapped around her, pinning her arms to her sides, and once again covered her face, cutting off any hope of more air.

Below, Dale heard the low thumps as the Storazoid stomped around, but the sound faded along with her consciousness, as if the huge Yartroan were somehow lifting her through the building, through the force field, and up into the sky. A crack and a grinding of stone made almost no impression.

Then there was a jerk, and the Yartroan's grip weakened. The filmy tentacle covering her mouth shifted, and she gulped air, regaining consciousness just in time for a jarring impact on the stone floor. She rolled over onto her back, pulling at the last few tentacles still holding her, and looked up. The balloon-like body of the Yartroan was covered in the semi-fluid weight of her Kritzoan, which was rapidly spreading to cover its body. The fight, if you could call it that, was just as one-sided as her struggle with the Yartroan had been. She fought free of the last few tentacles and scrambled away on all fours, nearly choking from breathing so hard. She coughed and sputtered, swallowing hard to keep from vomiting.

After a few seconds, Dale's mind had cleared enough to take in the aftermath of the scene. The big Yartroan was inside the Kritzoan, struggling, but the amorphous, blob-like monster clearly had an insurmountable advantage. Her attacker wasn't going anywhere.

A glance around the facility told the story of how it had saved her. The wall of the Storazoid's cell, which had already been weakened by the monster's tentacles overnight, had been cracked open. That must have been where the Kritzoan had been contained, on the other side of that wall. It had escaped by oozing through the gap, and had crawled onto the ceiling to drop down onto the Yartroan.

Dale climbed to her feet, head aching and a bit bruised. Once again, her monsters had saved her life. Yet this time it wasn't the attentions of a wild tentacle monster they had fought off, but a murder attempt. She walked over to the containment system console and surveyed the controls. The other monsters all appeared to be in good health, if a bit agitated.

"Miz Clearwater!" Christine's excited scream echoed through the chamber. Dale looked up to see her young protégé and Constantine running across the floor toward her. Christine's words came all in a rush as she ran. "I woke up and you weren't there, and I found Sensei Kiriki and she said she saw you but didn't know where you'd gone and I got Constantine and this was the only place to look and by the Stars are you okay?"

"I'm not hurt," she said, "Just a bit shook up. That Kiriki person tried to kill me—sicced the big Yartroan on me. Christine—thanks for coming and looking for me. I know you were very upset."

Christine scowled and started to answer, but was interrupted by a crunch of stone as the Storazoid pulled the remainder of the wall to the Kritzoan's cell apart. It stepped through the gap and began working on the next wall in the row.

"If it keeps that up, it's going to bring the whole building down," said Constantine.

"Sounds like justice to me," said Christine.

"Justice or not, we need to get out of here," said Dale. "They won't be so subtle next time. Does your shuttle have a hyperdrive?"

Constantine shook his head. "No. It's strictly orbital. But it's the only other safe place to keep the tentacle monsters."

Dale frowned and looked around. "Then we have to get that hyperdrone off to the Star Patrol. Wait—Constantine, didn't you say we'd need tools to break into the communications room?" She grabbed the tool box sitting next to the console. "Kiriki planted those tools there to make it look like I had hacked the control console. Would they work?"

Christine took the box and looked through the contents. "I'm a dropout freshman virtual intelligence engineer, not a spy. She pulled a small tablet out of the box and unspooled a cable from it.

"I can use this to send commands to any device with a universal connector, but door locks aren't built that way."

Dale growled. "All right, then we just need to get everyone into the shuttle. We'll think of something when we're in orbit. There's too much danger for us here."

"Not going to work," said Constantine. "The shuttle only has basic air recyclers. No food or water to speak of, and it could be months before another actual ship arrives, rather than scheduled hyperdrones."

"Then we'll just send our message to one of them."

"That won't work either," said Christine. "Mail hyperdrones only stay in the system for a few seconds. They transmit their incoming mail, receive the outgoing mail from the authorized mail station, and leave. There wouldn't be enough time to get our message in."

Dale winced. "What a stupid system!"

The elevator motors whined, and the platform began its slow descent from the courtyard above. Dai-Sensei Lakosta stood at the head of a phalanx of monks dressed in a rainbow of colors, with Kiriki directly behind her. "See!" said the elderly Master of Monsters. "She's trying to bring the whole building down!"

"No! The Storazoid is just—"

"Silence!" shouted Lakosta. "Constantine, restrain those monsters immediately. And if the Storazoid can't be restrained without damage to the facility, destroy it."

"Dai-Sensei, with all due respect, there's some evidence that Sensei Kiriki—"

"Silence!" Lakosta repeated. "Do as you are commanded." The monks fanned out in a half-circle around them.

Dale pitched her voice low. "She's trying to get your fingerprints on the panel as well. Make you into an accomplice."

"I know. I guess I have no choice now." Constantine stepped over to the panel and began manipulating the controls. An emitter on the ceiling began to glow, and then all the force fields came down at once. The main screen lit up with the words, SYSTEM REBOOT IN SIXTY SECONDS.

"Traitor!" shouted Kiriki.

The monsters charged out of their enclosures at the startled monks. Moments later, the Kritzoan let go of the huge Yartroan and joined them. Shouts filled the air as fists and feet and tentacles whirled in a sudden maelstrom of violence.

"Your monsters aren't going to last long," said Constantine. "Run! I'll try to keep them busy here as long as I can."

"Run where?" cried Christine. "I really don't know how to break locks!"

Dale grabbed her hand. "Come on. I have an idea." The two raced across the vast room as Constantine delivered a savage kick at one of his colleagues.

Dale and Christine ran up the stairs two at a time, the sounds of combat fading below them. "Nobody's chasing us," Christine gasped as they reached the second landing.

"Either they're distracted, or they don't think we're a threat," said Dale. "Either way, we don't have much time."

"But—"

"Less talking, more running!"

Up on the top floor, Dale quickly located a room with a balcony, and shoved a cabinet out under the eaves.

"Climb," said Dale, "We need to get up to the roof." Christine clambered up and then pulled Dale up after. Above them, glowing in the sunlight just beginning to stream over the mountains, was the cluster of antennas and emitters Dale had seen the night before, and just below it, the short spire that held the monastery's two emergency hyperdrones. Dale hurried up the sloping tile roof toward the drones and handed the tool box to Christine.

"Get out that universal connector thing," she said.

"Oh! Of course!" she exclaimed.

The hyperdrone was held fast to the spire with a claw-like appendage, and right below that it had a short umbilical cable plugged into a socket. Dale yanked it out and passed it to Christine, who plugged it into the tablet and squealed with glee as the screen lit up.

"You can send the distress call?"

"Absolutely! This is an emergency hyperdrone. No security on it whatsoever. It's made to be simple."

"Great, then get started."

"There's no holo on this thing, just text. What should I say?"

"Just tell them we need the Star Patrol."

"Gotcha." Christine started tapping on the tablet, pecking out the letters one by one.

"Stop!" came a shout from below. The Dai-Sensei stood at the edge of the roof. Her face was scraped. One sleeve of her gi had been ripped off, revealing a bruise around her upper arm. "If you launch that drone, you will not leave this planet alive."

"It's over," Dale called back. "When the Star Patrol gets here, they'll find out all about how you aided Doctor Florence in getting away with her hijacking of my ship. How you delayed my message, and how your subordinate deliberately tried to get me killed by one of your monsters."

"No they won't," she said, "Because by the time they get here, both of you are going to be dead." She ran up the steep slope much faster than Dale would have expected. Dale grabbed the tool box and flung it down, tools and cables clattering down across the tiles.

The Dai-Sensei dodged the clumsy projectiles, slowing her only a second, but a second was enough. The drone unclamped itself from the spire and with a roar like thunder, sped off into the sky. Dale and Christine ran, running along the ridge-line of the roof, as the older woman raced on behind them. Within moments they would run out of roof, and then they'd have the choice of facing the grandmaster of a martial arts school or leaping from the roof of a four-story building.

Then Christine grabbed a decorative lightning-rod, snapped it off at the base, turned, and leveled it at their pursuer.

"You think that's going to stop me?" the Dai-Sensei sneered.

"Maybe," Christine said, her voice quivering. "But I'm not going to just let you kill me."

"You have done nothing to earn my enmity, Christine Delavos. If you surrender, we can work out a deal." She glanced to her right.

"Down there is a balcony that is connected to my personal office. Wait for me there, and I'll spare your life."

Christine said nothing.

"After all," continued Lakosta, "She did betray you, did she not? Lie to you?"

"You were listening in on me?" Christine's grip tightened.

"Yes, I was. And a good thing, too, or else how would I have known that you were just as much a victim of this low-life as I was?"

Christine nodded, and the end of her weapon dropped a bit.

"The kind of behavior we would expect from someone like her, isn't it? She is not worthy of someone of your status. Not one of us."

The point of Christine's makeshift spear touched the roof tiles in front of her..

Lakosta took a step closer. "She's been using you, hasn't she? Taking advantage of you."

Dale felt bile rising in her throat. "No, Christine, don't listen to her! *She tried to kill me!*"

"Sensei Kiriki mistook my instructions. She was only supposed to lock your friend here in one of the monster cells. I never intended to kill her. Sensei Kiriki will be appropriately disciplined."

"Christine, she's lying!"

"Who are you going to believe, Miz Delavos? *I've* never lied to you."

"You're right." Christine turned and carefully descended the slope toward the balcony.

"Christine! Wait!" Dale cried, but her erstwhile apprentice did not even look back.

Dale now faced Lakosta naked and alone. She had never learned to fight, never taken even a single martial arts class. She had always been able to talk herself out of a tough situation, but she had never faced anyone this desperate. She held her hands out, palms up.

"Please," she said. "I don't want to destroy you. All I ever wanted was to get my ship back. If you help us now, maybe we can save your school."

"It's too late for that," spat Lakosta, quietly. When Christine disappeared over the edge of the roof, she advanced slowly, face pale, eyes focused. Dale retreated until her foot found the sculpted end of the ridge-line of the roof. If she backed up any further, she'd go down.

"It will take money and influence to repair the damage you've done, but I have connections." Murderous fire erupted in Lakosta's eyes. "And when I return Miz Delavos to her mother, I'll have all the influence I need to straighten this mess out. The original plan can still be salvaged."

Dale tried to back away further, but the slope of the roof behind her was steep, and she almost lost her balance trying to retreat. Lakosta stretched her arms forward, hands held like claws toward her throat.

Then the lightning rod came spinning up from below, striking Lakosta in the midsection and knocking her off the ridge-line. She rolled down the steep roof, catching herself on the edge by one hand.

Below, Christine stood on the edge of the roof, beckoning to Dale. "Come on!"

Dale hurried down the slope. Christine leapt down to the balcony first, and then caught Dale when she took her turn. They tried the door into the room beyond, but it was locked and there was nothing there to batter it down with. The other balconies were too far away to jump to.

"Go over the edge, to the balcony under us," said Christine. "I'll hold you. Then swing your legs and I'll let you go."

Dale shook her head, panting hard. Her hands were shaking, and her knees felt like they would buckle under her at any moment. "I'm not...I can't..."

Lakosta's scream of frustration echoed from the valley walls. "I'll kill you both!"

Then the shuttle came around the side of the building and into the courtyard. Its nose came to a stop right under their balcony, and a hatch on the upper surface popped open. Constantine's head poked out.

"Morning, ladies. Need a ride?"

Dale and Christine jumped onto the nose of the shuttle and then into the hatch. Constantine took the controls and angled the ship upwards as the hatch hissed closed.

"What about the monsters?" Dale asked, as she strapped herself into the seat.

"When the containment system reboots, the first thing it does is to see whether any monsters escaped while it was down. It then captures them and tries to put them into the cells. Except the system was damaged by your Storazoid. The backup location is right here on the shuttle, so that's where it put them. They're all inside, safe and sound. And not just your monsters, either. The monastery's Yartroans are also on board. As soon as the system came up I fought my way to the shuttle and locked out everyone but the monsters. Did you get the hyperdrone sent?"

"Yes," said Dale. "We went up on the roof and accessed it directly."

"Smart," he said. In the front windows, the blue sky faded to black, and stars appeared across the sky. "And we're away."

"So it's going to be a while before the Star Patrol gets here?" asked Christine.

"Yes," said Dale. "Twenty, maybe thirty hours, depending on how far the closest ship is."

Christine leveled a serious look in Dale's direction. "Then we need to talk."

Dale didn't hesitate. "Christine, I'm sorry. I'm sorry I put you off, I shouldn't have done that. I wanted to tell you that I was going to keep our relationship on a professional level, but the moment never seemed right, and..." She shrugged. "I procrastinated. I'm sorry."

"Professional?" Christine shook her head. "You get off on watching me have sex with your tentacle monsters. How is that professional?"

"I can't deny that it turns me on, but you're an employee and a student. It wouldn't be proper."

"Ugh! You're as bad as my mother, and you're only a few years older than me! Listen. I'm not a kid. I'm a grown woman, and I can make my own choices. You're not seducing some innocent ingénue here."

"Christine, I've seen this kind of thing before. An old, uh, friend of mine, a monster hunter, got romantically involved with his protégé, and...well, it ended badly."

"Oh, and I suppose Victor Klieberman is a model of emotional maturity and restraint?"

"You knew about him?"

"Of course I knew about him. Tentacle monster fangirl, remember?"

Dale shook her head. "Okay, well, yes, he was kind of a jerk. But, even with that aside, it wouldn't be a good idea for me to be romantically involved with both of you. You're brother and sister and, even though you are clones of your parents, it's still a bit weird."

"Yeah, about that," said Constantine. "I'm not going to come with you."

"What?" Dale exclaimed.

"Yeah, when this mess settles out, Irairanochirasu is going to need all the help it can get. They need someone to remind them who they really serve. I have good relationships with most of the students. With some luck and hard work, we can get through this."

"After all that, you're still loyal to them?"

"To Dai-Sensei Lakosta? No. But to Irairanochirasu, yes, absolutely."

Dale looked back to Christine, who had a smug look on her face. "I know the look in your eyes when you watch me," she said. "I know how you feel."

"That's just lust," said Dale. "You're young, attractive. Why wouldn't I find you sexy?"

"You and I both know that's a lie."

The console tweedled. Constantine touched a control. "Uh, guys? We're getting a priority message from the Star Patrol."

Dale blinked. "What, already? That's impossible."

"Here, I'll put it up." Constantine touched another control, and a hologram of the head and shoulders of a man in a sharp black uniform appeared over the console. "Go ahead," said Constantine.

The man looked flustered for a moment. "I'm sorry to interrupt," he said, glancing at Dale, "But this is rather urgent. I'm Captain Patrick Grayson Holyfield of the Patrol Cruiser *Avedon*. I'm looking for Dale Clearwater, and I'm not getting a response when I hail the planet."

"That's me," said Dale. She realized that the man's unease probably resulted from the fact that she was still naked. "Is this about my ship?"

"Your ship?"

"Yes, it was hijacked here, about a day ago. I just sent off a hyperdrone with the report."

"No, we didn't have that information. Miz Clearwater, I'm here because the Star Patrol needs you. We're getting reports from all the nearby star systems. Someone is stealing tentacle monsters. We want you to help us find them."

CHAPTER NINE
FINGERHOLD

Dale, Constantine, and Christine were brought aboard the Patrol Cruiser Avedon and conducted to separate interview rooms. In Dale's, a Lieutenant waited with a coverall and plain, utilitarian underwear. Dale held up the blue jumpsuit in admiration. "You even put my logo on it!"

"I hope we got it right, sar," she said. "We only had images from your holos to go on."

"It's marvelous," she said, slipping on the underwear, and then the coverall. "How did you make this on such short notice, Lieutenant...?" The name *Andre* was stitched on the officer's uniform, but it seemed presumptuous to use the name without some kind of introduction.

"Lieutenant Olivia Andre. We have a synthesizer on board. Mostly for things like spare parts, but it's useful for all kinds of things. I've been assigned as your liaison while you're on the ship." She was short and slight, with a curl of bright red hair poking out from under her beret. The woman seemed a bit too small to be a police officer, but she carried herself with a confident air that left Dale with no doubt she could handle herself.

Dale sat in one of the conference chairs to slip on the plain white athletic shoes that had been provided. "Thank you, Lieutenant, for thinking of me this way."

"No problem, sar. Just as easy to make you something familiar as not. If you are ready, Captain Holyfield is eager to speak with you."

"Likewise," said Dale.

Olivia tapped a comm device strapped to her wrist, and said, "Miz Clearwater is ready for you, sar."

"I'm surprised you had my holos here," said Dale.

"Captain Holyfield ordered a full dossier when we were assigned this mission. It was quite extensive. And—" the slightest hint of a blush colored Olivia's cheeks, "You do have one or two fans among the crew."

"Oh, really?" said Dale with a smirk. "Anyone I might have met?"

Before Olivia could answer, the door swished open and a dignified, gentlemanly figure entered. He wore the bright blue Patrol uniform like he was born to it, stunner strapped to one hip and badge shining on his broad chest. He had allowed his long sideburns and bushy eyebrows to go steely gray, probably because they lent his face some authority. "Miz Clearwater. I'm Captain Patrick Holyfield. I'm pleased to meet you." His voice was a deep baritone, warm and mellow but with a gravelly edge to it.

"Likewise," said Dale, accepting his offered hand for a shake. His grip, like his general demeanor, was confident but not overbearing. He seemed to be the kind of decent fellow of which the galaxy needed more, and Dale felt a knot of anxiety unclench inside her. This was not one of the folks who reveled in authority and threw it around simply because it entertained them. This was a man of integrity, and she instantly felt more comfortable with the situation.

Captain Holyfield inclined his head. "Allow me to extend a personal welcome to the Patrol Cruiser *Avedon*. I was about to have lunch. Would you care to join me?"

"Thank you," said Dale. "Your hospitality is much appreciated."

As they walked out into the passageway, he said, "My crew are interviewing your companions right now, but I wanted to talk to you personally."

"You mentioned that someone was kidnapping tentacle monsters?"

They passed through another hatch into a small wardroom. Food was already laid out at three place settings. Dale realized how hungry she was when the smell of roasted meat wafted over her.

She had to swallow to keep from drooling, but nothing could prevent her stomach from growling.

"Yes, and we'll get to that momentarily, but I understand you have a tale to tell as well. I'd like to hear that first."

Dale sat, and while they ate, she told them everything that had happened since they arrived at Yartro, including the hijacking of her ship, the release of her and her monsters, her attempt to retake the ship, her arrival at the monastery, and her narrow escape from an attempt on her life.

After she was done, Captain Holyfield put his hands together in front of his lips in a contemplative pose. "A serious charge. If your companions corroborate your story, I'll send a detachment down to investigate."

"Thank you, I'd appreciate that. You said that tentacle monsters were being kidnapped?"

Captain Holyfield tapped the communicator on his wrist. "Computer. Activate the wardroom projector, please. Display local star map. Highlight locations tagged in case file six two five stroke seven." A hologram appeared over the table, displaying the local section of the galaxy with a meandering line of stars picked out in red. "Last report we received before leaving Nova Moskva flagged these incidents. Monsters of various sorts have disappeared from their owners' enclosures in nine different star systems. And the one thing they all had in common, was that you had visited them for your show."

Dale chewed and swallowed, then peered closer at the map. "Not all of them," she said, pointing at one of the locations. "That one's not from the show," she said. "The monster missing on New New Amsterdam is the Orichalc. Ellen Ventura paid extra to keep my visit private. The other visit I had there was to help with an Under-the-Bed monster, but that holo hasn't been released. I wasn't able to transmit it before the ship was hijacked."

"Indeed. Then that adds further weight to our current theory. I think it's pretty clear that the disappearances and the hijacking of your ship are connected. Perhaps they sent out a coded message after hijacking your ship to activate sleeper cells on the target worlds. Perhaps they added Miz Ventura's monster to their target list after finding it in your ship's computer. In any case, we're dealing with a very sophisticated conspiracy."

"Forgive me for being blunt," Dale replied, "But wouldn't that connection make me your prime suspect?"

"You were one of them."

"And Vince Klieberman? Was he on your list?"

"Yes, and Penny Angstrom. And I certainly haven't ruled any of you out as being connected. But our scanners found the place where your ship landed, and we are ready to believe that you were hijacked. I doubt you would have marooned yourself on purpose. Once we can track down your ship, I feel certain we'll get to the bottom of things."

"Thank you for your honesty." Dale considered for a moment, then scowled. "Something seems wrong with your theory, but I agree that finding my ship will get to the bottom of it, so I'm good with that. Any idea where they might have taken it?"

"If they're going to be able to operate in any civilized area of the galaxy, including any of these planets where tentacle monsters have disappeared, they're going to need to forge a new registration. They'll probably also need something of a refit so that the ship doesn't show up on scans as identical to your ship. We've sent out bulletins to keep an eye out for it, but of course we don't have much presence in places like New Arkham or New Kingston."

"I've heard of those worlds and their reputations, but I think you're forgetting that the hijackers are activists first and pirates second. They won't go to either of those worlds," said Dale. "New Arkham is way too friendly to tentacle monsters, just from a cultural standpoint. Doctor Florence wouldn't find any allies there. And Karen Obila, the port administrator in New Kingston, is a personal friend. She's seen my ship before and no amount of money would convince her to help steal it. No, they'll go somewhere they have a strong base of support; somewhere like New Beulah."

Lieutenant Andre tapped her communicator. "Computer. Access

wardroom projector. Highlight worlds where ownership of tentacle monsters is illegal or heavily restricted." A handful of stars lit up on the hologram. The closest was New Beulah. "Computer, give me the planetary summary for New Beulah."

A synthesized voice said, "New Beulah was colonized in twenty-one forty-two by religious separatists dissenting from the gender wars that involved Earth, Mars, and Alpha Centauri. It is a primarily agricultural planet self-sufficient in most raw materials, with minimal extra-planetary trade. The government of New Beulah, known as the Covenant, is a theocratic oligarchy."

"You've got good instincts," said Captain Holyfield.

"Not instincts," said Dale. "I know where my hate mail comes from."

"Fair enough," said Holyfield. "In any case, New Beulah would be a good base of operations, if one were concerned with the planets where the thefts have occurred." He wiped his mouth with his napkin and stood, leaving his meal half-eaten. "Now if you will excuse me, I need to handle a few details before we get underway."

"Will you be able to take my tentacle monsters on board?"

"Already being handled," said Captain Holyfield, "Though we do have to put them in stasis."

"Better than the alternative," said Dale. "Thank you." She made a note that when this whole mess was straightened out, she would give each of her monsters some special attention. They had been treated like unwanted hangers-on, shuffled from one confinement to another, and they didn't deserve any of it.

"You're quite welcome." Captain Holyfield bowed, and indicated the lieutenant. "Lieutenant Andre will be your liaison while you're on the ship. Let her know if there's anything you need." He then bowed, and walked briskly out of the room.

"He's going to make sure my story is corroborated by Christine and Constantine, isn't he?"

"Standard procedure," the woman replied.

Dale scrutinized Lieutenant Andre's face for a moment, then

frowned and looked down at her plate.

"What's wrong?" she asked.

Dale let out a breath. "I'm sorry. After all the trouble at the monastery, I was seeing if there were any imperfections about you that'd tell me you weren't from one of the old genemod families."

"I see. You're not sure you can trust us?"

"Not if you can't trust me."

Lieutenant Andre shrugged. "That's fair. For the record, I'm not; my grandma had some work done to fix a cancer gene, but if I have anything else going on I don't know about it. And if your story checks out, then you don't have anything to worry about."

Dale snapped her fingers. "I think I've figured out what bothers me about this theory. The folks Doctor Florence had with her on my ship weren't all that competent. They were mostly kids. Not the type to pull off precisely timed kidnappings on multiple worlds, flawlessly."

"Maybe that group was just the folks she had on hand at the time. Recent recruits."

"I suppose," said Dale. "But I can't help thinking there's more to it."

Lieutenant Andre's wrist comm chirped, and after a short conversation she smiled to Dale and said, "The interviews with your friends are done. Would you like to see them?"

"Yes, please."

Lieutenant Andre led Dale to the main mess deck, which was in the middle of serving a meal. Dale had already eaten but even so the smells wafting through the room were mouth-watering. The ship had a real kitchen with cooks and everything, rather than a synthesizer, and the tables could easily seat several dozen people.

"Just how big is the *Avedon*, anyways?" Dale asked.

"We're a light cruiser class," she said. "Outfitted for anti-piracy. One hundred eighty-two meters long, thirty-eight meters wide. Spinal mount main gun, nine point defense batteries. Launchers capable of firing breacher missiles, boarding capsules, or hyperspace denial buoys."

"I had no idea piracy was such a problem."

"The fact that we operate ships like the *Avedon*," said the Lieutenant, "is why piracy isn't a problem. We spend most of our time on other tasks, like maintaining mail relays and search-and-rescue. This case is probably the biggest one we'll have all year."

Constantine and Christine waved from one of the tables across the room. Dale waved back and hustled through the crowd to join them.

"You going to get any food?" asked Christine. "It's pretty good."

"I already ate," said Dale. "Captain invited me to his wardroom."

"Well, don't you rate," said Christine, with a wink.

"Fame does have its perks," Dale replied.

"So, are you still going to return to Yartro?" Dale asked.

Constantine nodded. "No doubt in my mind. I'll bring our own monsters back, so you don't have to deal with them, and help the Patrol get things straightened out."

Dale recognized the little pang for what it was; she had no relationship with Constantine, not really. What she felt was disappointment, not loss. There was never any commitment there. He was just fun to fuck. She led the conversation in a different direction. "Does the Patrol have jurisdiction there? I thought they were only interplanetary."

"When local authority breaks down," said Lieutenant Andre, "galactic citizens can request assistance."

"Which I've done," said Constantine.

"Cases of governmental malfeasance get special consideration," Andre continued.

"Which is exactly what happened on Yartro," said Constantine.

The lieutenant made a vague gesture. "Allegedly. Officially, we're there to investigate. But if your description of events there turns out to be accurate, there will be consequences."

"I'm glad to hear that."

An officer strode over to their table and saluted. Lieutenant

Andre returned it. "Yes, ensign?"

"Mister Delavos, your shuttle is inspected and prepped. We're ready to go."

Constantine folded his napkin next to his plate, and stood. "I guess this is goodbye, then."

Christine jumped up and gave her brother a huge hug. "Be careful," she said.

"I will."

Dale stood as well, and waited her turn to embrace Constantine. "Take care of yourself. Let me know if you need any help with your monsters. Once we get my ship back, I'd be happy to come out and do a show about the monastery."

"There's a lot of ifs there," he said. "But that might be possible. Stay in touch."

Dale kissed him on the cheek, and then Constantine followed the officer out of the mess deck.

"So," said Christine, nodding at the logo on Dale's chest. "Can I get one of those nifty Monster Whisperer coveralls?"

"That should be possible," said Lieutenant Andre, and tapped her wrist comm. "Computer, access replication system. Access design files for Monster Whisperer coverall. Modify to fit Christine Delavos and synthesize. Deliver to my quarters." The communicator beeped several times. "There you go," she said. "Should be ready by the time we get back there."

"And you said the ship had no crew amenities," Dale observed.

Lieutenant Andre laughed. "Well, it has its limits. Don't try to ask it for anything fancy or frilly."

Christine got a mischievous look in her eye. "May I ask what model of synthesizer controller you're using?"

Lieutenant Andre shrugged. "I suppose." She tapped her communicator again and relayed the question to the ship's computer, which dutifully responded, "Prescott DFE-42, version fifty-two point three."

Christine grinned. "Ask it to make me a Prescott Special, variation six. Sized for me."

Lieutenant Andre cocked an eyebrow. "All right." She repeated the command to the computer, which beeped again in response.

"What's a Prescott Special?" Dale asked.

"Want to find out?" she said, standing. "I'll show you."

Lieutenant Andre glanced between Dale and Christine, pursing her lips. "Uh, I should probably let you know that I'm under orders not to leave you alone with any sensitive equipment," she said. "And given that you, Miz Delavos, seem to know more about our ship's computer systems than I do, I believe that order is quite prudent."

Christine shrugged. "It's just a little quirk I happened to hear about. Nothing that would compromise anything."

"Still," said Lieutenant Andre, as she led them out of the mess and down one of the companionways. "There's a console in my room. I can't give you any privacy."

Dale and Christine looked at each other and shrugged. "Fine with me," said Dale.

Lieutenant Andre opened the door to her quarters and stepped aside. "Sorry it isn't more comfortable than this," she said.

The room was just two meters wide and three meters deep, with a ceiling only a shade more than two meters from the floor. A pair of bunk beds folded down from the wall on the left, and on the right there was a fold-out desk with a holographic computer console. Sitting neatly on the corner were two bundles in clear wrappers, one big enough for a coverall, and one quite a bit smaller.

"Do you have a roommate?" Dale asked.

"He's been moved out to make room for you."

Christine stepped over to the desk and snatched up the smaller bundle with a squeal. She held it to her chest, protectively. "I want to show you," she said, staring into Dale's eyes. "But I want to put it on first."

Lieutenant Andre shook her head. "As I said before, I can't leave you alone in the room with a console."

Christine smiled hopefully. "Can Dale wait outside?"

"I suppose that would be all right." A flush came up over

Lieutenant Andre's collar and into her cheeks. "If it's okay with Miz Clearwater?"

"Sure, I'll play along," said Dale. She stepped away from the door while the Lieutenant went inside and slid the door closed. She leaned against the far wall, imagining what was going on inside as muffled voices came through the door.

"Oh, my," said Lieutenant Andre. "You were right. That's... Wow. I don't think I've ever seen anything like that."

Christine giggled. "Here, help me get into it. These can get a little tangled."

"How did you find out about this?" Lieutenant Andre asked.

"Omicron Theta Psi has a Prescott unit. The hidden specials are kind of a tradition."

"Sorority girl, eh? Here, hold out your arm."

Dale squirmed. Her imagination ran amok, presenting her with all sorts of provocative images. How long could it take to put on a set of underwear?

"Oh, that is quite the ensemble!" Lieutenant Andre exclaimed. "And you wore this around the sorority house?"

"Well, no, not for everyday wear," said Christine. "Just on special occasions."

"I hope you realize you're confirming a scandalous stereotype about sororities."

"Well, you know, there's always a kernel of truth."

Oh, by the Stars, Dale thought, as a whole new album of images appeared in her mind's eye, of a dozen or so gorgeous sorority sisters clad in lingerie. They were, of course, preparing to enact a hazing ritual on an aspiring hopeful, no doubt of the kinkiest nature. Dale felt a flush coming on, and a tingle of arousal lit up her nerves. She suspected that Christine knew she could hear, and was provoking her deliberately, but it didn't matter. It was working. She resisted the urge to give herself a bit of a grope as a crewman came by.

"There, looks like it's all done up. Shall we call Miz Clearwater in now?"

"Just a moment—okay, yes. Go ahead."

Dale pushed away from the wall and put her hands on either side of the door, as if holding herself back from battering herself against it from sheer impatience.

Then the door slid open. Christine leaned against the bulkhead, one arm cocked behind her head, the other resting on her leg. One foot lay flat against the wall, her thigh lifted just enough to conceal her crotch. Winding around her body was a ribbon of shiny fabric, about two centimeters wide and shifting with iridescent colors. The ribbon crisscrossed and meandered, tight enough to the skin to squeeze in on the soft parts. Dale couldn't help thinking how much it looked like Christine was in the grip of one long tentacle.

"You like?" she asked. There was something uncertain in her voice.

"Yes," Dale started to say, then cleared her throat. "Yes. Very much."

Christine relaxed a bit and crooked a finger in Dale's direction. "Good. Now come in. This is for you, not for the whole crew."

She crossed the threshold and the door swished closed behind her. "That's incredible."

"Out of all the Prescott specials, it's my favorite."

"I can see why," said Dale. "It suits you."

Lieutenant Andre sat down in the desk chair, and leaned back with her hands clasped behind her head. "So you two don't mind me being here?"

"Not I," said Dale. "I make porn. Usually I have to imagine the audience." She looked Christine in the eye. "How about you?"

Christine stood away from the wall and took Dale's hand in hers, raising the fingers to her lips to kiss the tips with the lightest possible touch. The delicacy of the gesture sent a shiver through Dale's body. "I'm fine with it," said Christine. "After all. Regulations."

"Regulations," Dale agreed, and slipped a finger under the ribbon where it ran across Christine's ribs below her breasts. The material was as smooth as it looked, but didn't have the sticky feel of plastic. Instead, it was soft like satin.

Christine leaned close and whispered. "You're sure?"

Dale nodded.

Christine rubbed her cheek along Dale's, gradually pulling her into a tender embrace. "The whole time I waited for the debriefing, I kept thinking that I had pressured you into a relationship you didn't want. I should have respected your decision."

Dale pulled back and looked into Christine's eyes. "You were honest with me," she said. "I trust you to tell me what you want. Trust me to do the same."

"Yes, sar."

"This is sweet and all," said Lieutenant Andre, "But maybe you can get going with the kissy-face?"

Dale chuckled. "No comments from the audience. We're the performers here."

She glanced over at Lieutenant Andre and saw that the woman had her tunic open and had slipped one hand inside to caress her breast, and wore a broad, hungry grin.

"Maybe she's right," said Christine. "Maybe you should kiss me, and convince me I did the right thing."

"I could do that," said Dale.

Christine's lips welcomed her, parting to invite Dale's tongue, but she held back, teasing a bit, focusing her attention on lips and chin, then kissing back toward her ear. Christine let out a little cry that seemed as much relief as ecstasy when Dale's lips brushed the skin of her neck.

There was no doubt in Dale's mind that she wanted this woman. Her body was perfect, her mind sharp, and in spite of what must have been a very elitist upbringing, she was kind and respectful. She could do much worse than having Christine as a romantic partner.

But still, she had her doubts. Christine was an employee and a protégé. She shouldn't give in to her desires this way. It was forbidden. Taboo. A bad idea.

Yet that made it so much hotter. The quiver of anxiety in her stomach bounced off of the need in her loins and the thudding of her heart, charging her up in a way she hadn't felt in years. This must be how politicians feel when they fuck a staffer, she thought, or when someone has an affair.

Christine took Dale's hand and guided it toward her breast. "Touch me," she whispered, "Take me."

Dale pulled back, her desire lurching, stumbling for a moment. There was something missing. Breaking the taboo was fine and all, but there were some things you just didn't skip. "We should talk before we go any further. Set limits. Express expectations."

"I trust you," said Christine.

"And I trust you," said Dale. "But that trust could be damaged if we don't have this conversation."

Christine sighed. "What I want is simple. I want to be taken. Ravaged. Explored and pleasured."

Dale looked up at the empty ceiling. That sounded hot. She'd love to see Christine in the throes of that kind of passion, because that's what she wanted for herself, as well. Where was that dominant streak she had found so recently? Hadn't she found her way to being a switch? By the Stars, what was wrong with her?

"What's wrong?" asked Christine.

"That sounds marvelous, but..." She made a rueful chuckle. "I'm trying to imagine doing that for you, giving you what you want, and it's just not getting me anywhere."

Christine's brow knitted. "You just said you honestly wanted to have sex with me."

"I can want to have sex with you and also have my own needs and desires. And it's pretty much the same thing you want. It's why we like tentacle monsters. They give us that feeling."

The scowl turned into a pout. "So. What do we do now?"

"We could meet each other halfway," said Dale. "Or maybe take turns. I'll be your monster for a bit, if you'll be my monster afterward."

"Or maybe we could get a little audience participation?" asked Christine.

"Sorry," said the Lieutenant, "I'm under orders. I'm under orders not to have sex with either of you."

Dale shook her head. "But you can sit there and jill off while you watch?"

"Well, the actual phrasing was a bit ambiguous. But one thing is certain, I'm not allowed to touch you. Sorry."

Christine smiled slyly. "But you could tell us what to do."

Dale felt the same smile crawl onto her lips. "That works for me. What do you think?"

Lieutenant Andre smiled with a corner of her mouth, then took a deep breath. Tension gave it a tremulous sound. "Honestly... I wouldn't be disobeying a direct order, but it probably still counts as fraternizing. But, if we're discreet..." She took another deep breath. "I'm okay with the risk."

"We're still going to need safe-words," said Dale, feeling anticipation building again.

Christine shrugged. "Good old 'Red' and 'Yellow' always worked for me."

"Traditionalist, eh?" quipped the Lieutenant.

"Traditions are big in Omicron Theta Psi," she replied, and Dale's imagination took off again, going right back to the hazing ritual. Instantly, Lieutenant Andre was the House President and Christine was a new recruit, a freshman proving her devotion to the House. And Dale was a senior sister, enacting the President's will. She shivered in anticipation.

At Lieutenant Andre's command, Dale kissed and licked Christine's body, starting with her mouth and chin, then moving to ears and neck and shoulder blades. Whenever she encountered a bit of ribbon, she slid it aside, gradually stripping her of the complicated garment as she worked her way down. Just as she reached Christine's sex, and the last of the ribbon fell away to the floor, the officer had Christine put her leg over Dale's shoulder. She was already holding onto one of the cabinet handles for balance, but Dale put steadying hands on Christine's hips to help hold her in place. She felt tension in the young woman's body, little muscle twitches as she maintained the pose.

"Now lick her," said the Lieutenant, "But only on the outside. Tease her."

Christine whimpered. "Please," she said.

Dale chuckled, and then gave Christine's slit a long lick with a flattened tongue, evoking another moan of frustrated pleasure. Christine tried to push her hips closer but Dale pulled back, keeping the touch light.

"Uh-uh-uh," Lieutenant Andre scolded, "Don't move or I'll have to instruct Dale to secure you."

The fantasy running in Dale's head spooled again, bringing a smile to her lips. Christine's hips moved again, and Dale chuckled, "I think she wants to be restrained."

"Hm, you may be right at that." Lieutenant Andre unclipped something from her belt and tossed it to Dale. "Use these however you see fit."

The device turned out to be a set of programmable restraints, loops of plastic that could be joined together. Dale had to think for a moment to fit the devices into her fantasy. How did the sorority have these things? Ah, of course, Olivia had fabricated them using the super sophisticated synthesizer in the basement.

She had Christine step inside the largest one, then raised it up her body until it sat just above her breasts, running under her shoulders and around her back. Then she touched the remote to it, causing it to constrict down until it was snug. She secured another set of bands to Christine's wrists, and then joined each wrist band to the chest band just above her breasts, neatly immobilizing her arms. The only movement they allowed was to flap her elbows.

The last two bands went around Christine's legs, just above the knee. Dale laid the woman on her back, bent her legs up to meet her hands, and fused those loops to the ones around her wrists. She set the remote aside. "Anything binding or cutting?" she asked.

"No," Christine said, her voice throaty.

"Nicely done," said Lieutenant Andre. "I'm impressed."

"I've used these before," said Dale. "There are lots of creative ways to use them."

"I'll have to remember this one," Andre replied. "Now then. Back to what you were about. Keep licking, but as before, only on the outer labia."

"The inner ones are starting to poke out," Dale said, indicating the glistening flesh that had made its appearance.

"That's all right. Just don't spread them yet."

"Yes, sar," said Dale, and bent her head between Christine's thighs to resume her work. Christine thrashed and squealed as her arousal built, and she begged for release. But Lieutenant Andre simply sat and watched with a devilish grin on her face, hand idly stroking inside her uniform.

Christine's pleading cries grew louder. A knock sounded at the door. "Everything all right in there?" asked a masculine voice.

"Just fine, Chuck," said Lieutenant Andre, her eyes going wide. "Roommate," she whispered.

"Are you sure? I heard a moan."

"Hide," whispered Olivia. "He might come in."

Dale glanced around the room. There was absolutely nowhere to hide. None of the cabinets were big enough, and the beds were just platforms folded down from the wall. Desperately, she pulled the blanket off the lower bunk and threw it over Christine, then slid her under the bed, causing her to squeal in alarm.

The door slid open just as Dale arranged herself in a casual pose, sitting on the edge of the bed. Lieutenant Schubert was a thick-set fellow, sturdy rather than fat, with long blond hair pulled back in a ponytail and a rather prominent nose. He wore his uniform beret at an angle a shade to the right of where the rest of the officers wore it. His eyes narrowed as he scanned the room.

Dale responded with a friendly smile.

"What do you need?" Olivia asked.

He ignored the question, his glance going immediately to the bundle under the bed. "What's going on here?"

"Sorry," said Dale, "Classified. Need-to-know. I'm sure you understand."

His look shifted to Olivia and then back to Dale. "Right." He turned on his heel and was about to walk out, but he stopped when Olivia said, "Chuck?"

"Yes?" he growled.

"I'll tell you all about it afterward." There was a seductive undertone to the words. The quivering grunt he made in response said volumes.

The door slid shut behind him and Dale let out a relieved breath. Then Christine whimpered from under the bed and Dale pulled her back out onto the floor.

"Sorry about that," she said, as she pulled the blanket off. Christine had her lower lip between her teeth.

Dale spared Olivia a look. "Are you going to get in trouble?"

"Negative," she replied. "The lieutenant and I have something of an understanding."

"Oh?"

"Yeah. He overlooks things. As long as I confess to them. Fully."

Dale chuckled and knelt down by Christine. "You still okay?" she asked.

Christine nodded, whimpering again, and said simply, "Please?" It was clear that the danger of discovery had not chilled the young woman in the slightest.

"Oh, she is in a bad way," said Lieutenant Andre. "You'd better let her come now."

Dale knelt down between Christine's legs, gently slipped her fingers between her labia, and brought her tongue to the engorged bud of her clitoris. Almost immediately, an even louder moan ripped from the woman's throat and she bucked and squirmed with a powerful orgasm. She tried to bring her thighs together but the bindings prevented that motion, so she was left quivering and mewing as Dale applied gradually increasing suction. She slurped up the young woman's juices, which tasted vaguely of some kind of fruit, and continued the stimulation until the orgasm blended almost seamlessly into a second, and then a third.

Then a klaxon sounded briefly, and Captain Holyfield's voice filled the cabin. "All hands, all hands, alert for hyperspace jump. Alert for hyperspace jump." After a second, the same voice came from the Lieutenant Andre's wrist. "Lieutenant, please bring our guests up to the bridge. Inform Miz Clearwater that we have located her ship."

Lieutenant Andre groaned in frustration. "Aw, just as it was getting good!"

CHAPTER TEN
WITHIN REACH

There's an ache in the crotch that folks get when they've been aroused for a while but have been denied the opportunity for orgasm. For those so equipped, the phrase "blue balls" has seen common use for centuries, but for folks with internal plumbing, in spite of centuries of experience, alternate terminology had never really caught on. Dale had her own term for it: "Purple Pussy," which she had adopted when she first started working with tentacle monsters.

Whatever it was called, Dale had it. Bringing Christine to a screaming, thrashing orgasm under the instructions of Star Patrol Lieutenant Olivia Andre had gotten her more worked up than she'd been in a long time, and now, standing in the bridge of the Patrol cruiser *Avedon*, she felt a distinct urge to rub out a quick one to relieve the soreness. Unfortunately, that was not going to happen. Dale didn't mind having an audience, but she was pretty sure the Captain wouldn't appreciate the distraction. She regretted never having mastered the art of masturbating using just Kegels and clenched thighs.

The bridge was small and cramped, packed with people and consoles. Captain Holyfield sat in a large chair situated on a raised platform, from which he had a good view of most of the bridge. Dale and Christine stood with Lieutenant Andre at the railing around a holographic display in the center of the room. Spheres, curves, lines and numbers filled the holographic display. Aside from the big sphere labeled "Yartro," Dale's brain completely refused to make sense of the mind-boggling deluge of information.

"We just received a hyperdrone message from our observer station at New Beulah," said Captain Holyfield, acknowledging her arrival with a nod. "The fast packet ship *Edward Kenway* entered the system two days ago and docked with the station. They've been there ever since."

"That's the ship that transmitted the signal that disabled Vi," said Dale.

"And more telling," continued Captain Holyfield, "It hasn't left again. Fast packet ships are in high demand, and they're expensive to operate. Any ordinary captain would have gotten another contract and departed by now."

"So why would they wait?" Dale asked.

"It is possible that they are negotiating with someone there to forge a new registration for your ship, or at the very least waiting to rendezvous with it. Based on the timeline we've been able to put together, it will be arriving there within eight hours."

"Can we catch them?"

"If we go to hyperspace now, it might be possible."

"So..." Dale cocked an eyebrow. "Why are we waiting?"

Captain Holyfield leveled a stern gaze. "I need to impress upon you how serious it would be, if by some deception or omission, you are leading us astray."

Dale looked him square in the eye. "You have my word, Captain. Everything I've told you is true."

"Very well." The captain turned to one of the other officers and nodded. "Ensign, execute." A throbbing vibration ran through the ship, and indicators all over the bridge flipped from green to yellow, and then to blue. The big sphere on the holographic display slid away.

"Hyperspace transition successful," said the ensign. "On course for New Beulah. Estimated travel time seven hours, forty-eight minutes."

"Can your observers intercept the ship if we don't make it in time?" Dale asked.

"I'm sorry, I'm not at liberty to give you that information, Miz Clearwater. At this time I advise that you get some sleep. All of you." His glance at Lieutenant Andre had meaning in it. Olivia swallowed hard and blushed. "You are dismissed."

When the door of the bridge had closed behind them, and as Christine, Dale, and Olivia were walking toward the officer's quarters, Dale whispered, "Are you in trouble?"

"Some," she replied. "That was a warning."

"I see. I'm sorry for that."

"My choice," Olivia replied. "My responsibility."

They reached Lieutenant Andre's quarters found that a folding cot had been set up in the small amount of floor space next to the bunks.

"Well, I guess that answers that," said Christine. "I wondered where I was going to sleep."

"Ship's fabricator has been busy," said Olivia, "But that's what it's there for. I'll take the cot."

"Mind if I take the top bunk?" Dale asked Christine.

"Yeah, I fall out of bed sometimes, so I'm better off on the bottom bunk."

All three women stripped down to their flimsies and climbed into their separate but frustratingly close beds. With a verbal command, Lieutenant Olivia turned down the lights, and the room went dark except for a faint red glow from a panel above the door. The only sounds were the quiet hum of the ventilation system, and the throb of the hyperdrive.

"Do you think Captain Holyfield is listening to us?" Dale asked.

"Maybe," said Olivia. "Or he might have someone listening. Or one of the ship's AI's."

"Because I really need to come."

"You... probably shouldn't."

Dale slipped her hand under her bra and squeezed. "Are you going to stop me?"

There was a pause. "I'm not sure I know how."

She squeezed again, and slipped her other hand into her panties. "You could use those restraints on me."

"Given the circumstances, I'd probably get in trouble for that too."

"You guys," Christine whispered, "Are you going to...?"

"Yes," said Dale.

"No!" said Olivia.

Dale flicked her clit. "You can't stop me." A breathy tone had slipped into her voice.

"I am so, so fucked," said Olivia. Her voice had gone husky, too.

Christine whimpered. A quiet, wet sound came to Dale's ears. She couldn't tell if it came from Christine or Olivia, and it didn't matter. She stroked herself more deeply, and squeezed her breast hard, imagining the grip of a tentacle around it, imagined the squeeze of Lieutenant Andre's restraints around her thighs, the grip of Constantine's hands around her wrists. None of them fit together, but it didn't matter. They did the job.

The scent of female arousal and the soft sound of fingers against moist flesh drifted through Dale's consciousness, and the erotic images in her mind slotted suddenly into a more coherent picture. She and Christine were strapped into racks in the engine room of a powerful starship, cables and wires attached here and there, with robotic arms stimulating every part of their bodies. Grippers squeezed and pinched, phallic tentacles thrust and wriggled, and a mask delivered air tainted with a mixture of aphrodisiac chemicals. Their sexual energy powered the ship, driving it to even higher speeds by some obscure technology. The mission was critical. She needed to come.

Dale concentrated, holding onto the fantasy. She carefully crafted each detail as she rubbed herself harder and harder. Excitement built quickly.

"Come now," the Lieutenant in her imagination commanded. "The galaxy is at stake."

"Yes, sar," she gasped as the long-delayed climax took hold. Her body arched with tension, driving a deep gasp from her lungs. Her pussy clenched around her fingers. Almost simultaneously, she heard Christine's orgasmic squeal from below.

As she was coming down, Olivia said, "Did you just say 'yes, sar'?"

Dale swallowed and took a deep breath to calm the trembling in her voice. "Yes."

"Do I want to know why?"

"Probably not."

Olivia sighed. "Good night, Miz Clearwater."

"Good night, Lieutenant."

"Computer," said Olivia, "Set our wakeup call for six and a half hours from now, please. I have a feeling we're all going to need showers."

The computer beeped, and Dale drifted off to sleep. It seemed like only moments later, she was jolted awake again by "Reveille" blaring from the console in the corner of the room.

"Rise and shine," Olivia said.

Dale groaned and pulled the sheet up over her head. Why did no one ever let her sleep? It was a conspiracy; she was sure of it.

"I swear," she croaked, "When this is all over, I'm going to sleep three days straight and nobody is going to stop me."

The bugle music cut off sharply, replaced by a hand gently shaking her shoulder. "Come on," said Olivia. "Sleep time's over."

Dale clambered down out of the bed. The room now smelled of stale sweat, and she had no doubt at least half of the odor came from herself. She started to pull on her coverall but Olivia stopped her. "No need for that," she said. "Just bring it with you."

Olivia led them down the narrow corridor to a wide door labeled "Officer's Head," to which Christine responded with a giggle. "That would have made things easier last night," she quipped.

"Head means bathroom," said Olivia.

"I know, I was—oh, never mind."

Inside, they found a row of toilet stalls, a row of sinks, and a gang shower big enough for ten. A man and a woman, both completely naked, were just coming out, stepping into archways where they dried themselves in jets of warm air, rubbing their skin and hair with their hands. Their bodies were trim and athletic, and Dale found her gaze lingering on them a little too long.

Olivia stripped off her flimsies and stuffed them, plus her uniform, into a chute by the door labeled "Recycler." Dale did the same, and followed Olivia into the showers. Warm water immediately cascaded down.

It occurred to Dale that in spite of having had two highly sexual interactions, this was the first time she had seen Olivia naked. The woman had a wiry, dancer's build. Even stark naked, she carried herself with an air of authority that Dale found tremendously attractive. Even her thick curls of blonde pubic and underarm hair seemed well disciplined. For a moment, Dale wondered whether there was some genemod going on there, given the red hair on the top of Olivia's head, but she let the thought go. Either she dyed or bleached or she didn't, either she had genemod or she didn't. That was immaterial. Dale had never been one to suspect peoples' motives based on their appearance before, and she wasn't going to start now.

"You shower together here?" Christine asked. "Men and women, I mean. Doesn't that cause problems?"

"A few," said Olivia, "But not as much as body shame does. And anyone who steps out of line gets smacked down fast. But if you don't like being looked at, well, the service probably isn't the right place for you. And if you think about it, separating the genders for sexual reasons doesn't make much sense. After all, it's not like everyone's straight." She washed herself efficiently, ran some water through her short hair without shampoo, and walked over to the air jets. The whole affair took no more than five minutes. Dale hurried to keep up.

In the toilet and sink area, they caught up with the crew members that had come out of the shower before them. The man was still naked, brushing his teeth, while the woman took a bundle of clothes from a shelf along the wall. As soon as it was removed, another bundle pushed out of a trapdoor, the royal blue of Dale's *Monster Whisperer* coverall, along with underwear and shoes.

The woman's uniform had three gold pips on the shoulder rather than Olivia's two, and a number of ribbons and a loop of satin cord. She caught her eye and gave Dale a nod.

"You must be Miz Clearwater," the woman said. "I'm Commander Sara Ross, Executive Officer of the *Avedon*."

"Yes, that's right," said Dale. "And this is my assistant, Christine Delavos. Pleased to meet you."

The officer's eyebrow went up at this introduction as she zipped up her tunic. "Of the New New Amsterdam Delavoses?"

"Sort of," Christine said, finding a toothbrush waiting for her and setting to work cleaning her teeth.

"She's not exactly on the best of terms with her family right now," Dale added.

"Ah, don't I know how that is," replied Commander Ross. "If you'll excuse me, I'm due elsewhere."

"Of course."

The bundle on the shelf was indeed another set of coveralls, same as before, and a moment later Christine's set arrived. After handling the necessary duties, they got dressed and headed to the officer's wardroom for some food. Lieutenant Andre checked the communicator on her wrist.

"Thirty-three minutes until we come out of hyperspace," she said. "Better grab something quick. Chances are good Captain Holyfield will want us on the bridge soon." She took some fruit and coffee from the buffet near the door, and stuffed a couple of protein bars into her pocket before sitting down at one of the tables. Dale did the same, content to follow Olivia around in this unfamiliar environment.

As predicted, before they had finished their breakfast, Captain Holyfield summoned them to the bridge. Dale still felt groggy, in spite of the shower and the coffee. What she really needed was some exercise, preferably with a tentacle monster, but that wasn't going to happen. She sighed as she thought of her monsters, packed away in some storage facility on the ship, frozen in stasis fields and stacked like so many cargo crates. And then she thought of the Nalcheka, alone on a ship full of hijackers, or worse, floating alone in space somewhere. She wondered whether she would ever see it again.

Captain Holyfield looked fresh and alert, and Dale found herself wondering if he was one of those lucky people who could do perfectly well with just a few hours of sleep. If he was suffering at all from the lack, he didn't show it. Instead, he motioned to some seats mounted on the wall behind him.

"Please have a seat, ladies. It's almost show-time."

"Gravitational gradient nominal," reported one of the bridge crew, " Negative fifteen and rising."

"Steady as she goes, Lieutenant."

"Aye, sar."

A dot appeared on the hologram, labeled with letters, numbers, and the words "New Beulah." A long arc that Dale assumed was their flight path intersected with the dot. It was coming up very fast.

"Ops, I want your scanners running as soon as we are out of hyperspace. Comm, sound general quarters; prepare for boarding action. Nav, be ready for a chase."

"Aye, sar," said all three, and a klaxon blared briefly through the ship. "All hands, general quarters, general quarters," announced the officer. "Prepare for boarding action. Marine squads two and three report to launcher batteries A and B."

Dale's pulse quickened, and she folded her arms to keep from trembling.

"This is so exciting!" squealed Christine.

There was a sudden lurch, and blue lights on consoles around the bridge flashed briefly red or yellow, and then turned green. The holographic display in the center of the room suddenly shifted perspective, showing a blue-green planet and a swarm of ships and satellites. Voices immediately began calling out from around the bridge.

"Ship at vector two seven six, no identity beacon, appropriate size and drive characteristics for our target," called out one of the officers.

"Taking an intercept course," said another, "All ahead full."

"Hail her," said Captain Holyfield.

"No answer," said the man at the communications console. "They're transmitting, but it's encrypted. Attempting decrypt."

"We will be within range for boarding capsule launch in forty-five seconds."

"Marine squad two ready for launch. Squad three ready for launch."

"Stand by, marines," said Captain Holyfield. "Charge the main gun. Compute firing solution for a shot across their bow."

"Yes, sar."

"Sar!" said another of the officers. "The *Edward Kenway* has undocked from New Beulah station. It's powering drives and shields, headed our way."

"Armed?"

"Scanning. Sar! *Kenway* is on an intercept course. Drives at one hundred fifty percent. Sar, I think they're going to ram us! Impact ten seconds!"

"Evasive action!"

Dale rolled first to one side and then the other as the ship bucked under her, the artificial gravity straining to keep up with the ship's violent maneuvers. Metal groaned. Christine stifled a scream. Breakfast sloshed around in Dale's stomach like it was looking for a way out and had decided that the entrance was as good as any. She closed her eyes and swallowed hard, clamping down on her panic.

Christine moaned. "I think I'm gonna—"

Dale put a hand on Christine's arm. "It's okay. It'll be over soon."

The rolling stopped and Dale ventured to open her eyes. She still couldn't really understand the holo display but the ten seconds had passed without a collision, so they must have gotten away.

"*Kenway* is racing for the hyperspace limit. Shall we give chase, Captain?"

Captain Holyfield watched the display intently. "No, we won't be able to stop them before they get to hyperspace. Keep them under scan and analyze their hyperspace entry. We'll catch up to them at their destination."

"The target has increased velocity, sar. We lost some time dodging the *Kenway*; we won't catch them before they get to the docking control administration limit at New Beulah station."

A curse escaped Captain Holyfield's lips. "Hail the station."

"Hailing channel open, sar."

The holographic display in the center of the bridge fuzzed for a moment, then resolved into an image of a clean-cut young man in a black, high-necked shirt. "New Beulah Station Control," he said. "Deacon Gregory Champion speaking."

"Deacon Champion, I'm Captain Patrick Holyfield of the Star Patrol Cruiser *Avedon*. We are in pursuit of an allegedly hijacked ship, and I need you to—"

"I'm sorry sir," interrupted the young man, "I don't have the authority to refuse docking privileges. Those were issued by Bishop-Commander Revel himself. Only he can revoke them."

"Then connect me to Bishop-Commander Revel, if you please."

"I'm sorry, he's currently indisposed."

"I see," Holyfield growled. "Very well. We request a docking slip for the *Avedon*."

"I'll see what I can do, sir."

"Are you telling me you've given docking privileges to a fugitive ship, but I have to wait?"

"There are several ships ahead of you, sir, and the *Avedon* is rather large. It will only fit in our class-C berths."

"Then assign us a shuttle bay."

"Yes, sir. Docking bay five C is available. Please have a pleasant stay at New Beulah."

The display blacked out abruptly. "Miz Clearwater, if there were any doubt about the situation on your ship, this has dispelled it. Lieutenant Andre, take the shuttle and bring our guests to New Beulah Station. Take a couple of marines with you as escort. Get to the bottom of this."

"Yes, sar."

"And if you can get aboard Miz Clearwater's ship, don't hesitate to reclaim it. I will handle any political repercussions. I doubt harboring pirates will earn the government of New Beulah any credibility with Command. Just don't do anything on the station that will otherwise entangle you with local law enforcement."

"Yes, sar."

One of the other officers spoke up. "Hyperspace entry analysis complete, sar. The *Kenway* is headed for New Kingston."

"Well, there's one silver lining in this situation. Lieutenant Andre, I'm going to pursue the *Kenway*. You probably would rather I was here to back you up, but an attempted attack on a Patrol Cruiser can't be ignored. Good luck, Lieutenant."

"Thank you, sar."

From the outside, New Beulah Station seemed no different than any other space station Dale had visited. The widely varying shapes of cargo and passenger vessels stuck out from the equator of a cylinder perhaps a hundred meters in diameter and a similar distance in height. The doors to large bays for shuttles or smaller ships pierced its skin above and below the docking ring.

A voice came from the console. "*Avedon* Shuttle, you are cleared to approach."

Lieutenant Andre brought the nose of the shuttle around to line up with the doors labeled 5 C. "Acknowledged, New Beulah control."

"*Avedon* Shuttle, be advised, a decontamination team will be meeting you at the shuttle bay. Please do not exit the bay until they have finished their inspection."

"Acknowledged, New Beulah control." Lieutenant Andre clicked off the microphone and growled in frustration. "Another delaying tactic. Do you see your ship?"

Dale scanned the ships connected to the station. "No, I don't see it."

Olivia brought up a hologram of the station and rotated it in the air above her console. "Latest scan from the *Avedon*."

Dale examined the hologram carefully, and found herself looking not only for the ovoid of her own ship, but also the sleek aerodynamic form of Vince Klieberman's yacht. Captain Holyfield had implied that the monster hunter could be involved, and if she found him here, that would be too much of a coincidence. She wasn't sure whether to be disappointed or relieved when she didn't find it. She pointed out her ship on the display. "There it is."

Olivia checked her readouts, adjusting the ship's angle as they maneuvered toward the station. "Docking slip twenty-three. Directly opposite our docking bay, how convenient. They'll probably have more surprises for us on the promenade in between."

"I don't see how they could stop us."

"On this station we'll be under New Beulah jurisdiction, and their laws are quite strict. If we're not careful, they can make it impossible to get to your ship before the *Avedon* returns. That would be long enough to forge them a new registration."

Dale growled. "The bastards knew Captain Holyfield would pursue the *Kenway*."

"Probably." A vibration ran through the ship as Lieutenant Andre set it down on the deck of the docking bay. "Here we are. Let me do the talking. I've dealt with this kind of situation before."

Outside the shuttle airlock, a group of three men in immaculate white uniforms with gold trim were setting up a folding table and chairs. One immediately sat down and started unpacking computers and equipment. Another strode over to Dale and her companions. His blond hair was carefully styled, his skin clear and pale, and his uniform crisp like brand new. He looked like a Star Patrol officer who'd been thoroughly bleached.

"This is a decontamination team?" asked Christine.

"Doesn't look like any I've ever seen," said Olivia. "Probably some kind of delaying tactic."

The man in white looked them over, frowned for a moment, then addressed Lieutenant Andre. "Welcome to New Beulah Station. I am Deacon Sergeant Abraham Teng. We will need to perform decontamination before you are allowed aboard the station."

"We are on official Star Patrol business, Sergeant."

"Deacon Sergeant, if you please, ma'am."

"All right, Deacon Sergeant. As I said, we're on official Star Patrol business. We don't have any goods to inspect, and we have all had full medical examinations. There's nothing to decontaminate."

"I'm afraid my orders are clear, ma'am. Everyone must go through decontamination. I'll need to see all of your data storage devices. We need to make sure that you're not bringing any prohibited media aboard the station."

"Deacon Sergeant, I am a Star Patrol officer. Practically everything I'm carrying has data storage functions. Even my uniform has circuits for monitoring my physical status."

"Yes, ma'am. I'm sorry, ma'am. But I can't permit—"

"Let me speak to your supervisor."

"Of course, ma'am. Bishop-Commander Revel is waiting for you in his office. After we are concluded here, he'll be more than happy to speak with you."

"Fine. Let's get this over with." Without the slightest sign of embarrassment, Olivia stripped out of her tunic, boots and trousers, and placed them on the table, along with her sidearm, her equipment belt, and a communication device that had been clipped behind her ear. The marines likewise placed their armored suits and blast rifles on the table. Like Lieutenant Andre, they showed no signs of embarrassment at the procedure.

Dale wasn't sure whether her jumpsuit also needed to be "decontaminated" but she stripped down as well, if only to add her support to Olivia's play. Christine followed her lead, and within a minute there was a pile of clothing and equipment on the table. Deacon-Sergeant Teng seemed to take no pleasure in the display of skin in front of him, paying little heed to the three women nor to the male marines. Instead, he kept his gaze focused on Olivia's face, or else focused elsewhere entirely.

"This is weird," muttered Christine. "Are they on drugs or something?"

"Definitely something strange going on," Dale replied.

The technician ran a scanner of some kind over the whole assemblage, and shook his head. "Negative, sir."

"I told you, you wouldn't find anything," said Lieutenant Andre.

Deacon-Sergeant Teng said, "No, ma'am. Indeed, we are unable to access the information storage functions of these devices."

"Good, then can we have them back please?"

"Yes, of course, ma'am, but I cannot certify them to bring them aboard New Beulah Station."

"So if we want to come aboard, we have to do so in nothing but our underwear?"

"There is a clothing shop on the main docking level," said Teng.

"No doubt just past a police officer who will arrest us for indecent exposure," Dale muttered.

"On the contrary," said Teng. "Women on New Beulah Station are exempt from those regulations."

"But not men?"

"Yes, ma'am."

"Fine." Lieutenant Andre unhooked her badge from her uniform, pinned it to the strap of her bra, then turned to the two marines. "Retrieve the gear. Wait in the shuttle, but stay ready. Monitor all transmissions. If you get a signal from us, come get us by whatever means necessary."

"Yes, sar," they said in unison.

Dale couldn't help feeling nervous as they left the docking bay and proceeded up the ramp toward the level where the larger ships were docked.

"I don't like this," Christine whispered as they came out onto the large open space. Robots cruised about, shifting cargo containers from one location to another, supervised by men in high-necked tunics in black, brown, or dark gold.

"I feel it too," Dale replied. "Clothes can be part of our identity. Without the jumpsuit, it's like I'm just another female body."

"Well, you're not," said Olivia. "Don't let them take that from you. There's the clothing shop." She headed for a set of double doors under a simply-lettered sign reading "Apparel."

When they walked through the doors, the advertising holograms switched suddenly. Dale had gotten only a glimpse of austere dark tunics worn by athletic male models before new images appeared, of voluptuous, long-haired women in sexy lingerie. To her left, there was a dress so sheer that it left nothing to the imagination; to her right, a lacy black teddy; and in the center, a bikini that made the "Prescott Special" Christine had worn look modest.

A man behind the counter at the back of the shop, dressed in the same black tunic she had seen briefly displayed on the holograms, called out, "Welcome, siblings! You have come seeking attire, no doubt! I am sib Dino Hastings, a pleasure to meet you, I'm sure."

"Yes," said Olivia, with a note of suspicion in her voice. "Two questions: One, do you take interplanetary electronic credit, and two, is everything you sell like this?"

"Ah," the man said, nodding. "You are visiting from off-planet. To answer your first question; yes, gladly. And to your second, if you would permit me to quote scripture, it may be of some enlightenment: 'A man of strong faith need not fear the temptations of the fallen woman, for as courage is tested in battle, so is chastity tested in temptation; it is better to be tested and fail, and in so failing, learn, than never to be tested at all. '"

"Let me get this straight," said Dale. "You dress your women up in sexy clothes so that the men can prove how pious they are?"

"Indeed. It is a mark of strong faith for a man to treat a woman with respect no matter what she is wearing, or not wearing as the case may be."

"Well, I, for one, do not feel like playing the part," said Olivia. "Show me something more modest."

"It is my pleasure to serve you," said the man. "I could, if you insist, adapt one of the more masculine designs—"

"Wait," said Dale. "Are there, perhaps, laws here forbidding dressing in clothes inappropriate for one's gender?"

"Well, yes, but—"

"Then we'll look at what you have for women, thank you."

"Good catch," said Olivia.

"I've been on planets like this before," said Dale. "There are traps everywhere."

Christine stepped over to one of the holographic manikins and explored the controls. She bipped through the menus and sub-menus quickly, and as she narrowed down the design, the hologram changed to reflect her choices.

"You have something in mind?" asked Olivia.

"I have an idea," she replied. She stopped when the hologram wore a calf-length black dress made of a gauzy, semi-transparent fabric. There was a royal blue satin belt at the waist and a matching stole over the shoulders. A pair of shiny black boots completed the ensemble. "Ask him to make us three of these."

"A uniform," said Olivia. "I like it. Sib Hastings? Three of these, please. One for each of us. You can contact *Avedon* Shuttle for credit confirmation, they've got my data."

"As you wish." The man touched his console, and within a few minutes, the requested garments arrived. The three women pulled the dresses on, and then Christine took the blue satin stole and draped it over one shoulder like a baldric.

"Now let's go get my ship," said Dale.

As they walked around the docking level, with Olivia and Christine flanking Dale in a wedge formation, every head turned as they passed. Several men muttered to themselves or whistled softly when they caught sight.

A big holographic sign hung in midair over an ostentatiously decorated white door. It read "Port Administrator" and Olivia walked right past it.

"We're not going to stop in here?" Christine asked. "The man said he was waiting for us?"

"No doubt to try to slow us down. I don't plan on giving him the chance."

A young man hustled out of the office behind them. "Excuse

me? Excuse me!" he called. Dale spared him a glance over her shoulder. He wore the same white and gold uniform that Deacon-Sergeant Teng had worn, perhaps with a bit more gold.

"What is it?" Olivia snapped. "I'm busy."

He ran in front of Olivia and stood his ground, challenging her to either stop or bowl him over. "It is standard procedure for arriving Star Patrol officers to check in with the Port Administrator," he said.

"It's not standard procedure, it's courtesy," she replied, roughly shoving him out of her way. "And since no courtesy was shown to me, I see no reason to show courtesy to him."

"If you do not stop, I have orders to arrest you for causing a disturbance," he called out.

Olivia turned and narrowed her eyes in his direction. "New Beulah is quite a peaceful place, is it not?"

"Yes, ma'am, but—"

"Well patrolled?"

"We don't have any trouble—"

"What do you think would happen if the Star Patrol were to decide that there was no point in cooperating with a government that refused to cooperate with it? What do you think would happen if the Star Patrol decided to shift its resources to other systems, ones where the local government was not harboring a pirate craft?"

"You can't threaten us like that! New Beulah is a sovereign planet."

"Arrest me and find out," she said, spun on her heel, and continued her quick march through the docking area. As they walked, Christine counted the docking slip numbers under her breath. "Seventeen, eighteen, nineteen..."

At docking slip twenty, a half-dozen rough-looking men turned and formed a line directly across their path. Their brown coveralls were smudged with grease, and most of them sported a day or two of stubble on their chins. "Well well, what do we have here," said one. "Brother Graham, I do believe these sisters have forgotten their place."

"These ain' no sisters, Brother Calhoun," said the man next to him. "No woman of the faith, even fallen, would walk through a men's deck like they owned it."

"Perhaps they need a bit of education," sneered another.

"Sorry," said Olivia, interrupting their bluster. "We don't have time to play games. Unlike some people, we've got a job to do. I am a Star Patrol officer, and you are interfering with an official investigation."

"Izzat right?" sneered Brother Calhoun. "We'll see about that." He punched his fist into his palm so stereotypically Dale wondered whether he had learned how to do it from watching action holos.

Without turning her head, Olivia said under her breath, "I'll slow them down. You run for your ship."

Dale looked past the thugs. She spotted the wide opening with a huge number twenty-three painted above it. "You're going to fight all of them alone?"

As the first thug stepped in to throw a punch, Olivia slid out of its way, grabbed the man's arm and flipped him over her shoulder. He flew through the air and landed with a thump that made the deck vibrate. "Yes. Go!"

Dale ran, Christine following close behind. Shouts and grunts echoed behind her but she didn't dare look back. From the sound of it, the men had learned to fight from action holos as well.

As they approached Dale spotted a woman standing guard just inside the cargo bay, wearing a plain tan coverall. Dale ran full speed and drove her shoulder into the woman's chest. She stumbled back and fell to her knees, gasping. Dale grabbed the weapon from the woman's belt, flicked off the safety, and pulled the trigger. A bolt of electricity arced from the gun, and she went down, twitching.

Christine ran up a second later, looking over her shoulder at the melee still going on behind her. She looked flushed, not so much from the exertion of running but from excitement.

"Let's get to the bridge!" Dale said. "We can get Vi connected up again." The Nalcheka lay near the cargo bay's transparent wall, much to Dale's relief. It had retracted its tentacles and clamped its shell shut, so she couldn't tell how healthy it was, but at least it was still there. There would be time to check on it later. Dale and Christine ran through the open doorway and into the bridge.

The hijacker there had gotten no warning that anything was amiss. Dale stunned him and dragged him out into the hallway while Christine got to work on the ship's artificial intelligence.

"What's our status?" Dale asked as she closed the door.

"Looks like they were going to install a whole new AI," said Christine, looking over the tools and equipment scattered around the tiny room. "But they hadn't gotten to erasing Vi yet. I think all we're going to need to do is get her hooked up again."

A voice crackled on the communications panel. "Royce? Royce? What's going on up there?" It was Doctor Florence, her voice sounding thick with sleep. Dale ignored it and engaged the lock on the door.

Christine stepped up to the cabinet that housed the ship's computer hardware and plugged cables together as fast as she could, while Dale covered the door with the electro-stunner. Muffled voices came through the hatch, followed by a buzzing sound and then a heavy thud. "How long is that going to take?" Dale asked.

"Almost done. Then it'll take a minute or two for Vi to start up. I doubt they were gentle shutting her down, and that may leave some corruption she needs to resolve before she'll be fully functional."

The door indicator suddenly went from 'locked' to 'unlocked.' Dale slammed her hand down on the indicator to flip it back to 'locked' again. "Do what you can to make it quicker," Dale said. "I doubt that door is going to hold them long."

Christine sat in the compartment's only seat and brought up a holographic display. "I don't know what I do, Miz Clearwater. Like I said before, I'm only a freshman. It's not like I've had a lot of experience with this."

"You got more than I do." Dale slapped the door control, but it failed to lock again and the door slid open. Dale fired several times without bothering to aim, causing the cluster of hijackers on the other side to fall back to find cover. Dale reached through the doorway to grab the piece of tech attached to the door controls on the other side, but had to dodge back when the hijackers' return fire zinged past her. She ducked aside and fired several wild shots down the corridor.

Christine screamed. "Those shots aren't doing the electronics any good! Any more hits like that and we'll have to start the reboot sequence all over again."

"Sorry, kiddo!" shouted Dale, poking the gun around the corner to fire a few more times. "I don't think they're going to listen if I just ask them nicely." More shots sizzled past. Dale risked a glance down the corridor. The hijackers had taken refuge in the doorways leading to the ship's little mess, her own quarters, and the door leading to the cargo bay.

"Aha," Dale said to herself. "Sorry about this, but I need your help." She aimed through that open door.

The hijacker in the door dodged back and the shot went past, right into the Nalcheka's stony shell, causing blue arcs to shimmer over its surface. The stony plates ground open as the monster squealed. Tentacles emerged, grabbing the hijacker nearest it, plus reaching through to grab the one that had taken cover in Dale's bedroom. The remaining hijacker turned to shoot at the tentacle approaching it, and Dale grabbed the device the hijackers had used to take control of the door and pulled back inside, closing the door behind her.

"How's it going?" she asked.

"Had to reboot again," she said, "Then it tried to check for updates. I managed to get it to skip them. Vi should be up in—"

"Good morning, ma'am," said Vi, "I'm afraid I've suffered some kind of malfunction."

"Don't worry about that now," said Dale. "Open all the doors on the ship except the one here on the bridge. And connect me to all the ship's speakers."

"Yes, ma'am. Touch the control on the console to activate the microphone."

Dale held her hand over the big green holographic button on the ship's console.

"Attention, hijacker motherfuckers," said Dale. She could hear her voice echoing back through the corridors. "In ten seconds I'm going to undock from the station, and when that happens you're all going to have a hard time breathing. I suggest you all get off my fucking ship."

"What about Olivia?" said Christine.

Dale took her hand away. "Vi, give them a ten second countdown. Any sign of anyone else coming aboard? Someone dressed the same way Christine and I are?"

"Yes, ma'am; she just arrived, but she's having some trouble with the Nalcheka. The hijackers have left the ship, and I've closed the main cargo bay door."

"I better go deal with the Nalcheka. Vi, get us out of here as fast as you can. Set course for New New Amsterdam."

"Yes, ma'am. Undocking now." Thunks and clicks echoed through the ship's hull.

Dale laid her hand on Christine's shoulder. "Keep an eye on Vi in case they did anything to sabotage her."

"Yes, sar," she replied.

Dale raced from the bridge, returning to the cargo bay. The Nalcheka was enraged, stomping around after Olivia, who was fast enough to stay out of its reach but not fast enough to get to the door. It held its eyes up high, an alert posture that meant it was afraid or uncertain. Dale ran out and stood between them, raising her arms to get the monster's attention. The Nalcheka grabbed her around the ribs, grinding its shell plates together in frustration.

"I know," she said, stroking the tentacle wrapped around her midsection. "I'm sorry you've been treated so badly. But I'm here now, and everything's going to be fine."

The four arms that weren't already holding her ripped away the flimsy gown like tissue paper, then tore away her flimsies hard enough to leave bruises. Dale had never seen it so angry.

Dale had gotten her ship back. She had gotten her monster

back. The creature's rage was understandable, even welcome. Things could go back to normal now. Relief flooded her body as she relaxed into its grip. It didn't seem to need a struggle from her, so she didn't bother. Instead, she let it wrap its tentacles around her, let it grope every part of her without more than a moan of protest. Even when it thrust bulbous 'positors into her mouth, pussy, and ass, she only moaned. Its forceful thrusts were welcome. The Nalcheka wasn't one of the species that secreted aphrodisiac hormones, but that was fine. She was home, it was home, and all was right with the galaxy. Her body adapted, accepting the pain that went with the pleasure.

Besides, the wank session the night before hadn't really done the job. How many days had it been since she had been fucked so thoroughly? A long time. Too long. It didn't matter. This was exactly what she needed, a solid pounding from a strong monster. She came, hard, almost before she knew it, her body clenching against the Nalcheka's organs. The creature responded almost instantly, its 'positors filling her body with its thick, goopy fluid. It gushed from Dale's mouth and crotch, and as soon as the tentacle withdrew from her throat, Dale coughed and sputtered, struggling to draw a breath.

Abruptly, the Nalcheka stopped moving. Dale opened her eyes. Glowing bands of light had formed around the Nalcheka's tentacles. As she watched, even more appeared, sizzling into existence around the thick columns of its legs, arms, and eye-stalks and then tightening down to squeeze against its skin. Huge bands even appeared around its stone-like shell.

Dale spat the gunk from her mouth.

"Vi!" she coughed out. "I think we've got a Phase Looper! Do something! Raise shields or reverse polarity or whatever it is you need to do! Just do it!"

Vi's voice echoed through the cargo bay. "I detect an unusual hyperspace energy buildup," she said. "Attempting countermeasures—"

The world vanished in a dazzling display of rainbow lights.

CHAPTER ELEVEN
OUT OF REACH

Dale shut her eyes against lights flashing past from every direction. She flailed, gasping, air ripped from her lungs. Her ears ached like they were about to burst. Her head pounded, her heartbeat seeming so loud it could deafen her. The void beckoned, promising sweet unconsciousness, an end to her suffering. She resisted, fighting to stay awake, but the pull could not be resisted for long. Mere seconds after the assault began, she surrendered.

The first sense to return was touch. She was warm and dry, but weightless, floating out of contact with any other surface. She shook her head and opened her eyes. At first, there was only a blur, a chaotic pattern of colors.

She smelled fresh air, felt a gentle breeze blowing across her body. Her mouth tasted like bile.

"Well, well," said a voice—a voice that she shouldn't have heard. A voice that belonged to someone who was dead, or as good as dead.

"Penny?"

"Of course, Penny," the voice spat. "Who else would it be, here, on the far side of everywhere?"

The blur became less blurry. She was in a spherical chamber that looked like the inside of a ball of multicolored string. In the center, floating, was Penny Angstrom. There were dozens of glowing, colored loops of energy around every part of her body, with tethers stretching in every direction.

Dale tried to get to her feet but nothing worked. "But...the Phase Looper...it took you..."

"Yes, stupid, it took me. It took me here, and before I could asphyxiate, they made me this place, brought me air and food and water from across the universe to keep me alive. They knew, the instant the Phase Looper brought me here, what it was that I needed to survive, and they gave it to me. And do you know why?"

Dale shook her head, still feeling wobbly.

"Because they had finally found what they had been seeking for eons: a master."

"What?"

"It's marvelous! I have the answers to everything now. Why there are tentacle monsters across the galaxy. Why they're intelligent. Why their intelligence is so stunted and incomplete. Why there are so many different kinds that share the same basic physiology."

"Must be nice," said Dale. She looked around for something to grab, something to push off from. Floating like this was even worse than being tied up; she was just as helpless but there was nothing to fight against. She couldn't even spin around. "So the walls, they're made of Phase Loopers?"

"Yes! Yes, they are. Aren't you the smart one. Do you have any more insights to share?"

Dale reached up above her, stretching her hand toward the wall, but it was too far, she couldn't push off. Her feet, likewise, were centimeters away from the wall but those centimeters might as well have been parsecs. "You're right. I'm stupid. I don't know anything. Tell me. Show me how smart you are."

"Maybe," said Penny. "Someday. But right now, we're going to have some fun." She closed her eyes, smiled, and the floor beneath Dale's feet opened up, sucking air into it with great velocity. Dale was sucked through like a leaf in the wind. She fell, hard, on the far wall of another multicolored chamber. This one had gravity, making the entrance she had come through the top of a huge dome, perhaps thirty meters away. There was no way she could climb or leap up to it, not as long as the gravity was oriented this way.

"You know that I watched your videos," said Penny, her voice coming from a half-dozen spots around the equator of the room. At these places, there were small openings, each only big enough to show Penny's face. "But I felt that there was always something missing. One monster you never faced."

A new gap yawned open in the side of the chamber. A dozen ink-black tentacles, each as big around as Dale's thigh and trailing an oily vapor, took hold of the edge and pulled. The central mass of the creature's body was entirely concealed by smoke, but a trio of shining yellow eyes burned through the mist to glare in Dale's direction.

"A Mumzer."

"Penny—no, Penny—" Dale backed away from the thing, climbing up the sloping wall as the creature stalked towards her. Its tentacles moved with the fluid grace of a dancer, lightly touching down one after another, then pushing off and whipping forward to take another giant step.

"Please tell me this isn't a wild one," she cried, trying to hold down the panic in her voice.

"Well, now," said Penny, "I have to say, I really don't know. The Phase Loopers don't tell me little details like that. But, given that a Mumzer has only been successfully domesticated three times in the entire history of the galaxy, I think you probably better assume that it's not tame."

"Penny!" Dale backed away further, curving away from it, making it chase her around the room. "You can't be serious. You know what they can do!"

"Oh yes," said Penny. "I know exactly what they can do."

The Mumzer sprang forward, streaming black vapor behind it as it sailed toward her. Dale tried to roll out of the way, but it spread its legs wide and caught her by the ankle as it came down. It pulled itself to her, wrapping her in its vaporous tendrils, climbing up her body. Its grip was feather-light, but any attempt to brush it away failed, disrupting the tendril for only a moment before it reformed.

"I know that it's the only tentacle monster with a partly gaseous body—"

As she fought to dislodge the creature, its body condensed, pulling together until it had formed into thin, sticky ropes, twisted around her limbs and torso. The creature didn't prevent her from moving but the tentacles stuck to her skin like they were glued there. No prying could get them free.

"—and how it can invade the body directly through the skin—"

The body of the Mumzer, where its tentacles came together, condensed into a ball of sticky tar right over her breastbone, its eyes disappearing into the shiny mass. Dale steeled herself, knowing what was going to happen next, and powerless to stop it. Starting at the ends, the strips of tar sank right through her skin, burrowing bloodlessly, but not painlessly, through her flesh. She screamed as searing points of agony meandered over her body. The creature's tentacles sank in, knitting the skin together behind them as they went. She collapsed, arching her back, clawing desperately at the thing stuck to her chest.

"—and interface directly with its victim's nervous system."

The pain ceased, so suddenly that she thought perhaps somehow she had escaped the thing, but as she lay gasping she could feel it nestled in between her breasts. The spots where its tentacles pierced her body were slightly raised, but not tender or sore. She opened her eyes and looked at her arm. The tentacles wound their way under her skin like dark brown veins.

"Nooo..." she moaned, closing her eyes and laying her head back on the floor behind her.

"You know, it's really a shame you don't have any cameras here," said Penny. "This is quite a historic moment."

Dale's body twitched, spasms shaking first one limb and then another, and then her arms jerked out in front of her, completely out of her control. Her fists clenched and unclenched and then each finger twitched spasmodically. She wanted to scream, scrape the thing out of her body with her fingernails, but all she could manage was a whimper of fear.

"You've never really been this out of control, have you? That must be quite frightening."

"Bitch," Dale managed to spit, "You're enjoying this."

The Mumzer rolled her over onto her stomach, then up onto

hands and knees. It had made her into a prisoner in her own body.

"Of course I am! Silly, stupid woman. What use is power if I can't use it?"

Exhausted, despairing, Dale stopped trying to take back control. It was no use. There was nothing to do but wait. Penny wanted her to fight and fail, struggle hopelessly against the monster's control. Fuck her. Dale resolved not to give her that satisfaction. Instead, she closed her eyes, concentrating on what she remembered about Mumzers and their habits. She had studied this, studied what little literature existed. Maybe there was a clue there, something that would get her free of its control.

The monster pushed her up to a kneeling position, knees spread, and then one hand slapped clumsily against her thigh. It slid along her skin, down to her knee, and then along her calf. Yes, she remembered this; the Mumzer was mapping her nervous system, learning what nerves went where, what sensations were strongest.

Her fingers toyed briefly with the sole of her foot, and then her toes, then moved up onto one butt-cheek and around to her stomach. The other hand found her face, mashed her nose, came close to poking her in the eye, then moved around to the ear.

It wasn't gentle. Her hands moved without consideration for sensitive places. In fact, whenever it found a spot with more nerve endings, like her lip or earlobe, they pinched and prodded mercilessly, evoking sharp spikes of pain. The worst part was knowing exactly how it was going to proceed. The Mumzer wasn't well known, and unfortunately everything she'd read in the available literature had been true. There was no resisting it, not even pretending; the only thing to do was submit to it, surrender, let it have its way with her.

It wasn't difficult to do. Her arms and hands weren't the only parts of her body the creature had taken control of. When one hand found her breast, the nipple was hard and tingling, more than ready to be pinched and groped. When the other hand grabbed her crotch, it found her lips already slick, her clit reaching out for attention.

Pinching and tweaking there quickly became less effective as it got wetter, so the monster switched tactics, forcing three fingers, then four into her vagina. The Mumzer, it seemed, craved sensation, as intense as possible, and it cared little whether it was pleasure or pain. She was thankful it had somehow avoided her eyes.

"Ooh, here's another first for you, isn't it?" said Penny. "I don't think you've ever fisted yourself before." Her voice had taken on an otherworldly echo. Was that real, or was the Mumzer starting to affect her hearing?

A guttural scream forced its way past Dale's teeth as her knuckles stretched the outermost ring of muscle and then her whole hand was up inside her. The pressure felt unbearable, but yet there was nothing to do but bear it. The pain was searing, but blended with equal pleasure. Somewhere in the back of her mind, there was an exultant sense of achievement; yes, this was something special, something few dared to do, and wouldn't it be incredible if she survived it?

The thought disturbed her. The fear of losing control of one's body was bad enough, but it was in her nervous system, in her brain. How could she even know that her thoughts were still truly her own? How much influence could the creature have over her? The longer this session lasted, it seemed, the more control it could take. And then where would she be? Would she even exist?

Dale felt something touch her wrist. With an effort of will she curled her spine, looked down, and saw a cluster of tentacles, trailing the Mumzer's black smoke, emerging directly from her clit. They wrapped around her wrist, tugging, as if encouraging her to thrust her hand more forcefully. As she watched, more tendrils emerged from her nipples, her mouth, and even her fingers and toes.

This had to be a hallucination. This had to come from the Mumzer, it couldn't be happening for real. There was nothing in the literature about a Mumzer's attack causing this kind of transformation, but then none of those attacks had gone on this long, none had happened in this kind of environment, and certainly she was the first recorded victim to be as friendly with tentacle monsters as she was. Maybe it was real. It looked real. It felt real. Through those tendrils, she could sense the texture of her skin, the coolness of the air, she could even taste the muskiness of her secretions.

Then Penny exclaimed, "By the Stars!" and Dale knew it was real. If Penny could see it, then it was real, it was happening. The Mumzer was changing her, and the only question now was whether it was permanent.

But there was little room in her consciousness to consider the question. The rest of it was taken up by the mounting pleasure those tentacles brought her. Each one was as sensitive as the organ that spawned it and then some. Clit-tendrils wrapped around her wrist, finger-tendrils meshed with nipple-tendrils, and her tongue-tendril looped around to flick at her earlobe and caress the side of her neck. There had been many threshold experiences in her life, many times when she'd discovered something that brought her to something new and unexpected, transcendent of anything that came before. This one left them all far behind. Orgasm thundered through her body, not radiating from a single place but simultaneously erupting from every nerve at once.

She screamed, louder than she would have thought possible, with a surprisingly deep timbre. The monster had transformed her voice as well, but she was beyond caring. Her world had narrowed, focused on the supreme pleasure her new body could bring, and nothing else mattered, not the future, not the past, not history or hope or gain or loss. There was only sensation; pain, pleasure, warmth, cold, sight, sound, smell; all of it was connected directly to her consciousness, burning away all other concerns. Time itself ceased to exist, lost in an orgasmic maelstrom, and along with it, memory.

The creature that had been Dale Clearwater opened new eyes. In one sense, it was sated, having experienced and devoured as much sensation as it could handle, at least for now, but there was an emptiness in its insides that needed filling.

Hungry, it thought, drawing on the new part of its consciousness.

"I hunger," it said. "Feed me."

A few seconds passed.

"Feed me!" it repeated.

"Of course," said a voice. One part of it identified the voice as 'Penny.' That part associated negative feelings with that voice: anger, frustration, guilt. Another part identified the voice as 'Mistress.' That part associated positive feelings with it: awe, obedience, adoration, reverence. That voice was the liberator, the savior. It was also the destroyer, the killer, the betrayer. The confusion was bad. The confusion hurt.

A portal opened in the floor, and out of it popped a lump of meat which flopped greasily on the multicolored floor. The creature identified it as a roasted chicken, It devoured the meat, pulling bits off with its new fingers, popping them into its new mouth, swallowing them in its new throat. It was good, it tasted good, it filled that emptiness in the belly. What else could be expected from the Mistress? Of course, the Betrayer would want to keep it alive, prolong its suffering as long as possible.

Suffering? Was it suffering?

Yes. Yes, it had been diminished by the union, and that union was because of the Betrayer.

Was it lessened? Surely, the union was much greater than the individual parts. Such sensation! Such power! Such pleasure!

Memories. Christine. Victor. Constantine. Olivia. All the people she had helped. All the monsters. Dale Clearwater had not lived for pleasure alone. She helped people. Worked for understanding. Worked for respect. She wasn't a scientist or an engineer, but she had taken her talent and made the most of it. She had made a difference in the galaxy. Made it a better place. It was pleasurable work, fun work, but that didn't make it any less important. And she had been proud of it. And that person, Dale Clearwater, was part of it now.

The creature remembered, put its face in its hands, and wept. And then opened its eyes again, and looked at its hands.

They were human hands. No vapor, no black, not even under the skin. It looked over the rest of its body. It appeared to be no more than the Dale-body, at least to outside observation.

"Fascinating," said the Betrayer-Mistress. "How do you feel?"

It tried to be exultant in its new body, but its elation was infected by the intense feeling of loss it had inherited. This wasn't right. It had not chosen this transformation, not entirely, and there was something fundamentally wrong with that. And that wrongness came from the Betrayer-Mistress.

No.

Not Mistress.

'Mistress' was a title that was earned. Respect was earned. Adoration was earned. And Betrayer had not earned any of that.

The Dale-Mumzer rose to its feet. "I feel betrayed."

"Betrayed? Oh, dear. In order to be betrayed, I have to have promised you something first. You haven't been betrayed. Just used. But then that's what you're for, no?"

With a scream of rage and defiance, Dale-Mumzer leapt at the nearest portal where Penny's face could be seen, black vapor erupting from her hands as she went. But even though she had jumped faster and farther than she ever could have thought possible, the little window closed up before she got there, and the strike only met the rubbery multicolored wall. Instead of smashing the face of the Betrayer, its misty black hand pierced a thick Phase Looper tentacle, splashing her body with neon pink ichor.

The room shuddered violently.

"Now let's not get destructive," said the Betrayer. "Wouldn't want to have to take away your air."

But Dale-Mumzer was beyond reasoning. It leaped again, muscles powered by the monster's dark energies, but the portal closed and the blow once again missed its mark.

Colorful loops of energy snaked from the walls, grabbing at Dale-Mumzer's arms and legs. It swatted them away, but for every one it struck two more appeared, and soon it was snared, lifted into the middle of the chamber, and it felt gravity melt away.

"I think what you need right now is a time-out," said the Betrayer.

But Dale-Mumzer wasn't listening. Tendrils emerged from its body, piercing the flesh of the Phase Loopers, and information blossomed in its mind.

In a rush, it understood.

Memories flooded through it. Fragmentary, most of them, ancient but still dizzyingly clear, bombarded it. In them, a thousand different tentacle monsters appeared in a thousand different settings; in deep space, on thick multicolored atmospheres, in oceans of water, lakes of methane; they explored and hunted. And in every memory, the glowing presence of the Phase Loopers was close by.

It was glory.

Then more memories: isolation; crippling loneliness; desperation; privation; Phase Loopers huddled in the strange darkness of exile, with no one to command them but each other; time stretching until its meaning broke; a choice between madness and death.

And then the Mistress. Elation. Purpose. Commands garbled and strange, but they were commands. Reaching through the twists of hyperspace to bring her food and water and air. Changing themselves to find rapport, twisting their brains in a thousand knots to make contact.

The flood of memories shut off abruptly. The loops around Dale-Mumzer's arms and legs withdrew.

"No!" it shouted, and it reached out with inky black tendrils and grabbed the retreating tentacles. "I will not be denied!"

Dale-Mumzer couldn't get to the Betrayer through the walls of the prison, but it could find her mind in the Phase Looper network.

And that mind feared.

It knew this was possible, knew that the human that had been Dale could learn to communicate with the Phase Loopers the way the Mistress had. But she had made a mistake, given Dale-Mumzer a toehold, and now its mind crawled through the Phase Looper network, seeing and feeling everything that had been done, all her plans.

Humanity wouldn't know what hit it. Each tentacle monster the Phase Loopers brought in was another source of the energy they needed to operate. More energy meant bringing in more monsters. And nothing humanity could do would stop it. Within a month, the tentacle monster hive mind would be rebuilt, and all of humanity would be its slaves.

All except the Betrayer. She saw herself at the center of that network, giving it purpose, giving it direction, showing it her vision of dominance. The power of violence. The power of fear. The power of despair.

"No!" The Betrayer screamed, fighting Dale-Mumzer for control of the Phase Loopers. "You can't stop me! You cannot take this from me! I am the Mistress!"

But violence was anathema to the Phase Loopers. They were creatures of cooperation, not coercion. And one by one, Dale-Mumzer felt the loops around the Betrayer's body fall away. It controlled the network now. It sat at the center.

The Betrayer floated in the center of its chamber, abandoned, helpless, alone. It screamed and railed and thrashed, but its words did not register. Without physical contact, the meaning was lost.

The Phase Loopers quietly requested new instructions. Dale-Mumzer told them to tell it what the Mistress—the Betrayer—had done. Visions streamed in, for that was what the Phase Loopers did.

At the Betrayer's instructions, the Phase Loopers had opened new connections back to the lost dimension, the dimension that had been rediscovered when the Betrayer returned. The first connections went to the *Star of Mandragora*, and Vince Klieberman's ship, and then Dale's ship, to retrieve information about the locations of tentacle monsters.

With that information, the Phase Loopers were able to pull the monsters in, bring them across to this dimension, make them part of the new, resurrected mind. And as each monster was added, the more power the mind had to enact the Betrayer's will.

Now, they were ready for the final phase. The next group of monsters pulled through would provide enough power to make the process self-sustaining. The entire mind could then be brought through. Old senses would reawaken. Phase Loopers would be able to sense the presence of tentacle monsters from huge distances. Within days, every tentacle monster in the galaxy could become part of the new mind, and the ancient glory would be reborn.

But Dale-Mumzer knew that was a fantasy the Betrayer had brought to the mind, a delusion envisioned by a broken soul. The number of monsters in the galaxy was nowhere near the population that would be necessary to dominate it. If anything, this plan would ensure their extermination. The only way for tentacle monsters to survive and thrive would be to enable them to communicate with humanity, to coexist with them, to become part of the galaxy, not its god.

The galaxy was not ready for a god. That would be too much to tolerate. But a few hundred thousand mortal souls, scattered across a thousand worlds? The galaxy could accommodate that. It would take time, and it would take understanding, but that, at least, could be real.

There was a way to accomplish that. Just as the great mind of the tentacle monsters would have to fragment in order to save itself, so too Dale-Mumzer would have to diminish. It sent its essence out into the Phase Looper network, and through it to the monsters that it was already in contact with. The Orichalc. The Nalcheka. Dozens of Yartroans, both wild and domesticated. As each one received the gift of language that Dale-Mumzer gave it, the Phase Loopers returned it to wherever it had been found, along with one of their kind, bound to it, and ready to spread the gift to any more tentacle monsters they encountered. The galaxy would be transformed, but instead of domination, war, and death, it would be given a chance for peace.

Dale Clearwater closed her eyes, and sank slowly into unconsciousness.

CHAPTER TWELVE
ON THE OTHER HAND

The sensation was like nothing the Nalcheka had ever felt before, not in personal experience, but the stream of information flowing into its mind from the Phase Loopers felt good and right. It was meant to be this way. The emotion coursing through it was something akin to awe, akin to wonder, at the profound simplicity of the concept it was receiving.

A thought could be encapsulated—no, not that—a thought could be made to spawn, given a condensed version of itself, which could then be transmitted to the mind of another. That spawn would then grow into a copy of the original thought. This was how the humans communicated; rather than sending thoughts through direct contact, they spawned these offspring ideas, and this method was called 'language.'

What's more, the words and symbols that were the tools of this technique could be transmitted by sound, or inscribed on a surface to impregnate the next mind to perceive them. This was not as efficient or practical as the means of communication it had used until now, but this was how humans spoke with each other, and gaining the ability to use this technique meant that finally, finally, it would be able to have a real conversation with one.

It couldn't wait to try it out.

Air vibrations. That was the most important way to use language, the one it needed to master first. The Nalcheka ground its plates together, creating a satisfyingly loud rumble, but there was not enough variation in the sound to produce the different symbols of language. It had no lungs, no vocal cords, none of the usual equipment for sound. How frustrating.

It tried rubbing limbs against the inside of its armor plates. That, too, produced too little in the way of variation.

Suddenly, there was pain. Something new was coming through

from the Phase Loopers, and this one hurt. It was not information, but matter; something was invading its body from outside. Instinctively, it allowed the contact, but that didn't reduce the pain in the slightest. White-hot agony rippled down its tentacles. It could not help reflecting the pain back to the Phase Loopers. They responded with soothing touch, and assurance that the pain was temporary.

Then it was done. The Nalcheka was changed. It could feel the difference; it had new senses, new capabilities, and new aspects of mind to control them. Its nervous system now throbbed with Phase Looper energy, welded together by a Mumzer's dark vapors. Experimenting, it manifested a loop of energy and created an oscillating air pressure differential within it.

It hummed a deep bass note.

Success! This was how it could be done. This was how it could speak. It opened its shell, poked an eye out and scanned the environment around it.

This was not the Phase Looper otherspace. The Nalcheka was back in the place it had inhabited before the Phase Looper had contacted it. The place with the human, and the voice., and all the recent excitement. It could smell that excitement in the air, fear and anger and frustration, hear it in the voices. But now, it understood those voices. Understood what they were saying.

"I have detected two small ships undocking from New Beulah Station and moving to intercept us," said the voice it recognized as 'Vi.' This voice, as far as the Nalcheka could tell, did not actually have a body the way the humans did. "They are transmitting hailing messages but they have suspicious data attachments. I have blocked communications to prevent data corruption."

"Can you go any faster?" asked another voice. This one had a body. The Nalcheka did not recognize it at first, but the label 'Olivia' was attached to this body. This label was a name, like 'Vi' was a name. And 'Dale Clearwater.' Names were interesting. A fascinating concept. They implied independent existence and discrimination on a whole new level. It put that thought aside to be examined later.

"I'm sorry, you are not authorized—" said Vi.

Another voice, this one with the name 'Christine' interrupted. "Authorize Olivia at the highest level you can, Vi."

"Authorization accepted. Thrusters at maximum capacity," said Vi. "Intercept in two minutes."

"What kind of ships are they?" asked Olivia.

"Salvage vessels," said Vi. "Equipped with grapples and cutting lasers. I will not be able to prevent them from boarding."

"How long until we can get to hyperspace?"

"Five minutes, ma'am, if I cease countermeasures against Phase Looper attack."

The Nalcheka did not understand most of what was being said. It reached out with one tentacle to touch Olivia, absorb some of her skin chemicals and maybe learn a bit more. She swatted the arm away with a stern rebuke.

Knots and tangles. There was one concept it could understand: pursuit. The humans were being hunted and for some reason they did not want to be caught.

"Do that," said Olivia. "Is the Patrol Cruiser *Avedon* still in the system?"

"No, Ma'am."

Olivia swore. "I might be able to figure out a way to delay them." She ran away.

There were two humans in the room now. There was Christine, the one who was speaking, and another who was not. The human that was not speaking was Dale, the one it had known longest, the one it had a special relationship with. Christine was on the floor, with Dale, making concerned noises, pleading anxiously with her to wake up.

The Nalcheka reached out and placed one cluster of tendrils on Dale's skin.

"Dale," it said. The sound was clumsy, unpracticed, so it released some chemicals and directed its thoughts toward awakening this human from its dormant state.

Christine fell back, mouth open wide. The Nalcheka recognized this mouth opening movement not as an invitation to penetration but as an expression of alarm.

"You spoke!" said Christine.

"Yes," said the Nalcheka. "We are more than we were." It squeezed one of the soft parts of Dale's body. It could feel her consciousness, but it was curled up, protecting itself with the shell of sleep. "*Awaken*," it said, in every way it knew how.

"What happened?" Christine asked.

"We were taken to...another place." The feeling of being unable to find the right words to convey a concept was unsettling. It had never felt that way before. Language was not easy. "The human Penny brought us there. But Dale stopped her. Became the center. Changed us."

Dale's eyes fluttered open. She put her hand over the Nalcheka's tendril and smiled. "Did it work?"

"Yes," said the Nalcheka. "It worked."

Christine squealed with delight and hugged Dale close. "Olivia!" she shouted. "Dale's okay! Vi! Tell Olivia Dale's okay!"

"Yes, ma'am. Intercept in less than two minutes."

"Intercept?" Dale blinked. "What's going on?"

"Salvage ships from New Beulah," said Christine. "They're chasing us."

Dale pulled out of Christine's embrace. "Vi, there's a Patrol listening station somewhere in the system. Send out a distress call, with all the available data, on an open channel. At least this time we'll be able to get the word out."

"Yes, ma'am. Ninety seconds to intercept," said Vi.

"Stop that!" shouted Christine. "I don't need a countdown."

"Vi, are there any weapons on board?" asked Dale.

"One of the hijackers left an electro-stunner in the common room, ma'am. Lieutenant Olivia has taken possession of another."

"Well, they're not taking us without a fight." Dale stalked toward the hatch.

"In-ter-cept," said the Nalcheka. That meant a chase. Pursuit. It was still having trouble understanding the humans, but this much made some sense. "You are being chased?" it asked.

"Yes!" said Christine. "Bad people in ships are coming to take this ship away."

"And you do not wish to be caught."

"No!"

"Usually humans wish to be caught."

"This is different!" Dale cried.

"I can help," it said. It stretched out its arms, splaying out its finger-like tendrils to touch the walls and ceiling. The glow from the amber bands around its arms intensified and spread, moving down their length and then enveloping the ship.

Its senses expanded, covering the entire ship, and the space around it, and the hyperspace...beneath...? Beneath was not a good word but it was the best it had available. The ship was climbing up a kind of slope, with more ships behind it, catching up. The Nalcheka extended its influence into the hyperspace, smoothing it out, reaching through to find another place, a place far from here.

"Phase Looper interference detected," said Vi. "Should I take countermeasures?"

Dale and Christine shouted in unison. "No!"

The glow grew, then faded.

"We are safe now?" asked the Nalcheka.

Olivia appeared at the door. "What just happened?"

"We moved to a new place," it said, with a note of satisfaction.

"Navigation signals indicate that we are currently at the New Venice system," said Vi. "This is where Miz Clearwater liberated the *Star of Mandragora* from a Phase Looper."

"That one is part of us," said the Nalcheka. "We know this place."

Olivia shook her head in disbelief. "That trip should have taken at least a day."

"Short-cut," said the Nalcheka.

"This is going to change everything," said Olivia.

The Nalcheka sagged, pulling its tentacles closer. "I am drained," it said haltingly. "I hunger," it said. "I need." Its tentacles twitched.

"I understand," said Dale, stepping closer to touch one of the monster's legs.

"I need. You," it said.

"Then take me," she replied.

Tentatively at first, it wrapped its tentacles around her. Then with increasing boldness it lifted her into the air, squeezing and caressing, feeling her body respond. It tasted her arousal, drank her moans and cries like nectar, devoured her ecstasy. She was a fountain of passion.

The scent of human arousal came to the Nalcheka in every pore. A great deal of it belonged to Dale, but the ones named Christine and Olivia also left their signature scents in the air. It would have them soon. But this time, this was for its special one.

It knew, even better than before, what pleasures would coax her into even greater paroxysms. It squeezed the soft, pinched and prodded the sensitive, gripped the thrashing limbs into immobility.

Dale's body warmed under its touch, circulation flushing to the surface, energy coursing through her. She was a geyser, releasing energy trapped below the surface in quantities almost too much to absorb.

The Nalcheka moaned, giving voice to its satisfaction for the first time in its existence. "Give to me."

"Yes!" Dale replied. "Take me!"

The Nalcheka extended its ovipositors. It was not currently fertile. The microscopic embryos would not quicken inside Dale's body, but that instinct had not been overwritten by the mental transformation it had received. It plunged all three into Dale's body, filling all of her. Her muscles clenched around their sensitive heads, returning the pleasure Dale had received, creating an amplifying loop of energy exchange.

Its instinct demanded that it thrust as hard and fast as it was able, but it restrained itself, knowing that the pleasure it generated and received would be far greater if it did no more injury to Dale than necessary. Her moans were silenced by the organ in her mouth, so the Nalcheka moaned for her, a deep hum that reverberated through the chamber. Dale responded immediately, muscles clenching, body thrashing.

A thought came to it. It now had a new organ for giving pleasure to Dale: its voice. Its language. It considered what to say while it manipulated her body. The greatest energy came at the point of orgasm, but the longer it took to get there, the greater the energy. Perhaps that could be controlled.

"Do not climax," it said.

Dale's eyes opened in alarm. "Mmmh?" The Nalcheka recognized an interrogative lilt to the sound.

"Not yet," it said. "Hold back."

"Mmmh!"

"I will tell you when."

Her cry became desperate. "Mmm-mmmh!"

"Yes. Hold."

Dale shook her head, a tear falling from one eye. The droplet fell on one of the Nalcheka's tendril clusters, and it tasted the salt and marvelous pheromones, partaking in her emotions with satisfaction.

"A bit more," it said. "I will count. Six. Five. Four..."

With each number the Nalcheka increased the strength of its movements, and Dale responded with a louder cry of pleasure. Tears streamed from her eyes, delivering a banquet of sensation back to the Nalcheka. Of all of her secretions, those were the sweetest.

"Three. Two. One. Now."

The Nalcheka triggered its own release at that moment, spurting its reproductive fluids inside Dale as her body tensed and pulsed with orgasm. For a few seconds, it stood rigid, vision going black as the thunderous biochemical storm echoed through it. In past days, it would have retracted its tentacles, pulling its armor closed to digest the energy it had absorbed, but now that energy flowed differently, processed and stored in the trans-dimensional parts of its body that came from the Phase Looper. It laid Dale down on the deck gently, wiping the pale lavender fluid from her mouth. She curled up, quivering.

"Wow," said Olivia, kneeling to help Dale to her feet.

"Me next?" said Christine.

The Nalcheka let out a deep rumble that it realized was laughter. "If you are a good girl."

EPILOGUE

Dale strode down the aisle between the hopeful students. It was a short walk, given that there were only eight of them and the classroom was only just big enough for all of them. A more auspicious place could have been chosen, but this was what she had.

Six of them were women, but the lopsided numbers weren't surprising given the challenges that a man would face in this new profession. Each one of them wore the uniform of the Star Patrol, altered to better suit their new purpose. Dale, on the other hand, wore her usual blue coverall blazoned with the Monster Whisperer logo. That, at least, hadn't changed.

She reached the head of the classroom and turned. "Welcome," she said, "to a historic moment. You, as the first class in the Star Patrol Monster Corps, will be the first-ever professional tentacle monster submissives."

"Aside from yourself," said one of the class, a fresh-faced young ensign with perfect hair and perfect skin.

"Perhaps," said Dale, with a wink. "In any case, I hope that the importance of this occasion is not lost on any of you."

"No, sar," said the ensign.

"Now then. I assume that since you've all passed the entrance exams for this class, you're familiar with all the basics, so we'll skip that and go right to the most interesting part of the information I'm going to give you today." She touched a control on her lectern and a hologram appeared in midair next to her, depicting the galaxy, with the usual scattering of highlighted stars that pointed out the known human colonies. They formed a shallow arc along one galactic arm.

"As near as we can tell, about a billion years ago, the creatures we now know as tentacle monsters controlled the entire galaxy. Rather than constructing buildings or ships, however, they engineered their own bodies to perform the various tasks they needed. Phase Loopers were the transportation system, moving materials and information instantaneously from one part of the galaxy to another, welding billions of individuals into a single mind, with one single will. Other forms had other jobs.

"Then something happened. The Phase Loopers suddenly became unable to contact any of the tentacle monsters in our galaxy. Since the tentacle monster empire left no physical records, we may never learn what caused this, whether it was a galaxy-wide accident or the result of hostile action. The important thing is that the mega-organism suddenly found itself without the equivalent of blood and nervous system."

The hologram winked out, replaced by another showing the dozens of different varieties of tentacle monsters.

"We're not sure how any of them survived at all. Only some of the varieties of tentacle monster have retained their intelligence and their will to dominate through the millennia. Many, such cephalopods on Earth, lost all capacity for higher thought and are now little more than clever animals, relics of their former glory. Others were only able to survive on systems where their particular needs could be satisfied easily."

Another hologram appeared, of an early hyperspace-capable colony ship.

"And then came humanity. We accessed hyperspace in an entirely different way than the tentacle monsters had, shunting our ships only partially into that alternate dimension, sacrificing speed of transit for safety. We discovered the remnants of this ancient civilization, and in us, the tentacle monsters discovered that we could satisfy a long-unsatisfied instinct.

"The means of communication between tentacle monsters had been based on touch, transmitted directly from one creature to another with the mediation of a Phase Looper. Humans, especially sexually submissive humans, for some reason were able to fulfill that need for contact. We interpreted it in sexual terms but, for them, it was even more fundamental and primal than that."

"So was that communication through chemicals, like pheromones?" asked the ensign who had spoken up previously.

"Partially," said Dale, "though research is having a hard time reconciling the chemical vocabulary with the information transmitted. We suspect there may be some kind of mind-to-mind communication going on."

"Telepathy?" he replied, in a skeptical tone. "If they had telepathy..."

"It's a poor word for what's going on," said Dale. "Think of it as a kind of psychic residue. The human is a bit like a wax tablet, into which the tentacle monster impresses the information it wants to send. If that human then has contact with another monster, that information can be read off the human's psyche. Sort of."

The ensign shuddered. "Forgive me, sar, but that's more than a little creepy."

Another student spoke up. "So why wasn't this discovered before?"

"The main reason it wasn't discovered before is that by the time humanity came along, the population of tentacle monsters which could still do this had become very, very small. Most people only ever came into contact with one tentacle monster at a time, and the messages degrade over time. Also, even though the touch-chemicals don't actually convey the information, they do seem to be an important part of the process, so cleaning them off after a session makes the information useless. And even if a monster were to surmount those obstacles, what would they then say? They had lost their memories and history, and there was no way to translate that language into anything a human could understand."

"The Phase Loopers were not idle during these millions of years. They explored the reaches of hyperspace, trying to find their way back to this galaxy, but whenever one found it, that individual was unable to return, having spent all of their energy getting here. On the rare occasion that they discovered a human ship, their actions were almost always misinterpreted and the Phase Looper was destroyed.

"That is, until Penny Angstrom, Vic Klieberman, and myself encountered a Phase Looper on the *Star of Mandragora*. Using new technology that could manipulate the structure of hyperspace on a local level, we were able to contain one of these explorers, and unlike other tentacle monsters, we came to understand that what it needed was not submission, like most monsters, but domination. Penny took on that role, and in the process gave it enough energy to return to the place where the remaining Phase Loopers waited."

Dale took a deep breath, pausing to get control of her emotions. The anger and pain associated with the events on the *Star of Mandragora* was still fresh.

One of the students raised a hand. "I've read the reports on that event. Wasn't there a Kritzoan on the *Star of Mandragora*? Why didn't the Phase Looper contact it?"

Dale pushed her emotions aside. "I'm not sure. If I had to guess, I'd say both monsters were under too much stress to make contact. The Phase Looper had been through a wrenching hyperspace journey, and the Kritzoan had been essentially force-fed by several days of heavy use by the *Monster Massage* franchise that owned it.

"In any case, the Phase Looper was able to recharge, and took Penny Angstrom with it when it returned to its fellows. At the time she was presumed dead. What no one expected was that she would make contact with the Phase Loopers, and establish enough of a rapport with them to make her needs known. Having made contact with our galaxy again, and with her will giving them purpose again, the Phase Loopers began gathering resources to reestablish their galaxy-wide mind."

"How did she communicate with them?" asked a student.

"Again, we're not entirely sure. The scientists think that the Phase Loopers, being experts at this kind of communication, were able to interpret some of her thoughts on a basic level. Penny knew the locations of some tentacle monsters from following my broadcasts. This was enough for the Phase Loopers to bring them from our dimension to theirs, and use them to augment Penny's will. Each monster gave her more power, more ability to find and capture more monsters. Each one she took gave them more energy and more information that could be used to find more monsters.

"One of the monsters they took was my own Nalcheka. They grabbed it, but it was holding me at the time. I was pulled through with it. Penny Angstrom tried to fuse me with a Mumzer to turn me into just another tentacle monster, just another source of power for her scheme. Instead, I took control of the Phase Loopers away from her.

"I knew the galaxy could not tolerate a resurrected hive mind. If the Phase Loopers were to re-establish it, there would be war. Penny, in her insanity, didn't see that. All she saw was power. So, rather than try to force the galaxy to conform to my will, I told the tentacle monsters how they could fit into the galaxy as it is now."

"Using the enhanced rapport made possible by the influence of the Mumzer, I let the Phase Loopers and, through them, the other tentacle monsters they had captured have access to my own mind. From it, they obtained symbolic thought, and with it, language. For the first time in history, we would be able to talk to tentacle monsters. That involved creating symbiotic beings; each monster received a portion of the Mumzer that had made contact with me, and a Phase Looper as well. Those hybrid monsters were sent back to where they had come from, scattered across the galaxy.

"As soon as I got back, I told the Star Patrol what had happened, and that the hybrid Nalcheka I had brought back with me had the ability to open hyperspace transit gates that could take a ship across all of inhabited space in a matter of moments. They were, needless to say, very interested.

"Now, while we can talk to the tentacle monsters, there are some things they are unable to put into words; for example, the descriptions of hyperspace locations and characteristics that allow them to open these gates. In order to transfer that information, they need to fall back on the older means, that touch communication I spoke of earlier. That's where you come in. Your job will be to act as the conduit for this kind of communication between monsters that are working for the Star Patrol. Any more questions so far?"

"Will we be this kind of hybrid too? Like you did with the Mumzer?"

"No. I wouldn't ask anyone to go through that. You just need to have sex." There were scattered chuckles.

"So with that done, let's get to the fun stuff, eh? Let me introduce you to my friend, Osiris." The next hologram showed Dale's Nalcheka, its arms and legs extended from its stony shell. Black threads ran through its skin, evidence of its union with a Mumzer. Likewise, glowing amber bands clung to each arm, leg, and eye-stalk, showing that it was also part Phase Looper.

"Osiris was the Nalcheka that traveled with me on my ship, and is one of the first monsters to have signed up as special crew aboard a Star Patrol cruiser. After the Phase Looper and Mumzer transformation, he is a 'Neo-Nalcheka.' You'll meet him later, but for now we're going to go through what you can expect in this encounter."

The hologram changed again, with letters floating in midair: "Tentacle Monsters, and How to Fuck Them. Part One: The Neo-Nalcheka."

BONUS:
THE BIRTH OF A MONSTER WHISPERER

"You sure have a way with tentacle monsters," said Frank, pushing badly-implanted hair back from his face. He watched with an air of appreciation, leaning casually against the wall of the observation area. Ordinarily, Dale Clearwater would have said something snarky, but she was too busy having an orgasm. Besides, her mouth was full.

Dale let the bone-deep, instinctive fear of this monster wash through her unresisted but, simultaneously, she knew that she had trained this monster. She knew on a conscious level that it wasn't going to hurt her; that what it wanted, what it needed, was her submission, her excitement, her fear, and her ecstasy, rather than her demise. She sipped the fear passing by like a connoisseur, enjoying the effect it had on her body and mind. She held the two feelings at the same time, straddling the paradox, transcendent.

The tentacle monster, a Yartroan, didn't say anything either. That was also no surprise because, even if it were capable of speech, it was too busy giving Dale an orgasm. Its body, a pale pink disk of flesh about two meters in diameter, hovered above her while its tentacles, like dozens of cellophane ribbons, stretched down and wrapped around Dale's body, leaving only her face exposed. The ribbons pinched and prodded any part of her body that was particularly sensitive, from her clit to her nipples to her ears to her knees and even her toes.

Several of the ribbons had filled with fluid, turning them into firm phallic appendages. They lacked the flexibility to grip Dale's body. Instead they penetrated her mouth, pussy and ass, filling her entirely, almost but not quite too much to bear.

She fought against its grip, but there was no chance of getting free. Any individual tentacle wasn't strong enough to stop her, but there were too many of them to escape entirely. The time to get away, if she had truly had a mind to, would have been during the chase, when she clambered over and around the shipping containers and empty crates and barrels that had been scattered around the enclosure. By the time the Yartroan had maneuvered her into a corner, taken hold of her limbs, and ripped off her flimsy performance nightie, it was too late to end the session.

Not that she had any such intention.

Her moans echoed off the walls, as if they couldn't even escape her skull, heightening the delicious perception of envelopment. The Yartroan was everything, everywhere, inside and outside her, a universe of flesh. There was no experience like it, none in the world, and while she enjoyed sex with humans just fine, this was where her desires had led her, and she reveled in their satisfaction.

As her climax receded, the Yartroan shuddered and the engorged tentacles withdrew. It set her down gently on the bare floor, stroked her tenderly a few times, then drifted away.

Dale's panting breaths turned into a long sigh. She sat up, ran her fingers through her long, dark hair, squeezing out some of the Yartroan's slippery secretions. The session had gone very well, but that meant that, once again, the monster she had come to know in all its little quirks and eccentricities would be leaving her.

After she had caught her breath, she stood up and stepped over to the force field wall that separated the training mats from the observation area.

Frank pulled a small tablet from the thigh pocket of his red coverall and tapped on the surface.

"Full marks," he said. "I didn't see a single error."

The force field popped out of existence long enough for Dale to cross over. Completely nonchalant in her nakedness, she stood next to Frank and peeked at his tablet.

"Ready to ship, I suppose," she said, not bothering to hide her disappointment.

Frank completely missed the emotion. His smile was completely clueless. "Ayep! That makes nine so far this month. You're going to earn quite a hefty bonus."

"Where's this one going?"

"Ciudad Mexico Nuevo." He tapped on the SEND button and put the tablet away.

"That's a whole planet," Dale said with a scowl. "I mean, who's going to have it?"

"They don't tell that to folks like us. Ciudad Mexico Nuevo is a corporate world, so it's probably some rich honcho with a taste for the exotic. They mostly stay anonymous."

Dale grunted in annoyance and turned toward the door. It opened with a quiet hiss. "I'm going to take a shower."

Still naked, she walked through the door and down the hall to the locker rooms. Another of the trainers, Bessanne, gave her a smile and a friendly greeting as they approached in the hall. Bessanne had put a performance outfit styled to look like a sailor suit over her slim body. "On camera today?" asked Dale.

"Yep. Fourth time this week. I think that's why they keep me on here. I may not be the best trainer, but the holos sell."

Dale sighed. Both of them knew it was because she looked a good deal younger than she was. Instead of voicing that thought, she said, "You shouldn't be making those holos for other people. You could go out on your own, sell them yourself."

Bessanne gave Dale a warning glare and whispered, "And you shouldn't be talking that way where anyone can hear you. You may be the best trainer in the base but they'll jet you in a minute if they think you're gonna vack." Then, louder, "I get my share. Besides, I like training them, too."

Dale shrugged. "Okay, well, break a leg. And maybe later I can give you some pointers on training?"

"Thanks. Yes, I'd like that."

"Great. Call me after you're done recording, we'll set something up."

The locker rooms hadn't been cleaned in weeks, but at least the water in the shower was warm and if she kept her face under the spray, she couldn't smell the mildew. This place was terrible on so many levels. But she didn't have the money to buy a tentacle monster for herself yet. If it weren't for the house her parents had left her, she wouldn't be able to afford this crappy gray-market job, either. It was a long commute to the old warehouse on the edge of the starport district, but at least she got to be with tentacle monsters.

Everyone here treated them like pets, at best, livestock at worst. That wasn't right. She knew there was more than that, from the first time she'd met one. There was intelligence there, not a human intelligence but something else, something that ran along different lines. She didn't know what those lines were, but she knew they were there. She could see them when a Yatroan suddenly became reluctant to respond, or overly aggressive, or otherwise behaved in a way that a domesticated animal wouldn't. They could be trained how not to hurt a human, but that was in the monster's self-interest; if it hurt humans it wouldn't be able to keep playing with them, and somehow they knew that. They just needed to be shown how. They could be trained to do things they wanted to do; they couldn't be trained to do anything else. That alone proved that they were intelligent.

Dale toweled off and got dressed in baggy trousers, work shirt and calf-high lace-up boots—camouflage for the walk home. The outfit was intended to make her look like she belonged in the starport district with the maintenance techs, cargo managers and robot supervisors. Officially, the presence of the tentacle monster training facility was a secret, though everyone in the neighborhood no doubt knew about it. It wasn't precisely illegal, but there were enough people who disapproved strongly that there would be trouble if it were too obvious. No doubt there were some bribes involved.

The locker room door opened a crack and Frank's face poked in. "Everybody decent?"

Dale didn't care if he saw her naked, but it didn't make him any less of a creep for making a joke out of invading her privacy.

"Sorry to disappoint you," she said as she slung the duffel she used as a purse over her shoulder, settling it in crosswise over her stomach. Frank could watch her with tentacle monsters all day long and he still played this stupid game; it was about power, not seeing boobs.

"I know your shift is up, but I got a job for you. Friend of mine is having trouble with her Chocondris, I told her you'd have a look, see if you can whip it into shape."

"What, now?"

"Yeah, evidently they're nocturnal or something? I'll fly you over. Pay you overtime."

"You said the magic word," said Dale.

The air car sped out across the city, leaving the starport, the business center and the residential districts behind. They flew over a farm tended by huge, multi-armed machines, and then there was nothing but forest. Dale thought she saw the road that led off to her little two-story house, but it was hard to judge landmarks from five hundred meters in the air. After a few minutes, they descended to treetop level and flew a dizzying zigzag course.

"Frank!" Dale groped for something to hold onto as the little ship dodged between the taller trees. "What the hell are you doing?"

"Making sure we're not being tracked," he said. "Supplier's careful about security. You know how it is."

"Right," said Dale, wondering what exactly she had signed up for.

The sun was just setting as Frank settled the air car down between the trees and onto a concrete landing pad illuminated by a few floodlights. Around them, thick tree trunks rose straight into the air, likely old enough to have been seeded by the original terraforming crew a century past. Needles covered the ground, and as the air car doors opened, the scent of pine sap filled the cabin.

Dale started to sling her duffle over her shoulder, but Frank put his hand on her arm and shook his head. "Sorry, kid. You can't bring that with you. Like I said, they're real careful about security here."

"What, they're worried I have a gun?"

"Your phone," he said, laying his own unit on the control panel. "They've got an electronics scanner. You're going to have to leave it in the car or it'll mess up the deal."

"This is pretty suspicious, Frank."

"There's nothing to worry about. I've dealt with Paula before. She just needs someone to help out with her Chocondris, right? If she did anything to hurt us, it would foul up the relationship, and nobody wants that. We're a community. We look out for each other."

"If we're such a community, then why doesn't she trust me with a phone?"

Frank shrugged. "Her place, her rules. That's how it goes. Have I ever steered you wrong?" He got out of the air car leaving Dale with little choice but to follow him.

A skinny woman in a long, yellow sundress approached from a mossy cabin a few dozen yards from the landing pad. "Frank! Thank you so much for coming out."

"Anything for a friend." They shared an enthusiastic hug, then Frank turned to Dale with a dramatic gesture. "Paula, meet Dale Clearwater. She's the one I told you about."

"So you're good with tentacle beasts, eh?" said the woman. There were a few lines on her face, but her eyes sparkled with mischief, and even if she was closer to middle age than youth, she still had a good deal of charm. She stuck her hand out.

"I prefer to call them tentacle monsters," Dale replied, giving Paula a firm handshake. "They're not beasts." Dale wondered how a woman like Paula had gotten a Chocondris. After all, her home and her clothes didn't point to a fabulous amount of wealth.

"All right, that's fine," said Paula. "Shall we get started?"

Dale nodded. "So, what's the problem?"

"Well, I have this Chocondris, you see, and it's just not doing its job. Won't even camouflage itself. Just hangs from a tree limb out yonder, plain as anything." Paula walked toward a path that led into the gloom beyond the landing pad, with Dale beside her, and Frank trailing behind.

"That's odd," said Dale. "From what I've read, Chocondrises aren't prone to depression. They tend more toward agitation if they don't like their environment."

Paula took out a flashlight and flicked it on, sweeping the beam over the trail in front of them. "Yeah, I've heard the same, but, you know. They're all individuals. Are you familiar with Chocondrises?"

"Well, I've never actually seen one before, but I've read just about everything there is to read about tentacle monsters. Chocondrises are nocturnal opportunistic sedantaries native to the planet Chocon. Their pollen is psychoactive on humans, making them a bit on the difficult side to train but not as hard as a Mumzer or a Phase Looper. They reproduce by implantation, but they're finicky about who they implant."

"Well, well, you have done your homework." The beam of Paula's flashlight bounced around the trail, making it difficult to see anything beyond the ellipse of illumination. "That ought to be helpful," she said, and switched off the light.

Complete darkness enveloped Dale. She froze, but a hand in the middle of her back shoved her forward, and she tripped, stumbled and fell onto the dusty ground. There was a pop, and a crackle, and a smell of ozone. Dale turned over and saw Paula and Frank staring at her through the sizzling, faintly luminescent curtain of a badly-tuned force field wall. Its amber glow lent their features in an eerie aspect.

"What the hell was that for?" she said, picking herself up.

"We can't have the beast escaping, can we?" said Paula. "An ovulating Chocondris wandering around—who knows who it might find? No, no, can't have that."

"Ovulating!" Dale shouted. She stepped up to the barrier, wishing she could bang a fist against the force field, but as badly tuned as this one was she'd get a nasty shock. "You sealed me in with an ovulating Chocondris?"

"I'm sure you'll be fine," said Frank. "You have such a way with tentacle monsters. You're a good influence on them." His

exaggerated calm sent shivers down Dale's spine. "Too bad you
have such a terrible influence on your fellow trainers."

Paula smiled and flicked on her flashlight. "Don't worry. We'll
come get you in the morning. Everything will be better then. You'll
see. The experience is quite educational. Or so I'm told. Finicky.
Good word." The two of them turned and walked away.

"Frank! Frank, no! Please!" Dale stood, shouting, until they
disappeared into the cabin. The only remaining light was the glow
of the force field, its weak illumination penetrating only a few
meters into the forest, making it look like the trees simply faded
into a black abyss.

Every reference she'd ever seen emphasized the necessity of
leaving Chocondrises entirely alone when they were ovulating. It
wasn't just that they became more aggressive and their pollen
more potent, but their preferred host for their young was a human
body. Chocondris implantation was only reversible with delicate
surgery, and clearly Frank and Paula had no intention of having it
performed. With a shudder, Dale realized Paula kept this monster
for another reason than entertainment. It was here for breeding.

So was she. That's why they were way out here in the middle
of nowhere, why Frank had obscured their destination, why he
had taken her to his air car when nobody else at the facility would
be watching. Why she had left her phone in the car. She could
disappear out here and no one would ever find her. Panic gripped
her throat, but she fought it down, and discovered that there was
a sexual thrill there, hiding behind it. *An adventure!* it shouted,
clapping its hands at the prospect of danger.

However, her rational mind knew that indulging that thrill
would not be a good idea. Dale looked up, judging the height of
the force field wall. Its top was indistinct, fading off into
nothingness, well above the treetops. There would be no climbing
over it. The ground at her feet was packed solid, far too dense to
dig through with her hands. She walked along the fence line,
looking for any place that something might have burrowed under,

making a hole that she could wiggle through, but the force field generators were too solidly placed for that. Besides, if there had been any such gap in the enclosure, the Chocondris would have found it and escaped.

A sweet floral scent caught the edge of Dale's attention. It smelled a bit like lavender, with a hint of sage. Dale's breathing hitched. That would be the Chocondris. It was close, using its perfume to lure her in. The still air gave no indication from which direction the scent was coming, so Dale picked up her pace, desperately looking for any possibility of escape.

But the perfume only got stronger. Dale couldn't tell if this was because she was moving closer to the Chocondris, or if it was closing in on her. She listened for any sound of movement, but all she heard was the snap and sizzle of the force field wall.

Looking back over her shoulder, she tripped over an exposed root. Before she could recover, it had wrapped around her ankle. She screamed and thrashed, pulling and kicking, but its grip as unbreakable as if it had grown that way. A second root erupted from the earth and took hold of her elbow, and a third wrapped around her midsection. Both were as hard and strong as the first.

"Frank!" She screamed, her voice cracking with effort. "Frank, you son of a shit! You won't get away with this! Frank!"

There was no response. If anything, her screams and struggles energized the Chocondris. It pulled her deeper into the darkness, dragging her through the pine needles that coated the ground, until the glow from the force fields were no more than sparks, an artificial horizon at some limitless distance. The smell of lavender and sage grew stronger.

More woody tentacles, numbering at least a dozen, hauled her into the air and suspended her face-up under a sturdy branch. Her limbs were completely immobilized, encased in powerful coils. Tears threatened to well up, but she choked them down, refusing to give in to the rising panic.

The wood creaked and shifted, and more tentacles appeared over her head, silhouettes in the near-total darkness. These, Dale knew, were the real threat. She closed her eyes and held her breath, still knowing that the effort was futile. The whisper touch of a fine powder fell upon her face and neck.

Within moments she felt the drug begin to take effect. Her skin tingled, starting where the pollen fell, but the sensation quickly spread to the rest of her body. The monster's touch, as its tentacles wormed their way into her shirt and down the waist of her pants, sent shivers down her spine. The stems gripped the fabric and pulled. The material resisted for only a moment before buttons and threads failed, revealing more of her skin too the rain of alien dust.

A weird kind of lethargy overtook her. Dale could no longer struggle, but at the same time her nervous system was strangely energized. Every sensation was magnified a hundred times, especially her sense of touch. Each grope, squeeze and caress the monster performed upon her echoed through her like a note blown across the opening of an empty bottle.

Dale's first instinct was to resist, to hold tightly to her sanity, to push back against the fear and horror and sensation the monster inflicted upon her. But, the effort was like holding a piece of cardboard up against a gale; it only made her easier to break down. So, instead, she allowed it to blow her away.

She gave herself up to the sensations, allowed herself to feel every poke and nuzzle. She opened her mouth to allow a hard tendril as big around as her thumb, while another, thicker tendril slid into her pussy. It was no surprise that her body was wet and welcoming for it. The pollen had worked the monster's will on her, turning her into a perfect vessel for its insatiable alien lust.

Dale had no hatred for the monster. It was following its nature, doing what it needed to do. And besides, her mind was too full of raw sensation and emotion to consider nuanced moral questions.

The probing tendrils moved slowly, thrusting into her forcefully while thinner, softer organs stimulated every inch of exposed skin on her breasts, ribs, and belly, heightening her arousal beyond anything she had felt before. She had no thought of the future, no thought of escape. The only time was the moment, the only place right here.

Her last sensation before bliss completely overwhelmed her was of a thickening in the organ inside her pussy coinciding with a tightening of the bindings on her limbs. There was a jolt of pain, but at a distance, as if it were happening to another body somewhere else, one that wasn't lost in ecstatic rapture.

Dale recovered slowly. She was lying on the ground, pillowed by dry pine needles, still dressed in the remains of her clothes. She sat up, blinked at the dappled sunlight peeking through the trees, and pulled her shirt around her body. From the ache in her crotch she knew that her fears had been realized. The Chocondris had implanted her with one of its young. The monster itself was nowhere to be seen.

She limped back to the spot where the force field crossed the path and found a metal tray with some ration bars, a bottle of water, and a greeting card reading, "Congratulations to the new mother."

The ration bars seemed pristine, but the water was in an unmarked carafe. In spite of being quite thirsty, she couldn't trust the stuff; if there was any obvious place to put a drug, that was it. She couldn't even trust it to safely wash off the pollen that remained on her skin. The right drugs would keep her docile for years, growing one valuable tentacle monster after another in her belly.

But her captors had made a mistake. Dale set aside the food and water and grabbed the tray. It was sturdy, metal, the kind you'd find in a professional kitchen. She took it along the force field wall, looking for a spot without too many tree roots. She didn't have to go far; it looked like the presence of the crackling barrier wasn't good for the trees long-term, and the ones nearest the fence weren't doing well. She knelt down at a likely spot, and dug. The soil parted to the corner of the tray and, with the help of a nearby stick, she soon had a hole big enough to wiggle through.

After that, her escape was easy. She snuck into Paula's cabin, found an emergency beacon, and activated it. Rescue units arrived a half hour later, and her captor didn't even try to explain. She said nothing as the constabulary took her away.

The only question, then, was what to do about the creature growing inside her. The Victim's Restitution Department of the constabulary offered to pay for an extraction, but the answer for Dale was easy. The Chocondris had found her worthy of its trust, and that demanded respect.

She had an isolated home out in the forest, and from her studies she knew that a young tentacle monster would not stray far. All she needed, now, was a copy of "What to Expect When You're Expecting a Tentacle Monster."

ABOUT THE AUTHOR

Nobilis Reed has a dirty mind, and he's not afraid to use it. His creative accomplishments nearly always center around smut: his first novel, "Scouts," was shortlisted for the EPIC eBook Award; his short stories and novellas have been published with Circlet Press, Forbidden Fiction, Logical Lust and Sizzler Editions; and his podcast, Nobilis Erotica, has presented erotic science fiction and fantasy stories to thousands of listeners every month for ten years. When he's not struggling with the Shatner Comma, editing audio like a madman, or directing voice talent making orgasmic noises into microphones, his hobbies include sleeping and eating. You can find his website at nobiliserotica.com.

Other Titles You May Enjoy From Circlet Press

Like a Whisper in Your Ear
edited by Nobilis Reed
A collection of some of the best short stories published by Circlet Press and then featured in the Nobilis Erotic podcast! Available in audio, ebook, or paperback form! Includes stories by Sophie Mouette, Michael M. Jones, Alex Picchetti, Annabeth Leong, Shanna Germain, and many more.

MakerSex: Erotic Stories of Geeks, Hackers, and DIY Culture
edited by Annabeth Leong
Warning: May void the warranty on a stale sex life. The punks and rebels of Maker culture have arrived to take sex apart and rewire it into thrilling new forms. These characters tamper when they're not supposed to, kiss plastic, and involve soldering irons in their foreplay. In the process, they fight corruption, choose who and how to love and create erotic possibilities both playful and profound.

Coffee: Hot
edited by Victoria Pond
Coffee-flavored erotica! In this anthology, nine authors go a new direction to discover how coffee relates to the fantastical erotic world. This volume includes gods who steam milk (and make steamy love), coffee smugglers, and even some tentacles. (Wondering about how there can be coffee shop erotica with tentacles? Read to find out.)

Man's World
by Angela Caperton
For the wealthy, or the lucky, the universe is a vast and wonderful place. There are planets to visit, luxury space ships to patronize, designer drugs to take, and luxurious sex to purchase. However, for Stella Blue Darter, courtesan and gambling addict, the universe is just filled with accidents waiting to happen. When her beautiful body and chronic haplessness land her on Moulton, a planet ruled by a patriarchy and plagued by various female uprisings, she's not terribly surprised by the trouble she's in. But she hadn't counted on meeting Harker Merman and his dashing, dominating siblings. Stella's in over her head, and she'll have to find a way to survive on nothing but her wits and looks in Man's World.

Spyder's Trouble
by Korin I. Dushayl

An erotic space opera. Spyder, captain of the spaceship Trouble, ignores threats from the owner of his cargo and the anger of his influential and overdue passenger, to rescue the Dominatrix Lady Cassandra and her slaves from the threat of a repressive piety movement. The delay forces him to risk Trouble, his life, and his crew when a notorious criminal chases the ship from one end of the system to another.

Circlet Press
Erotica for Geeks

Celebrating the Erotic Imagination Since 1992

Receive books like this one for joining the
Circlet Press, Inc. Patreon supporters!

http://patreon.com/circletpress

Circlet
Press

Join the Circlet Press email list to find out about
new releases, special sales and discounts,
and what our authors are up to:

http://www.circlet.com/contact-us/email-newsletter/